VANESSA
JOHNSTON
❦

EASY PEASY

EASY PEASY

LESLEY GLAISTER

BLOOMSBURY

First published 1997

This paperback edition published 1998

Copyright © 1997 by Lesley Glaister

The moral right of the author has been asserted

Bloomsbury Publishing Plc, 38 Soho Square, London W1V 5DF

A CIP catalogue record for this book
is available from the British Library

ISBN 0 7475 3509 4

10 9 8 7 6 5 4 3 2 1

Typeset by Hewer Text Composition Services, Edinburgh
Printed in Great Britain by Clays Ltd, St Ives plc

For Robert

ACKNOWLEDGMENT

I would like to thank Ernest Virgo for the loan of
his POW diaries, and both Ernest and Olive Virgo
for their generosity and help during my research for
this novel.

1 TEASE
2 TICKLE
3 LICK

TEASE

1

My father is dead. It is night. The phone rang. I did not answer it, I was dressing. We were going out to eat tonight, Foxy and me. And to talk, we had to talk, she said. She was going to tell me that she was leaving, that is what I think. Before the phone-call I was lying in the bath looking at my body in the greenish water, breathing in the scent of limes. Refreshing soak. Foxy was downstairs dressed already, her Biederbeck CD on, getting in the mood. We were going to Buster's where there is jazz on a Friday and they do chicken in a chilli crust and a searing red wine for next to nothing. Foxy and I are vegetarian except for Buster's chicken. I was lying in the bath, wet and sad, imagining what she might say and how she might say it. *Sorry Zelda, but it's over*, or, *I do not love you any more*. No, not that. More likely she would say, *I need space, a temporary separation, see how it goes*. She is kind, Foxy. That's how she'd choose to do it, by gradual let-down, slow realisation, the actual moment of separation blurred. Because there must be an actual moment, an actual tear in the fabric: one minute you're a couple, one minute you're not.

Lying in the bath in the green scent of limes, I did not cry. She hadn't said it yet, she might not. She is older and that worries her. She was one of my lecturers and although our affair didn't begin until after I'd graduated she still thinks it's wrong, well *dubious*, she says. She is only fifteen years older, only forty-four, but you'd think she was Methuselah the way she goes on. She thinks I am very young for my age.

I hauled myself out of the bath and the misery, got dried and perfumed and started to dress – in my silky 40s' camisole and knickers. I was hesitating between dresses when the phone rang. I took no notice – Foxy there to answer. I paused by the mirror arrested by my reflection oh so pretty, so enticing, my skin pink from the bath, against the ivory silk.

The music suddenly switched off. And more than that – somehow a stilling of the air. I don't know how else to describe it. What was missing? Foxy's loud and cheerful voice or . . . I don't know, but I shivered. Only September yet a real chill in the air: my green dress, then, with its long sleeves – or maybe the red? Foxy's voice too quiet. My mind spinning on to jewellery and hair and chilli chicken and tonight, after, if everything's all right and tomorrow . . . what tomorrow? A lipstick trembling between my finger and thumb. And then Foxy's feet on the stairs, pausing by the bathroom.

She entered the bedroom; I flirted for a desperate second, thrust one hip towards her, pouted my lips, fluttered my eyelashes. But she didn't smile.

'What?' Almost afraid. She put her hands on my upper arms. She is taller than me. She looked down at me as if I was a child.

'That was your mum,' she said.

'What did she want?' Still with the smile hitched to my lips though my heart like a bird falling.

'It's your dad. Sorry Zelda.'

'What?' Frightened, angry at the slump of time, the way a beat can stretch for hours, the way a heart can plummet.

'He died. He is dead. He . . .'

What got into me then? I do not know. I have never been violent. I beat her with my fists, I kicked, lucky my foot was bare so I did not badly hurt her shin. 'No!' I pulled away from her arms. I was on the bed. I screamed, I really screamed, not a strangled dream scream, a real hurting scream that raked my throat raw. Then I was still. We were sitting on the edge of the bed. Foxy put her arm around my shoulder.

'I thought you were still in the bath or I'd have called you.'

'Didn't she ask for me?'

'She didn't want to speak she only wanted to say.'

'Hazel?'

'She got the answerphone – but she couldn't say *that* on it.'

'Huw?'

'Ringing him next.'

'I'd better go . . .' I stood up, looked around for clothes, caught my own eye in the mirror, thought my hair is a mess, thought *that* then?

'Zelda.' Foxy took my hand and pulled me down again. 'She said not to come tonight, wait till morning.'

'But I must . . .'

'No. Wait till morning. I'll drive you.'

'Daddy . . .' I felt my heart moving in me again like a stunned thing returning to life.

'Oh, poor love.' Foxy's arms tight around me, her hair soft on my shoulder.

'What?' I pulled away realising what she hadn't said. 'I mean . . . heart attack . . . or what?'

Foxy's fingers dug into my arm. 'Your mum found him hanging in the garage, Zelda. It was suicide.'

*

She is asleep now. In the light from the landing I can see her face quite clearly. Her hair is spread out on the pillow to one side as if it's blowing in a gale, thick brown hair. Round her temples there is some grey. I lean over her to smell her breath, faint cigarette smoke and the mint of toothpaste. She has the most perfect nose I have ever seen, small and straight, a nose so perfect you want to pinch or pull it, or bite it off.

Anything, I had thought, almost prayed, lying in the bath.

Please make something happen, anything, so she cannot finish it. Finish with me. Please God. Anything.

But I did not mean this.

Suicide. I did not believe it for a moment. No, that is a lie. Before she said the word I knew. Can that be true? I felt anger before the stun kicked in. Anger? Yes, to do *that*. Suicide is so utterly selfish. What is it? It's a last *up yours* to everybody, a last flounce out, the only sure way to have the last word.

If I did it that's what it would be.

But not my dad. That's not it. That is not good enough.

*

Nights. It was not just one night, it was many nights all through my growing up. Daddy's dreams were the worst thing. Asleep, head on my cool pillow, my sleep childish and sweet, pastel colours to float in, all ripped apart by a sudden scream. A man's scream – Daddy's – but not like Daddy's voice which was quiet and grey in the everyday, this scream like the bellow of an animal, shapeless, or like the cry of a man without a tongue. He had bad dreams often. Sleep became less pretty as I grew more aware, knowing that this could happen any night.

I slept in the top bunk. Hearing the scream I would jerk up, my nightdress suddenly damp, my neck prickling cold. Underneath I would hear Hazel stirring. The scream woke me up so completely that I could not sleep again, not for hours. My heart would skitter and in the feverishness of my mind stupid rhymes would jump about, skipping rhymes thudding like feet in my head: *Teddy Bear, Teddy Bear turn around, Teddy Bear, Teddy Bear touch the ground. Teddy Bear, Teddy Bear say good-night, Teddy Bear, Teddy Bear turn out the light.*

We had a night-light in our room in the shape of a red toadstool with white spots. It stood in the corner and I'd fix my eyes on it whenever I was awake, the red-and-white spotted glow a babyish comfort that Mummy sighed about but let me keep.

Hazel would have her head under the pillow. I could never

understand how she could do that, why she did not suffocate or die from the heat, but that is what she'd do and she'd go to sleep again quickly and leave me horribly awake, my thumb jammed in my mouth, my mind sharp – and always, urgently, needing to pee. But I would have to wait.

Because after one of Daddy's dreams, after the screams, there would be footsteps on the landing, running water in the bathroom, Mummy's voice crisp and rustling as paper, talking to him sensibly. Not quite the words, but her tone of voice. And then, after a while, the click of a light switching off, and silence.

And then I'd climb out of my bunk, my feet damp and slippery on the metal rungs of the ladder, quietly, *quietly*, because if I made the bunk beds shake or creak Hazel would be furious and would pretend I'd woken her and she would hate me. She never would admit that Daddy had woken us. She'd say I made it up. She never would admit she'd heard him screaming too.

And in the bathroom a horrible sweetness, air-freshener hiding the smell of sick so that I had to hold my breath.

*

Being awake at night, the only one awake at night, is a terrible thing. I am frightened of the night. I do not sleep well. I want someone to talk to, someone to hold me, someone to tell me it's all right. But I also want to be alone so I do not disturb whoever that someone is. It is so hard to be sprung with energy, with thoughts like a whirling flock of starlings in your head, and to have to be still. In the winter in the town centre as it is darkening the starlings flock and squeal like a million rusty wheels come loose. And I don't like that. That is what my thoughts are like, my night thoughts.

Foxy is deeply asleep, turned now, her arm flung over her head, a surprisingly solid arm for such a slim woman, white like marble, little wisps of darkness underneath. How can she sleep tonight of all nights? My father is dead. I do not know

7

which way to turn. I must not wake her but I cannot keep my body still, my mind, I cannot still it. How can she sleep? Doesn't she love me? Doesn't she care?

Yes, she loves me. Yes, she cares.

It is only the brandy that makes her sleep.

Oh, my dad. Oh Daddy, Daddy.

2

Our house was called 'The Nook' and the garden was big and full of trees. The apple tree had a swing slung from a horizontal branch. There was a flowering cherry too and a silver birch – but the best tree was right at the bottom of the garden. Its branches reached up and pressed almost against the upstairs window of the house behind. The tree was special because of its colour – it was a copper beech – but also because, high up in its branches, was our tree-house.

The tree-house had not been built for us, it had been there when we moved in. It had a rope ladder that you could haul up once you were inside so you could not be reached. Its floor was made of planks cut to fit round the trunk and incorporating one smooth grey limb that made a kind of sloping bench, quite comfortable with a cushion on it. The walls had been woven from willow branches, like a basket, and lined with cardboard. Hazel and I Sellotaped the walls with postcards and pictures cut from magazines. We had half the wall space each – hers full of ballet dancers, mine of ponies.

The two windows were round. We'd tried taping polythene bags over them to keep out the draughts but that meant you couldn't see properly, so we left them empty. From one window you could spy on the house – keep an eye on the back door to see who was coming out; the other was only a few feet away from the window of the house behind. One day I looked out and saw a face gazing out of that window, staring straight at me in the tree-house. That was my first sight of Puddle-duck, a thin, wedge-shaped face, yellow as cheese, staring out from between two curtains, staring, just staring it seemed, for hours.

I kept my pets in the tree-house. My pets were ants, big brown ones, wood ants. Because Daddy hated insects, I wasn't allowed to keep them in the house. He didn't even know about them. The formicary had been in my classroom at school, a plastic aquarium in which lived a whole colony. When we had finished studying them, Miss Bowen asked if anyone would like to take them home to keep. Mummy said I could as long as I never brought it into the house, and never mentioned it to Daddy. So I smuggled it straight up into the tree-house, a place where he never ventured.

At one end of the tank was the nest, a heap of soil and leaf fragments laced with holes and tunnels and secret chambers. A ramp led down to it from the rubber-teated feeder bottle from which dripped a sugar solution for my ants to feed on. I used to drop leaves in for them and sometimes treats, a shred off the Sunday roast or the corner of a biscuit which they'd negotiate, cleverly, three or four of them together into a hole they'd widened for the purpose.

I felt like God giving gifts when I dropped things into the tank. I almost felt love. They were so busy my ants, so clever. I delighted in watching them scurrying up and down the ramp from the feeder to the nest, sometimes making forays up the sides of the tank, walking upside down on the lid. Sometimes on their journeys they'd meet other ants and stop, heads together, feelers waving. A whole colony of ants, of lives going on, in a plastic aquarium in a tree-house. The ants didn't know they were imprisoned and balanced in a tree for the amusement of a child. They thought that they were free and that their tank was the whole wide world.

*

The night is terrible. Thoughts are more urgent, fears are greater, the darkness muffles me, it makes me helpless, breathless. The landing light is on. Foxy likes it dark but she lets me leave the landing light on and it shines through the little strip of glass above the door. The door is closed. I would have it open – but for the landing light to be on and the door closed is a compromise. The stuff of our relationship. I would prefer the window and the curtains to be open, she'd like both closed. So we have the window open a little, but the curtains pulled.

It is midnight, just gone. All the hours of the night. I keep my eye on the strip of light. Foxy is beside me, I can feel her warmth, the feathers of her breath, but she is sealed away in sleep. I must not wake her. When someone is asleep they are not *there*. It is not fair. Was she going to tell me it is over between us? I do not know if this is better.

*

The swing was made of thick twisted rope with a slab of wood for a seat. The rope was greenish in its twist as if the green from the apple tree had run down it. I would hardly have been surprised if the rope had sprouted leaves and apples. The apples from the tree were sour and covered in scabs. Mummy made chutney from them and apple sauce and baked apples sometimes, from the biggest of them. I did not like to eat the skins, the scabs were like the crusts of grazes on our knees but inside the flesh fizzed soft and hot and sweet with golden syrup.

Food was complicated. Daddy was funny about it. He ate too much. He'd get fat, diet until he was gaunt, get fat again. He took pills to help slim and when he was taking the pills he was angry. He'd roam round with a spanner looking for things to tighten up. I preferred him fat. When he was fat he was quiet, unless he'd been drinking then he was scary. At least I was scared of him, Hazel too, I think, although she'd never admit it to me. Not scared because he would hit us or hurt us, only scared because . . . just because the air crackled and we sat on the edges of our seats and our nails dug into our palms . . . just a feeling . . . just because.

Daddy liked spice. Chilli powder, curry powder, hot-pepper sauce. 'I can't taste it,' he'd complain, trying one of Mummy's concoctions and putting down his fork. Mummy would get up sighing and fetch the Worcester sauce, the chutney, the Tabasco, and watch him smother his food.

But Mummy had her own funny ideas about food. She is Swedish, so we used to eat things with dill and soured cream, raw pickled herrings, gravadlax, things that no one else I knew would ever eat. Sometimes we went vegetarian, but none of us could manage without bacon for long so that would founder. Food should be fun, she used to say when we would not eat as children. Once she got us to eat our dinner blindfolded to see if we could tell what it was by taste and smell alone. It was something with red sauce I remember because of the mess on the tablecloth. Daddy was not there that time. He didn't believe that food was fun. He was often away when Mummy had her ideas, but if he was at home he'd eat alone, boiling up something from a tin and sloshing in half a bottle of Tabasco.

*

Tonight we didn't eat. I cannot believe the rage that swept through me, the way I flew at Foxy and beat her to try and beat away the truth: as if the news of my father's death was a buzzing thing, a dreadful fly, and if I screamed enough and fought enough it couldn't settle on me and his death could not be true.

We didn't go to Buster's and we didn't eat. We sat on the bed, her arm round my shoulders, until I was shivering. She helped me out of my underwear but we did not make love. I almost thought we would. I almost wanted to but she pointed out that I was chilled and made me put on my white satin pyjamas. We went downstairs and sat by the gas-fire drinking brandy. Metaxa, bought with the last Greek money at the end of our holiday, hot gold. Foxy brought in a tray of cheese and biscuits but I could not think of eating. It was like Christmas night after too much lunch, the brandy glasses warmed by the fire, the cheese, the crackly wrappings of the biscuits. Only no joy and no presents and no tree in the corner winking.

'I feel useless,' Foxy said, rolling yet another cigarette. 'I don't know what to say.'

'There's nothing.' The first shock was like the sea, like waves rolling in like I suppose labour to be. Engulfing waves of grief, of physical trembling and sickness and then a lull, a moment of reflection, even momentary forgetting as the mind gathers itself for another wave of grief. In one of these lulls I studied Foxy's face trying to read her thoughts. If she had been planning to finish with me, then she'd be feeling thwarted, frustrated. Because how could she finish with me now? Maybe that hadn't been in her mind at all. Maybe she loves me, maybe she needs me as much as I need her. But her face was inscrutable and all I could read in her eyes was concern.

I had tried to ring my mother back but every time there was just the engaged tone. Later on I rang Hazel, just in from dinner with Colin, and I had to tell her. I just said it straight: 'Dad's dead . . . Mum found him hanging . . . it looks like it . . . yes . . . no.' Hazel's voice faint, a little drunk, already thickening with tears. Hazel wouldn't rage or beat Colin with her fists. Hazel would accept. We made arrangements. Both of us would go to Mum first thing. I'd be there by lunchtime, Hazel, who lives further north in Durham, by mid-afternoon. We said good-bye.

'What did she say?' Foxy, avid for detail, as ever.

'Nothing much.'

And that is so. She'd said nothing much and nor had I. And nothing of any significance had been said between Foxy and me. The only significance, my violence and the tenderness of her response.

But there should be significance in words. There should be words that are profound. There should be more than train times and the beep beep beep engaged-tone of a mother's phone. There should be more.

All so ordinary and so strange. Foxy eventually giving way to hunger and snacking, apologetically, on biscuits and cheese. Both of us drinking too much Metaxa. The sound of next door's television through the wall, a commercial jingle, the sea-roar of laughter.

3

After seeing his face between the curtains peering at me in the tree-house, I met him. He was the new boy at school: Vassily Pudilchuck. He stood in front of the class, narrow shoulders hunched, a frightened smile on his yellow face, long teeth crossed at the front as if they were too tightly crammed in his mouth. His jumper was too big, rolled up at the wrists. Because he was deaf he had to sit at the front to make sure he could at least see. He had a funny smell, and big hearing-aids in each ear with wires going down his neck to a bulky rectangle under his sweater.

'Because Vassily is hard of hearing', Miss Bowen said, 'you must make sure he can see your lips when you speak to him. And enunciate your words clearly', she stretched her own lips as she said this to demonstrate, 'so that Vassily can lip read. Perhaps Vassily would teach us all a bit of sign language?' She looked at him but he had his head bent over the lid of his desk.

'What's sign language, Miss?' said someone from the back.

'It's a system of hand signals,' Miss Bowen explained, and there were sniggers as some boy did a V sign.

My desk was behind Vassily's. The knobbles of his spine showed right through his jumper and shirt as he leaned over his desk. The hearing-aids were pink and stuck out so that from behind he looked like some kind of robot with wires in its head. Later I was to learn that he hated the hearing-aids – that did little good anyway, but then they seemed an absurd, deliberately peculiar part of him. I didn't recognise him, then, as the face that stared out of the window into our tree-house, down into our garden. But I disliked him in the fierce way children can dislike weaklings or misfits – with a sort of fear.

By the end of his first day he had been christened Puddle-duck, a name that suited him because of the way he walked with his too-big feet splayed outwards and his head down. He was ten but he couldn't read properly. Not hearing makes reading harder, Miss Bowen said, but still, he *was* ten. When he spoke it was very loud and sounded as if he had a bath sponge stuffed in his mouth soaking up the edges, the points and angles of his words. By the look of it, he never washed his hair. It looked solid like brownish clay and sat on his head like a dull corrugated lid. He made friends with a boy called Simon, or maybe not *friends*, but they stood together in the playground and shivered. Simon had eczema absolutely all over him and wore glasses with pink sticking plaster over one lens. He'd never had a friend before. But even Simon called Vassily Puddle-duck.

I didn't recognise him as the boy who spied on us from his upstairs window until, a few days later, something terrible happened. Something that jolted me into recognition.

Puddle-duck hadn't got a PE kit.

'Never mind,' said Miss Bowen, leaning towards him and enunciating, 'just strip down to your underwear.' It was a rainy day and we were doing indoor PE – throwing bean-bags, climbing ropes and apparatus, jumping over wooden horses on to spongy green mats. If we had no kit we were not let off but made to show off, to all the other boys and girls, our pants and vests. Fear of this humiliation ensured that we never forgot. Miss Bowen was wearing a short navy skirt and white ankle socks for the lesson. She jogged up and down on the spot waiting for Vassily. Her big red legs were haloed with white fuzz. He handed her his hearing-aids, great handfuls of pink plastic and curly wires that seemed horribly a part of him. Miss Bowen took the aids and stopped running.

'Take off your jersey, Vassily,' she said. He looked down at the floor. Miss Bowen put a hand under his chin to make him look up. 'Take it off.' She plucked at his sweater. His face went dark red. I thought he would refuse, but he took off the sweater. Everyone was ready now, gathered round him watching and that made it worse. Under his sweater he was wearing a crumpled and much-too-big shirt tucked into his shorts. 'And this,' said Miss Bowen, touching his shoulder. I think Miss Bowen was cruel, *now* I think that. Everyone was staring at Vassily. She should not have let us all stand and stare at him like that. He undid his shirt and took it off. He had no vest on and what we saw, we could hardly believe. Nobody said an audible word but there was a stunned murmur.

'Griselda, perhaps you'd be kind enough to fetch Vassily an Aertex shirt from Lost Property,' Miss Bowen said. I hurried off, important. I was picturing his chest as I went down the gloomy, dinner-smelling corridor and I can picture him now. A puny boy with a flaming face and six nipples on his skinny concave front. It looked like the belly of a dog. Among the odd plimsolls and the rain-hoods in the Lost Property box I found a shirt for Vassily and took it back to the hall. Miss Bowen was holding Vassily's hand and peeping her whistle between her teeth as my oddly quiet classmates scrambled on the apparatus and queued for the ropes. I handed Puddle-duck the shirt and made myself smile. He smiled back, a grateful narrow smile that made me queasy. And that is when I recognised him as the spy.

If nobody liked Puddle-duck very much before, that day confirmed it. Puddle-duck was scarcely even human.

*

The brandy has given me a thirst. It's hot in the bedroom with the door closed. The window is open but muffled behind thick curtains. So the air in the room is still. The room is filled with breath. Foxy's breath is slow and even and rises up the walls until I fear I will drown in it. My own breathing is fast. I should relax. Breathe deep, breathe slow. But all I am inhaling is old breath. It is stale air. The room is full of dead air. Now I am starting to panic. Stop that. Stop. Breathe. The air is fine. The window is open. You cannot drown in Foxy's breath. You will not drown. Lie still. Oh my heart.

Like the nights of Daddy's dreams. Having to be still, hearing that scream but having to be still for Hazel. Having not to speak of it at all.

Breakfast after those nights was awful. My father would sit with his hands clasped round his cup of tea as if he thought someone might snatch it. His chin would be rough and his curly hair wild. There would be a greasy sheen on his glasses so you could not see his eyes. The breakfast room was sunny with windows on two sides, but however much sun streamed into the room on mornings after a dream, the room would contain a cloud, a chill. My mother would be the same as ever, serving up poached eggs or bacon or kippers, the sun bright on her blonde hair, but she would seem like an actor on those days, someone on the stage with rouge and spiky lashes while the rest of us were grey. But even she didn't speak to Daddy, just topped up his cup with tea and kept a nervous eye on him as she chatted to us.

I am angry with my father for dying. For choosing to die. How dare he? It is the most selfish thing. *Dad! How dare you? Eh?* I was going to know him. There are things I do not know, secrets. There are things I wanted to ask him. I wanted his story from him. I wanted to know what was in his nightmares, what was the fear behind the screams, the fear that threaded itself into my own sleep and into me.

The nightmares were never spoken of. Until I talked to Foxy I didn't think that strange. They were a part of my childhood, not normal perhaps, but not strange. No stranger than my mother's food fads, or the time she made us go barefoot for weeks to strengthen our arches. No stranger, I suppose, than the things that happen behind the curtains and the doors of every house in every street in every town.

But Foxy said 'What? You never asked him what he dreamed about?'

'No,' I said, 'you couldn't.'

'Why?'

I shook my head.

'What about your mum? What did she say?'

I tried to think. My father had been a prisoner of the Japanese for five years. He'd worked on the building of the Burma-Siam railway. I didn't think that was a big deal. I had seen the film *The Bridge on the River Kwai* and vaguely associated it with Daddy. Strong men, sweat and stiff-upper-lips. Daddy as Alec Guinness. Did I know the nightmares were about that? No, I didn't. Terrible things happened in the war, but the war was over. It was nothing to do with me. It was history. He was whole. My dad.

A holiday: the beach, Llandudno, North Wales. I noticed hollows on my father's legs, the fleshy calves, deep hollows big enough to cup an egg in. I put my finger in one of the hollows. I must have been very young. It was warm and smooth inside, purplish like the skin on a newborn mouse, not hairy like the rest of his legs. I wanted to ask him what the holes were but he jumped up and pelted down the beach, ran splashily through the shallows until he reached deep water and then he swam. He swam out and out like always, arm over arm over arm. I was afraid when he swam out like that, out towards the middle of the sea, towards nothing. His dark head grew smaller and smaller, sometimes vanishing altogether. When I could see him no longer and I thought he had drowned, I did not scream or shout or point, I turned over on to my tummy on the beach-towel, fear beating in my veins. I lay still on the beach-towel, eyes shut, the chill of the sand striking up through the towel, shutting out the voices of Mummy and Hazel who were oblivious to the danger, until I felt the sprinkle of cold that meant that he was back. I turned over and looked up at him, towering against the sun above me, all the hairs on his body cradling glittering drops. I got up off the towel to let him use it. I didn't say a thing but I was so relieved that he was safe I needed to pee. I walked down the beach and into the sea until the cold water gripped me by the waist and then I peed blushing as the invisible heat flowed out between my legs into the cold.

'I can't believe you didn't ask your mum about his dreams,' Foxy frowning at me, an edge of criticism in her tone.

I shrugged. Close as you are to someone, up to your eyes in love, it doesn't mean that they will understand you. No one from outside can really understand a family: it is a culture it takes a lifetime to acquire.

'If that was part of *my* family history, I'd have to know,' she insisted. Foxy is a historian, her special interest oral history, family histories, the quiet stuff, the detail. She still teaches a little but most of her time and energy are concentrated on writing and research. Her study is piled with boxes of tapes, faint crackly voices recounting memories from the beginning of the century, Victorian and Edwardian voices. She gets quite frantic sometimes when she thinks of the dying resource, the most direct primary evidence. But skewed, I say, for how can a memory not be skewed that is eighty or ninety years old, that has either lain dormant or been continually embroidered for the best part of a century? It's Foxy's turn to shrug at this and talk about intelligent and selective interpretation, about empirical corroboration. I criticise, but I think it's wonderful, what she does. I think she is wonderful, asleep now, awash in the tangle of her hair.

She is so much cleverer than me. Cleverer and more patient. My degree – not a bad one, 2:1 in history and philosophy – has fallen off me like so much dust, all that learning. I prefer the day-to-dayness of my business, selling second-hand and period clothes. Second Hand Rose is the name of my shop, a popular shop in the centre of York. I spend much of the week travelling to

markets and auctions collecting stock. I wash and press and mend
while listening to the radio most evenings, turned down low so
as not to disturb Foxy when she's working at home. I open my
shop five days from midday to six. Connie works in the shop and
lives in the upstairs flat. My guard-dog she calls herself, giving a
big husky bark of laughter. I can't pay her much but she has the
flat rent free, a pokey hole, admittedly, and the odd outfit. And
I mean odd. When I'm buying I keep Connie in mind. She's in
her mid-fifties. 'Mutton dressed as lamb, I know me duck,' she
says cheerfully, though I wouldn't say lamb exactly. She likes
spiked heels and patent leather mini-skirts, tight neon-coloured
satin blouses. She wears her hair in an orange beehive and her
legs are sensational. She has a stream of lovers, thirty years
her junior at least, whom she treats kindly – 'I give them the
time of their life, darling' – and then in the nicest possible way
discards before they become attached. Her voice is a deep sexy
purr and we fight constantly but amicably over the Gauloise she
will smoke from a long tortoise-shell holder so that the clothes,
when you shake them out, all have a faint reek of France.

My working life is markets and motorways, the shop and
Connie and clothes. Image. It is all surface, unlike Foxy's working
life which is earnest and burrows beneath the surface. But clothes
are important, they are part of it, Foxy says so herself. She likes
to get her subjects to talk about their clothes, the fashions, the
costs, the difficulties, it is a rich seam to mine, she says. Oh
Foxy. She is glamorous – even naked. The clothes she wears
are severe, her spectacles too, stern ovals, but her chestnut hair,
that is long and slippery. She wears it in a French pleat that will
not stay properly in. She is often to be seen, both hands behind
her head, her mouth full of hair-grips, recapturing it. She wears
too much lipstick and it never quite matches the shape of her
lips. It is always bright – vermilion or cherry or scarlet – and
always too big, slipping over the edges of her mouth. It is her
only design fault and I love it. All our cups and glasses have
red grease-marks on the rims, because unless you scrub, it will

not come off. Still, I don't mind, I like to drink from the very place where her lips have been. God, I am besotted! No wonder she wants . . . no! She has not said she wants to go and she is sleeping so sweetly beside me, how could she sleep so sweetly if she was not happy? If she did not want me beside her?

4

My mother has met Foxy, although I did not introduce her as Foxy. That name too pungent and feral to be taken into my family. My friend, I called her, my friend Sybil. It makes me laugh that she is really called that, Sybil – prophetess, fortune-teller, witch. She is none of those things – except in her capacity to bewitch me. She is the most rational and pragmatic of beings. Sybil Fox. It is only me who calls her Foxy, to most of her other friends she is Syb, quite inappropriate: a numb little snippy snub of a name. And she calls me Zelda. She has made me Zelda, a desirable grown-up woman when before I was a child, Griselda, known to my family, and even a lover or two, as Grizzle.

I have never told my mother, in so many words, that Foxy, Sybil, is my lover, but I know she knows. She is not shocked. She has an open, Scandinavian, streak in her. She has visited me, us, three times in this flat. Christmas shopping in York has become a new ritual. We wander round the shops until our feet are aching and then have lunch followed by tea and wicked cakes in Betty's, her treat. It is the most mother-and-daughterish thing we do.

She has seen the bedroom with the double bed, the double wardrobe, the two pairs of slippers on the floor. Foxy's study has a single bed where she sometimes snoozes in the afternoons among her papers so Mummy *might* think she sleeps there, if she wants to think that then she can. But I know she knows we

23

are a couple because last year her Christmas card to us read: *To Griselda and Sybil with love from Mum and Dad* as if we are a married couple.

Mum and Dad. That is the last time and I did not treasure it. This year the card will read only *love Mum* to her family, *love Astrid* to everyone else. How will she do it after forty-two years? How will she stop her hand writing *and Dad* or *and Ralph*?

I wish I had got through to her tonight. Why was her phone engaged so long? Who was she talking to? She should have been talking to me or Huw or Hazel. I could get up. I could get up quietly and phone her now. At this time? On a night like this?

My father is dead. This is the only day that he will die on. September 9th. No. It is past midnight, the 10th. Yesterday he died. Already it is yesterday, the past. September 9th. Last September 9th he didn't know he only had a year to go. You have a deathday just like you have a birthday, the only difference is you do not know it. It is a secret like so much else.

Daddy never knew about Foxy and me, of course he didn't. I never said to Mum, don't tell him. I couldn't, since it was only tacitly known by her. But as well as that it is implicit in our family code that we don't tell Daddy things he wouldn't like. Didn't tell. Soon the past tense will catch up with him, but, despite midnight, today is still his deathday, he can still be present tense today.

'What did he tell you about his war?' I asked my mother once, egged on by Foxy. Until I knew Foxy I had never noticed my mother's reluctance to talk or think about my father's past.

She moved her hand in a dismissive gesture. 'Hardly a thing. He used to try and talk but . . . oh, I really don't remember. Best not to dredge up the bad memories, best to bury them. Look forward not back. That's what Ralph does. You should respect that, respect his privacy.'

I repeated that to Foxy.

She choked on her coffee. 'Respect his privacy!'

'Yes.'

She wrinkled her nose so that her spectacles rose up indignantly. 'It's like letting gold flow down a drain,' she said. 'It is treasure, Zelda, it is part of you.'

I wonder if Foxy would feel differently if she knew who she was? She was adopted at the age of six weeks. She tried once to discover the identities of her natural parents, she found only that it was a private adoption; her mother a young girl, her father an American GI. That's all she knows. Her adoptive mother told her on her sixteenth birthday. I thought that must have been traumatic but, 'No,' she said emphatically, 'not in the least. I *liked* to know that. I always felt I didn't belong.' I didn't say that nor did I. I didn't feel I belonged to my family either. I am short and solid and dark haired while Mummy and Hazel are tall and slim and blonde. If someone had told me I was adopted I would have been delighted, excited to shed part of my identity.

Even now?

A fantasy: my mother rings me up. She confesses that Daddy wasn't my real, my biological, father, that she had an affair with someone – oh, Paul Newman, say. That used to be my fantasy. How would it make me feel? I don't know. I am so tired. And anyway it's stupid because although I haven't inherited my mother's Scandinavian looks, I *am* like Daddy.

Foxy still loved her parents after they told her the truth although she started, immediately, to call them May and Reg instead of Mum and Dad. May is her best friend. They talk on the phone for ages every Sunday night, gossiping and guffawing with laughter and often meet in London for a drunken lunch followed by a stagger round Harvey Nichols or Harrods, daring each other into ever more extravagant purchases. May knows about Foxy and me, treats me like a daughter-in-law. I am Foxy's third live-in female lover. Third time lucky, I say, and Foxy flicks her eyes to heaven. Even the slightest allusion to superstition gets up her delectable nose. And it *has* lasted longest. Five years almost. I wonder how many women she has made love to? And men too. None of my business.

But, an anomaly: although Foxy is almost obsessive in her plundering of other people's pasts, while she salivates at the combination of a Zimmer frame and a memory, she has not bothered with the background of May or Reg. When I ask why, she bats the question away with her hand and will not say. Why is she not interested in their past when she's fascinated by everyone else's?

I have not told Foxy about the envelope. I don't know why, it's just . . . I needed to dwell on it alone, let the idea settle. I am afraid of her eagerness, what she will do. I was afraid to let her loose on my dad. Not only because she would have doubtless given the game away, somehow, about the nature of our relationship, but because she would have tried to turn him inside out, upside-down, shake all the memories from the pockets of his mind and . . . And I feared what would happen to him, then. What would be left.

Foxy has such tenacity, such fierceness – she is more of a hound than a fox when on the scent of the past. I cannot imagine her in the same room as my father. Her energy would suck his out. They are like different species.

Now I exaggerate! The night is getting into my head. How I hate the night. I would like to live in the land of the midnight sun, but all year round, to have no division between night and day, no boundary, never a time when you look out of a window into the dark to see that every door is shut, every pair of curtains drawn, every light extinguished.

'You could train to be a nurse,' Foxy suggested once, 'and work nights.'

It made sense, but I could never be a nurse. I'm squeamish and I don't like touching people, except people I choose to touch. And working nights, whatever the job was, would rob me of Foxy for whom night-time is luxury. She is the deepest sleeper I have ever known and the quickest to switch. She is rarely sleepy, either awake or asleep as if there is a very efficient valve in her, no leakage either way.

The envelope. A fortnight ago my mother rang me. 'I've had a letter,' she said.

'Well?'

'Well, since you seem so determined to waken the dogs . . .'

'Sorry?'

'The sleeping dogs. All this pestering about your father's war . . .' I gasped at the unfairness of this, I had only asked her once or twice. 'I've had this letter. I don't know what to do with it. Should I send it to you?'

'What is it?'

'It's from a Mrs Priest writing to tell me of her husband's – who incidentally I don't know from Adam – death. The Reverend Priest would you believe! He knew your father in the war.'

'A letter about Daddy?'

'She's been through his papers and found some things. To do with, you know, the Japs and so on . . .'

'Shouldn't you give them to Daddy?'

'I don't want him all stirred up unnecessarily. Night after night of it I'm getting at the moment. He's worse. I don't want him more upset. And I don't want to open it. Shall I send it to you? You see what you think.'

'Yes do,' I said. I was touched that she had chosen me, not Hazel, touched that she had taken me seriously when I'd asked about Daddy. I'd thought she only considered it silly, and me a childish nuisance.

A bulky envelope arrived two days later. I picked it up from the mat before Foxy could see. She is insatiably curious about mail and phone calls. Nosy bag, I call her. It's not that she's suspicious or jealous, she's just plain nosy.

Inside the envelope, there was a note written on blue paper and addressed to my mother, this was folded round a fat manila envelope stuck down with parcel tape. I read the note:

Dear Mrs Dawkins,

My husband, the Rev. Priest, passed away three months ago. While going through his papers recently I came across the enclosed envelope, which, as you see, has your husband's name on it. I apologise for the delay in forwarding it to you. I have decided to send it to you rather than to Mr Dawkins directly as I know how sensitive some veterans are to the subject of their POW experience. Certainly my husband still suffered the scars – both physical and mental. Early on, I used to urge him to talk to me, or to remain in contact with fellow POWs, but to no avail. I wonder if your experience with Mr Dawkins was similar?

Sadly my husband died without, I believe, having addressed himself to the forgiveness of his Japanese captors. An oddness I think in a man otherwise so wholly Christian in outlook and behaviour.

So, in accordance with what I believe my late husband's wishes to be, I enclose these papers and leave to your own discretion what you do with them next.

With very best wishes,
Yours sincerely,

Mrs Anthea Priest

The brown envelope was thick, packed with papers. In faded ink I read my father's name written in fountain-pen by an elegant hand. I began to open it, my heart beating hard. My fingernail was under the edge of the brittle parcel tape when I heard Foxy's footfall in the hall, coming to see what the post was. I pushed the whole package into the bookcase.

'What was it?' she said.

'What?'

'The post, I heard it come, anything for me?'

'No. Just some Reader's Digest win-a-fortune sort of thing.'

'Your lucky day then.' She poked me in the stomach with her

finger and went back to work, grinning. If I'd shown her she would have ripped the envelope open and seen it all, explored it all. By nightfall she would have been full of plans for books and documentaries. She would have been on the phone to my father arranging an interview. I could not face it.

I had to go to an auction then, and driving on the motorway to Leeds gave me pause to consider. I did not open the envelope. I still have not, though my fingers have strayed to the corners where the tape is coming up; though I have often stroked the old faint grittiness of it and breathed its dusty smell.

I decided I would not open the envelope. It was not mine to open. No, I decided that I would give it to him. Not send: the thing appearing on the breakfast table, where Mummy always dumps the post, might come as too much of a shock, whatever its contents – which could, after all, be trivial. My plan was to take him out to lunch. Next month is, would have been, his birthday – his sixty-eighth. I have never had a meal only with Daddy, without Mummy there to smooth all the prickles, fill all the gaps. I thought I would take him out for lunch and if we sat in silence throughout the meal then so be it. But at lunch – a pub I thought, nowhere formal, somewhere with a fire and home cooking – I'd ease into the subject of the past and give him the envelope. I'd thought that maybe then he would confide in me, open up little by little. That I could learn his story not by sneaking behind his back into his private things but through his words, through what he chose for me to know. Because I am interested. Foxy may have nudged me at first but now the interest is my own. And if he chose to say nothing . . . which was quite possible, likely even, then I'd have to live with that. But I would have given him a chance to talk to me. Which was also a chance that I could get to know him, have some sort of relationship with him, which is something, despite growing up in the same house, I don't think I've had.

5

It was a long walk to school. Hazel was supposed to walk with me. We would set off together but Hazel's friend Bridget would be waiting for her halfway, chewing gum, blowing bubbles the size of eggs, oranges, grapefruits even, that never popped on her face the way mine did, but withered gracefully and shrank, grey and wrinkled, back into her open mouth. When Bridget was there, Hazel was completely different. Whenever they were together they talked in these stupid American accents and called me 'kid'. 'I'm only fifteen months younger than you,' I'd object, from behind, speaking to Hazel not Bridget, but Bridget would turn, eyes narrowed, gum snapping between her teeth. 'But honey,' she'd say, 'those fifteen months *count*.'

I didn't care anyway, I didn't want to walk with them. Bridget was allowed to wear shoes that were almost high-heeled and made her wiggle when she walked so that I wanted to kick her up the bum. She and Hazel would link arms and walk in step and, just before they reached the school gates, Bridget would spit her gum into someone's hedge.

My best friend, Elaine, lived in the other direction. Hardly any other children lived our way. Most families with children lived on the new estate the other side of the village. Our house was big and dark. Mummy hated it. She longed for a bright new house. 'Where we can inscribe our own personalities on the pristine walls,' she said, 'instead of battling against the dust of ages. A sort of architectural tabula rasa,' she added, and Daddy flapped his paper and belched in the way he did when most irritated.

Nobody lived our way, on the gloomy outskirts, separated from the village by a couple of flat, windy fields, nobody except old people. One of the houses was actually an old people's home and some were divided up into flats. Nobody I knew lived our way – until Puddle-duck arrived.

He used to appear at the end of the path that led up the side of our house to his, just as Hazel and I came out of our door every morning. I think he must have been bobbing down behind the fence, waiting, for whether we were late or early he would always step out smiling at me in a way that made my heart clench. A pleading smile. Just because I'd fetched him an Aertex shirt to cover up his dog's belly, he liked me. Hazel would ignore him, sweeping past as if he was nothing, her straight blonde hair swinging below her ears. I would smile back sometimes, but hurry past, leaving him behind.

When we met Bridget at the other side of the fields, I was supposed to drop back, but if I dropped back too much, Puddle-duck caught up with me. I couldn't stand it. 'Oh, it's lover boy,' Bridget would shout. 'Going steady, Grizzle?' My face would go tight and hot. At least Puddle-duck was deaf, that was a blessing. It was difficult walking far enough behind them and far enough in front of Puddle-duck. But I *couldn't* walk with him. When he said hello he sounded like a seal. If he was behind me I couldn't see him so my hardness couldn't be chipped away by the sad sight of him. Only sometimes he was close enough for me to hear the slap, slap, slap of his big feet in their plimsolls – he always wore the sort of plimsolls with stretchy elastic fronts – and sometimes I could hear him breathing too, he breathed so loudly because he couldn't hear I suppose, incorporating little squeaks and grunts.

Then, one morning over breakfast, Hazel mentioned Puddle-duck.

'Who?' Mummy asked.

'The boy who lives in one of the flats at the back,' Hazel said.

Mummy picked Huwie's spoon up from the floor and sat down, intrigued. 'The little fellow who stares out of the window?' Huwie, sitting in his high-chair, threw his spoon back on to the floor and jammed a Marmite soldier into his mouth with a pudgy fist. I remember that, because suddenly I became aware that Puddle-duck had been a baby once, not as sweet and fat as Huw I'm sure, but still . . . a baby boy. I felt a sort of surge of compassion for him. What if everyone hated Huw when he was older like everyone hated Puddle-duck? Compassion I tried to swallow with my mouthful of egg.

'I've often wondered about him. Have you noticed him, Ralph?'

'Eh?' Daddy emerged from his *Daily Telegraph* and took a bite of toast. It was smothered in marmalade that he made himself, the bits of peel as thick as caterpillars. I wouldn't eat it.

'The boy who lives at the back.'

'Little waif. Stares from the window?'

'That's him.' Mummy hooked a bit of egg-shell from Huwie's mouth.

'He's in Grizzle's class,' Hazel said. I kicked her under the table.

'His mother's that *piece*.' My mother widened her eyes at Daddy who wasn't looking.

'Piece?' I said, but they ignored me.

'You must invite him to tea,' Mummy said.

Hazel and I looked at each, panic stricken. Hazel was so stupid, sometimes. Couldn't she see what she was getting us into?

'I can't,' I said.

'No such word.'

'I mean, I don't know him, not really. He's not my friend. He never speaks to me.'

'He's deaf,' cut in Hazel. 'Don't know why he wears those hideous hearing-aids, they don't do any good.'

'How do you know? Anyway his mum makes him.' Miss Bowen was always telling Puddle-duck to put them back on or she'd write a note.

'Poor little so-and-so.' Mummy retrieved Huwie's spoon again. 'Invite him on Saturday. He can come to play in the garden and stay for tea.'

'But I don't want to play with him!'

'Do it.' Daddy folded his newspaper in quarters with the crossword on top and went off to the toilet.

'Grizzle . . . if he's in that top flat, no garden . . . just think . . .' Mummy's voice was hollow with the pity of it. She stuck a final soldier into Huwie's mouth. 'Just think of him gazing down at you children . . . with this lovely garden. And deaf, too.'

The next morning we didn't see Puddle-duck when we left the house. When Miss Bowen called the register he was not there and I went giddy with relief. If he was absent then I need not invite him, and if we kept quiet about Puddle-duck, if I could make Hazel keep quiet, Mummy might forget all about it. Her enthusiasms, so overwhelming when you were in the thick of them, blew over fast, like tornadoes.

At break-time, I told Elaine. 'Blinking heck,' she said. She'd been to my house many times and knew about my mother.

'*You* come on Saturday,' I pleaded, 'I'll tell her *he* was away and I invited you instead. We can have tea in the tree-house.' Elaine loved our tree-house and our whole untidy house and garden. Her house was on the estate, small and brand new. The front garden was just a lawn with a concrete lip round the edge, not even a wall or hedge, and the back garden was a lawn with a path straight down the middle and a rotary dryer in the middle set in a circle of cement. Our washing-line was hung loopily between trees, uneven, so that the clothes slid down towards the middle and dried all corrugated and spattered with leaves and bird-droppings. Mummy would have loved Elaine's house, every room was a neat rectangle with a big window, sort of *simple*, unlike any single room in our house.

'Please come,' I begged.

'Can't. We're going over to Nanny's.'

'Can't I come?'

'We'd never fit you in.' This was true. Elaine's father had a bubble-car that just the three of them, all fortunately slight, could squeeze into. Once Elaine's dad had driven round to pick her up from our house and Daddy, who had been clipping the hedge, had stood, arms folded, watching it drive away.

'Messerschmitt,' he said.

'What?'

'Cockpit of. Fighter plane. Minus the wings.'

'And the guns,' I added.

It wasn't until Puddle-duck was absent that I realised how aware of him I had been, how much time I had been spending day-dreaming him away. Not that I wanted anything bad to happen to him, but that his mother – the piece – and Vassily would move. Or that he would go to another school. A special school for deaf children where he'd fit in and be happy. Then everyone would be happy.

When I got home from school that afternoon, a woman in orange bell-bottoms was sitting in the kitchen drinking tea.

'Ah, Griselda,' said Mummy, 'this is Wanda, Vassily's mother.'

'Hiya,' I said. She didn't look like anyone's mother to me. Her hair was a big blonde afro – I could see a greenfly trapped in its frizzy ends. She wore white patent-leather platform boots and a cheese-cloth smock over her bell-bottoms, with nothing underneath. I had to keep my eye on the greenfly struggling in her split ends for fear of glimpsing the round dark nipples that showed through the thin material. Mummy seemed not to have noticed, or, at least, not to mind. I looked affectionately at her smooth hair and her neat blue shirt-dress that covered everything so decently – even if it was spattered with Huwie's Ribena.

'Cup of tea?' Mummy indicated the teapot. I shook my head and helped myself to a glass of water.

'So, you're in my Vassily's class, I hear.' Wanda said.

'Yes.' I smiled thinly at her.

'Your mum's invited him round, Saturday.'

'Oh good.' I went over and plucked Huwie from his high-chair. 'I'll take him outside.'

There was a funny dull musty smell surrounding Wanda, the same smell, only fainter, that hung around Puddle-duck. Later I learned that it was patchouli oil.

'Aren't you going to change?' Mummy said. Already Huwie had dribbled on my blazer.

'In a bit.' Mummy gave me a look. 'Oh all right.' I dumped Huwie on her lap.

Upstairs, I ripped off my uniform and flung it on the floor. There was no way out now. How could I play with him? I couldn't bear anyone except Elaine to know. Dressed in an old summer dress, I crept downstairs to the hall and dialled Elaine's number. We had only just had the telephone installed and were supposed to ask before we used it. If Daddy was there he stood and timed us, holding his sleeve up and gazing darkly at his wrist-watch.

'He's coming,' I whispered into the receiver. 'Mum's arranged it with his mum – who's wearing see-through. You can see everything. What shall I do?'

'Nothing,' Elaine said. 'You poor thing. You'll just have to stick it. What can you see?'

'Her bosoms. Ginormous. Promise not to tell anyone else he's coming. I'd die.'

'Cross my heart.'

'On your mother's life?'

'Course.'

I went back into the kitchen. Huw was standing on Wanda's lap grabbing handfuls of her candy-floss hair.

'Is Pud . . . is Vassily ill?' I said.

'Tests,' Wanda said. 'He has to have these tests up King's Lynn, for his ears and that.'

And that. I wanted to ask her about all his nipples. Whether he had to have tests for them.

6

Now I can't give the envelope to Daddy. I never can. Now there is nothing to stop me opening the envelope and reading what's inside. Nothing to stop me knowing. Knowing what? Knowing something about him that I do not know. That I want to know. Do I? Truly? There could be nothing in the envelope anyway, nothing of any significance. What *do* I know about my father?

Born: 10th October 1920, Ralph Harris Dawkins – an only child.

Parents: Harris Edmund and Eugenie May Dawkins – both dead before my birth.

Schooling: don't know – but bright. Oh yes, there's a book of Longfellow's verse awarded to him on Prize Day in 1932. Can't remember the name of the school. West Mersea?

Started reading Classics at Durham but joined up (called up?) in 1940.

Then, I don't know. Prisoner of the Japanese until 1945.

Employment: Civil Service, Ministry of Agriculture. Why didn't he return to university? Don't know.

Marriage: My mother, Astrid Larson, 1948. Astrid the daughter of Professor and Mrs Larson. Mummy has told me about their first meeting. A September afternoon tea-party in the garden of the Larsons' home. Select undergraduates invited. Mummy only twelve, a serious tall girl, with wispy white plaits.

I've seen photographs. This young man with his curling black hair the first man she had ever noticed in *that* way. He talked to her as if she was grown-up and untangled the string of her kite.

Eight years later, they met at a reunion organised by her father. She had never forgotten him. She had been fascinated by the black hairs on his wrists and hands that grew even down the backs of his fingers. Her father was blond and his hands and wrists were smooth. She had another boyfriend then, someone called Patrick who still writes to her occasionally, but when she saw Daddy again, she knew he was the one for her.

Family: Hazel born June 1959; Griselda, December 1960; Huwie, 1969. Why so long before they had the children? Unusual then. Mummy had no intention of having children, she said, and Daddy hadn't felt strongly. She had her work: she's a writer, magazine articles and stories, a couple of light novels, travel books – they travelled whenever they could – Egypt, Canada, frequent trips to Sweden – before we came along. When Mummy said this it made me feel as if we had spoilt their fun. Hazel was a surprise, she said, and Huw a downright accident. But I was planned. They wanted a companion for Hazel, another girl preferably, and, obediently, along I came. It made me smug when I was little to know this, that out of the three of us, only I was chosen. So why was it that I seemed the odd one out? That Hazel looked like Mummy and had this air about her, still has, as if she has a right to be here and that whatever she says or does is correct? And Huwie has always been happy-go-lucky, a cheerful fat baby with a plume of white hair, growing into an affable lanky young man who couldn't care less, I shouldn't think, whether he was planned for or not. But me, why do *I* find life so hard?

But anyway, my father. What else? Various promotions which meant moves from district to district and house to house. Three years at 'The Nook'. Only three? It seems longer. What else? Little. His dreams. His fondness for fiery food and his terrible digestion. His moods. He played golf at every opportunity. He drank whisky and smoked a pipe and, sometimes, cigars. He and my mother played a mean game of bridge, I believe. What else? A handsome face, in photographs, eyes that were very wide and dark, but I only remember his glasses and the way they reflected me back at myself, didn't let me through. I didn't like to see him without his glasses, he looked too exposed, vulnerable. The growling of his electric razor in the mornings. The *Daily Telegraph* that he read in the toilet every morning with Biro scribbles round the edges where he tried out anagrams for his crossword. Cigar smoke hanging like a blue cloud in a lamplit room. Holding on to his legs once, I must have been small, my arms round the two warm tweedy pillars, peering through the gap, and feeling safe. My Daddy. Safe. Did I? Puddle-duck. The time he was so angry with me, over Puddle-duck. Don't think of that now. His tears when the next-door neighbour ran over our cat. No. Did he cry? Surely not. We never had another pet.

So that is him. Oh the little things. One tiny thread attached to another. Could I reconstruct him from the tiny threads? His fear of insects, ants and flies. Not fear, surely, but profound distaste – disgust. The fly-papers in the pantry at 'The Nook'. Fly graveyards. I couldn't bear to look at them. I don't mind insects but I too hate the sound of flies, a filthy whine.

Is there a fly in here? I think I heard a fly, but it has settled. I could not sleep if there really was a fly in here. Foxy has turned over so I cannot see her face. She could sleep through anything. I want to see her face. She is breathing so softly I'm afraid that she will stop. She doesn't dream, she claims, or only rarely. But she must dream. It is just that she sleeps so soundly her dreams are sealed in. She doesn't remember them but they are there. I've seen her dream, her eyes moving beneath their lids, her lips twitching, sometimes a smile, even a chuckle or a squeak of fright. I have never known her to have a nightmare. Because I sleep so badly, maybe, the sleep I do have seems full of dreams, always vivid, often anxious, sometimes bad. I wake up with a scream jammed in my throat like a fist and my heart pounding. But sometimes they are only tedious. I used to recount them to Foxy over breakfast, long sagas of missed trains, strange encounters, falling or losing my keys, or standing on a stage with the curtains opening, the orchestra striking up – and no idea what I was supposed to sing. She used to listen patiently, one eye on the *Guardian*. I try not to bore her with them now – and anyway, I like to save them for work and let Connie, the expert, get her teeth into them. But I wish I knew what was in Foxy's dreams. I wish I could climb into her head and watch them and tell her what I've seen. 'Don't you ever dream about me?' I used to plead before I knew her better.

Her hair feels cool. I could snuggle up to her, mould my fretful body round her warm, solid sleep, soak it up, perhaps catch sleep from her like a bug, breathe in time with her breaths. No, that does not *work*. I cannot hold her because then I would have to be still and I cannot be still. If I buried my face in her hair then I would drown. Not drown, suffocate. What is the matter with me? I must be calm.

Calm! This is the day my father died. I want to cry but it is stuck.

The bar of light from the landing falls diagonally across the bed, across my waist and up to Foxy's shoulders, lighting up strands of her hair. Warm shiny brown. The green sprig pattern on the quilt cover is the only other colour. Everything else is black or grey, the colours leached by the greedy night. Not greedy, Foxy would say, that's a pathetic fallacy. It is only *night*. But Foxy loves the night, loves her sleep. No cars have passed for a long time, when they do pass the lights illuminate the deep pink curtains, a brief glow of rose and then dark again.

If I could have a wish, one wish, what would it be? That Foxy never leaves me, of course. But if I had two wishes, I only ask for two not three, the second wish would be for sleep, not just for tonight, but for the continued ability to sleep. I cannot do it. I cannot sleep a whole night. I don't know why. I don't have the confidence to slip into it. That's what it takes: confidence.

Confidence that you'll wake again and that everything will still be here. Sometimes I sleep for a while but then I wake and once awake, I cannot get back again. It's like trying to sink a plastic duck in a bath, it will not sink, it will bob up to the surface. That is my mind and sleep. It will not sink.

I must get up. The room is stuffy with Foxy's sleep. I need to pee. I'm too hot, woozy. Too much brandy on an empty stomach. I need to drink water and I should eat something. Softly, softly, I move to the edge of the bed, sit up gently, gently, so I do not make the mattress bounce. I put my feet to the floor. My dressing-gown is on the chair. Quietly I walk, soft steps lest the floorboards creak. My hand on the door knob slowly turning, the door opening a crack, yellow light spilling in.

'You all right?' I've woken her.

'Fine, fine,' I slip out, push the door shut, turn the knob slowly so there's not a click. She'll go back to sleep. But I will stay awake.

It's 1:30 by the kitchen clock. Not even late, not for a Friday night, some people still out drinking, dancing, romancing. I drink water from the tap like I did when I was a child, my lips touching the chrome. The floor is cool under my bare feet, cool and a little gritty. It is Foxy's turn to wash the kitchen floor, so it will wait for weeks. She is a terrible slut, my Fox. Washing the floor is something I could do. Tomorrow she will give up most of a day's work to drive me for four or five hours, to my parents', to Mum's rather, house on the windy coast. I wish it was still 'The Nook'. That was the best house. After that we moved several times, but nowhere had a garden like that, nowhere else had a tree-house. When I think of my childhood it seems all to have taken place there, not just three years of it.

When Daddy retired, they moved back to Norfolk to a tall shabby terrace in a village on top of crumbling cliffs. Because of their position, sideways to the sea on a headland, all the windows front and back look out across the cold North Sea. It feels a restless place to me, where sea-birds scream and splatter the roof with their droppings; where the wind never stops blowing and the short grass is bleached and spiked with sea-pinks. They had a fight about the decision to move there, which my mother lost. The sea is eating away at the coast, there are sudden cliff falls where yards of land, ends of gardens, sometimes a cliff-top chalet, are gone, just like that, plunged into the beating sea. My father wouldn't listen to advice, he liked the house, which is in no immediate danger itself. Because of the erosion the price of the house was minimal and that appealed. Also there is a golf-course nearby and more fresh air than anyone could possibly ever want. It does not feel like home.

'A good place for you children to come back to,' Mummy said rather doubtfully, once the move was made. 'A good place for grandchildren.' Which the three of us have failed to produce, so far.

Since Foxy is kind enough to drive me there tomorrow, I'll do the floor. I run hot water into the blue bucket and sprinkle in some Flash. I lift the chairs on to the table and sweep up the crumbs, a paper-clip, a penny, some peanuts and a dead wasp. I don't want a strange and windy coastal home to visit, I want somewhere I have lived. And I want Daddy to be there.

Daddy! When I thought what I would wish for I never asked for him to be alive! I asked for sleep, *sleep*, when my father is dead. And I asked for Foxy. If I had had a wish it should have been for him to be back, for this to be a mistake, all a mistake. I would do anything, give anything, to make him alive again. Would I? Yes, yes. Would I give up Foxy?

No.

I dip the sponge mop in the bucket and slide it across the floor making shiny wet paths across the cork tiles. Here and there a corner is broken and liquid settles in the dips. My nostrils twitch with the clean brisk smell. Not wishing for Daddy to be alive makes it seem that I've already accepted his death, so quickly, so easily. I feel traitorous and tears are on my cheeks, though I am not crying. Remembering Daddy three summers ago on my first visit to the new house. August Bank Holiday. Foxy living it up somewhere else with May. Daddy greeted me wearing a yellow-and-orange flowered shirt, a holiday shirt, short-sleeved and voluminous. I'd never seen him in such a thing before. He was making an effort for *me*. I was the only visitor that weekend but he dressed as if for a holiday, as if for *company*, in a hideously cheerful shirt. It made me cringe. I felt sorry for him, not sorry but . . . seeing him as small somehow. I don't know, but what is the expression? My heart went out to him. Good expression, a sensation like the heart unfolding, unfurling towards him. And is that the same as love? I don't know.

Neat wet stripes. I push the lever and squeeze black water from the sponge into the bucket. *Really*, Foxy, what a disgrace. I should leave the dirty water in the bucket as a reproach. *See* how dirty the floor was. But the floor is clean now and my feet leave prints in the damp, the soles of my feet tacky with detergent. Down the cold concrete stairs to the outside drain. The night air is cold and full of the charry smell of someone's barbecue gone cold. The water gurgles darkly away. And the sky is prickled with stars.

I switch the kettle on for tea. But tea is not what I want. There is something I would like, a comfort drink. I don't know if we have black treacle – but yes, a sticky tin in the back of the cupboard. Posset: one teaspoonful of black treacle stirred into hot milk. I sip it in the sitting-room, curled up on the futon. But it is not the taste of here with its stripped-pine floor, kelims and paper lampshades; it is the taste of a cracked leather Chesterfield you can hide behind and tapestry cushions with fringes you can plait or suck; a carpet you can stretch out on and trace its faded patterns of birds and flowers with your finger-tip.

I do not know what to do. Now I could open the envelope. But it would seem more of a betrayal of confidence than ever. I could burn the envelope unopened. Is that what my principles demand? But curiosity has got its night claws in me. What harm could it do to have a look? What harm now? I should not.

I nibble a piece of cheese from the plate we didn't put away at bedtime. A sliver of Cheddar, a strong taste, male, and then a corner of creamy Brie, its thick white skin velvety between my teeth. Foxy doesn't think you should eat the skin because of the mould but I think it's the best bit. I lick my finger and pick up cracker crumbs. Now I'm hungry. I sandwich two crackers together with Brie and munch, scattering crumbs down my pyjamas. What shall I do? I am startlingly wide awake, more awake than normal daytime awakeness. It is as if I'm wired up. Or like the feverish wakefulness I'd get as a child sometimes, if allowed to stay up late. 'She's over-tired,' Mummy would say, which seemed stupid when I felt so frantically awake – but fragile and very, very likely to cry. Sleep seems like a foreign country now, but there Foxy is and here am I, marooned in the night.

At least the kitchen floor is clean.

There is a pile of mending and ironing for the shop, delicate silk 20s' blouses and camisoles. An orange sateen jacket I bought with Connie in mind.

Or watch TV? I flick through the channels but there's nothing, only a dreary looking film with subtitles. A video? I pick two or three off the shelf, mostly Foxy's, documentaries she's taped, nothing I fancy watching now. Except, except . . . I had forgotten. This is so strange. Weeks ago, I taped it, even though I thought I'd never watch it. I slip the tape into the machine. I was wrong, I will watch it. *The Bridge on the River Kwai*. Nothing could be more stupid or appropriate to watch. I find the beginning, pause it, go into the kitchen for a bottle of wine and some bread and tomatoes to finish the cheese with. I pick up Foxy's woollen sweater from a chair. I loop it round my shoulders for extra warmth. The sleeves hang down on either side of my neck as if someone is holding me. The wool smells sweetly of her and there are long coppery strands of hair tangled in the black.

I settle down to watch. At first I cannot concentrate. The prison camp seems quite civilised, the huts spaced out and clean, the noisy tangle of jungle standing back from the clearing. The Japanese commandant of the camp is harsh but reasonable, vulnerable even. He cries after giving way to Alec Guinness's character. It is Alec Guinness as Colonel Nicholson who is the real danger. He would have himself and his officers shot rather than join in manual labour with the ranks. *Why not?* I shout at the television, then clamp my hand over my mouth. Mustn't disturb Foxy. The volume is low. Yes, Colonel Nicholson's honour is the most dangerous thing, worse than the jungle, or the Japanese who seem mild and humble in comparison. Watching the film makes me angry. Stupid man, with a rod up his back and a bee in his bonnet about a bridge.

Was Daddy an officer? I don't even know *that*. How can I be so ignorant? Not ignorant. But where was my curiosity all those years?

I eat my way furiously through half a loaf of bread and swallow a couple of glasses of red wine.

Then, a funny thing. It is over-tiredness surely, and drink, and the way I am focusing my mind. My eyes are on the television, the tape isn't good, keeps jumping, fizzy lines passing across the screen, but still I can follow it. The American, Shears, with his bronzed muscular chest, has survived an escape and stumbled into a Burmese village where he is treated like a king, decked in a flowered garland with a red-and-white-checked tablecloth tucked decently round his waist.

It is not cold in the room. I'm curled up on the futon with Foxy's thick jumper round me and the fire on. But suddenly *I* am cold. Goose-pimples rise on my arms and the back of my neck. My scalp crawls. There is someone else in the room. I can't move. How do I know someone is here? I don't know. In the room with me is a presence. I keep my eyes on the screen. I am frozen. Then I see him. I am not looking at him and I don't move my eyes but in the corner of my eye, by the bookcase beside the television, I see him. Not him exactly but a thickening of the air that is him. I force breath into my lungs. I dare not move my eyes or even blink. I don't want to frighten him away but I am frightened. Very, very slowly and slightly I turn my head and for a moment I do see him. Not his body but the essence of him and I smell his pipe smoke and spicy aftershave.

'Daddy,' I whisper.

He is standing by the bookcase, one hand – or where one hand would be – is on the top of some books.

'Daddy,' I say, not a whisper this time. My mind is scrambling. This is my chance to speak to him, to say good-bye. What should I say? What is the most profound thing to say? I love you, it should be. But I cannot quite . . . 'Daddy . . .'

He is gone. The chill is gone, the sense of a presence, the tenseness in the air, gone. 'Dad!' I call. But I know that that is it. I will not see him again.

And I said nothing.

I get up and go to where he was standing. I sniff the air but even the smell of him has not lingered. It feels as if life had stopped, was suspended for an instant and has restarted. Everything is ordinary.

The television seems louder. The soldiers are whistling 'Colonel Bogey'. I can't hear that without the rude words coming into my head. *Hitler had only got one ball, the other is in the Albert Hall. His mother, the dirty bugger, cut it o – off, when he – e was small.* When I used to sing it I didn't know what it meant. Ball? Or who Hitler was even. I thought it was to do with cricket. Elaine's mother smacked her for singing it.

Daddy has gone. The wave rises and I clutch thin air. A hot tear rolls down my cheek. I haven't started on the crying yet, the crying that surely there must be. I stand where Daddy stood, one hand on top of the books. My tongue catches the tear and draws it into my mouth. Hot salt. It is the only one. My hand is just where I think his hand was, on a book too big to go on the shelf vertically, that lies horizontally on top. And then I understand. His hand was resting on the Atlas where I left the envelope last time I looked at it. I had been looking at the buff and green page that was South-East Asia, a sprawling land-mass surrounded by grey ocean and pale lacy island trails.

The door opens suddenly and I cry out with fright and drop the Atlas. But it is only Foxy. She is tying the belt of her dressing-gown.

'You all right?' She comes to me. 'I thought I heard you shout.'

'You must have been dreaming.'

'No . . .' She looks at me curiously. 'What are you watching? Oh . . .' She recognises the film and pulls a face. Jack Hawkins limps along on a bloody foot, nubile young Burmese women fluttering around.

'Did I wake you? I'm sorry.' I pick up the Atlas and return it to the shelf, the fat envelope is tucked down the side of the bookcase. She puts her arms around me. She is all warm and silky, I rub my face in her hair.

'I shouldn't have gone to sleep and left you.' She squeezes my waist.

'It's all right, Fox, honestly.'

She yawns. 'Shall I make some coffee or something? Want to talk?'

'What I want is for you to get your beauty sleep. You need it.'

'Cow!' She pinches my waist and laughs. 'Sure you're all right alone?'

'Absolutely.'

'Is that my marching orders then?'

We kiss. One side of her face is all creased from the crumpled pillow, there are smudges of mascara under her eyes. She eyes the bottle on the table.

'Only a couple of glasses,' I say.

'You don't want to be hung over.'

'No.'

'Later then.' She closes the door behind her. Part of me yearns to join her in her sleepiness; to get lost in her soft skin and the fragrance of her hair. But that simply cannot be. And I cannot talk to her now. I will tell her about the envelope, everything. But now I have to be alone. To think about Daddy. But thinking about Daddy always makes me think about Puddle-duck. I should not call him that. Vassily. A man now. He may be at the funeral. No. Could he be? The funeral. I had not even thought. That must be arranged. Suicide. What happens when someone commits suicide? Is there a normal funeral? Daddy . . . why? No, no, NO. I cannot think of that.

7

Puddle-duck came to play on Saturday, as planned. He wore his school uniform. I could hardly believe it. On a *Saturday*! I was wearing jeans with flowery triangular inserts to make them look like bell-bottoms. Hazel had Bridget round. I could have killed her. I *told* Mummy not to let her come but she said 'The more the merrier – invite Elaine too if you like. You could have a tea-party.' 'She's at her Nan's,' I said, grumpily reflecting that Mummy had simply *no idea*. Tea-party! With Bridget and Puddle-duck!

'Bridget'll tell everyone we had Puddle-duck here,' I hissed to Hazel.

'*Who* had Puddle-duck here? Not me.' She tossed her head. Hazel had the sort of hair that always falls in the right place, fair, smooth and shiny, so when she smugly tossed her head, her hair went smugly back into place. Hazel's hair was just like Mummy's, only shorter, and Mummy cut it for her with a long fringe and the rest hanging beautifully just below her ears. 'It's a *dream* to cut,' she'd say, pausing between snips with the silver scissors splayed, and Hazel would smile at me with narrowed eyes. Hazel wasn't *pretty*, I'd rather have died than said that, but she had blue eyes and what Mummy called *regular features*, all of them neat and small. My hair was wiry and brown, not exactly curly but not straight either so that when she cut it Mummy was always tutting and frowning at me with her head on one side.

'I feel like the Ugly Duckling,' I said once, meaning for Mummy to deny it and call me pretty.

But, 'Never mind,' she said, giving me an annoying hug. 'You know what ugly ducklings have a habit of doing when they grow up.'

Hazel who wasn't supposed to hear, had heard, and on the way to school for weeks she would sing. *'There once was an ugly duckling, with feathers all tattered and torn'*, and Bridget would sing it too in a stupid American whine.

When Puddle-duck arrived, Hazel and Bridget were already up in the tree-house. Mummy had decided to bake some cakes and Puddle-duck stood in the kitchen gazing at her as she weighed flour. 'Grizzle, take Vassily out to play,' she said. I knew what would happen and I was right. The moment we were outside there were giggles from the tree-house, the creak of movement, Hazel playing 'The Ugly Duckling' on her recorder and then wolf-whistles.

Puddle-duck, who had taken his hearing-aids off and left them on the kitchen table, heard none of this, of course, and he stood looking round the garden with an expression of stupid wonder on his face. Every so often he'd catch my eye and smile expectantly as if I was suddenly supposed to produce *fun*.

I went back into the kitchen. Mummy didn't look up, she had the tip of her tongue caught anxiously between her teeth as she rolled up a strawberry jam Swiss roll. Daddy had just returned from a game of golf and was foraging in the fridge.

'I don't know what to do with him,' I complained. 'And Hazel and Bridget are being *foul* up in the tree-house. Teasing us. Teasing *him*.' I thought that would bother her, but I didn't expect Daddy to react. Usually he took no notice of us and our squabbles. But now he pushed past me into the garden. I followed him. There was a sudden silence from the tree-house.

'Hazel,' Daddy's voice was stern.

'What?'

'Could you come down and let Griselda and her pal up there.'

There was a stifled guffaw from Bridget, 'Pal!' Hazel shushed her.

'Would you like to?' Daddy smiled at Puddle-duck and pointed up at the tree-house, a question in his face.

'Yes,' Puddle-duck answered in his loud spongy voice, 'please.'

'It's my turn today. We're all set up,' came Hazel's voice. 'Isn't it, Grizzle? My turn.'

Daddy looked at me. I shrugged. There was no such arrangement, I only knew that if Hazel had Bridget round the tree-house was automatically hers and I wasn't allowed in. I should have backed her up but I was too interested in seeing what Daddy would do.

'I don't care,' he said. 'Griselda's visitor would like to look round.'

'*My* visitor is looking round,' Hazel said. I held my breath. How *dare* she cheek Daddy like that? She was only showing off in front of Bridget.

'I have said come down.' Daddy's voice wasn't loud but it was very dangerous. This had never happened before because Daddy never got involved.

'I'd leave them to it, Ralph,' said Mummy from the kitchen doorway.

'Down!' Daddy repeated. I suddenly wanted to laugh. He was looking up at the tree-house as if at a massive and disobedient dog. 'Down!' Puddle-duck's head was swivelling backwards and forwards between Daddy and the tree.

After a moment, the hatch opened and the rope ladder flopped and swung to the ground. Bridget came down first, blowing a rude gum-bubble at me, and then Hazel. She had red marks on the backs of her thighs where she'd been sitting on the crumpled rug. Hazel didn't look at me or Daddy but stalked past towards the kitchen door.

'Upstairs,' Daddy said.

'But . . .'

'Bridget can go home now.'

Hazel tossed her head as she went in but I could see the brilliant red of the backs of her ears.

Mummy, in the doorway, let Hazel past and then stood frowning at Daddy. She had flour in her hair that made her seem old. The happy smell of fresh cakes floated out and I felt sorry for Hazel. I could see that Mummy wanted to object: *she* would never have sent Bridget home, but she didn't let herself. She pursed her lips at me, then went back into the kitchen and shut the door.

'Up you go then, Vassily.' Daddy held the ladder still for him. I watched. Daddy never did this, took any notice of our friends, took any part in our activities. I'd hardly ever seen him so much as looking at Huw, even though he was so utterly sweet, and yet here he was helping Puddle-duck up the ladder, pulling it taut so it didn't swing about too much while the skinny yellowish legs in their long grey shorts climbed up. When Puddle-duck had disappeared through the trap-door, Daddy nodded to me to go up. He didn't hold the ladder still for *me*. But it didn't matter, I was used to it.

'Your mother will send up some cake,' he said. From the window I watched him go back into the kitchen. He would go up the stairs to our bedroom where Hazel would be waiting, her head held very high. She would not be crying, even if her face was very pink, she was much better at not crying than me. I looked at the bedroom window and thought I saw the oval of her face between the curtains, then it was gone. I could not imagine what Daddy would do or say to her. I liked television programmes, especially American programmes, where the mother says to her naughty children 'Just wait till your father gets home.' I thought there was something thrilling about that. Not that I wanted to have it said to me. Daddy was not like one of those television fathers. His anger was too deep and unknown.

Puddle-duck was hauling up the rope ladder, the way Hazel and I did. We'd haul it right up and put a sheet of wood over the trap-door so that we were unassailable. I was annoyed at the way he did it: the eager familiarity, as if he had been *just waiting* to do it. How does he know what to do? I thought. But looking out of the other window I knew. It was because he watched us, spied on us.

'Spy.' I accused, pointing to the window. He nodded vigorously. I don't know what he thought I'd said. When he'd settled the piece of wood over the trap-door, he sat down on the branch and gave me an expectant smile. What was I supposed to do with him? In the enclosed space I could smell Wanda's horrible clinging perfume.

I had an idea. I might as well get something out of this. 'The alphabet,' I said, stretching my mouth enormously round the separate syllables. 'A.B.C.'

He had such a narrow face that his grin was somehow shocking. But I also saw in it an impishness, the sort of thing that might be likeable, even lovable – if you were his mother.

With one index finger he pressed the ball of his other thumb. 'A,' he said in his tuneless way. He made finger and thumb circles and pressed them together to look like a pair of glasses. 'B,' he said. He made a cusp of his thumb and forefinger and held it up to me. 'C.' It was logical and absorbing. For a few minutes I forgot that I hated him. If I could learn to speak in deaf language I might teach it to Elaine and then we could talk in front of Hazel without her understanding. It would drive her mad. That reminded me of Hazel and I looked out to see that the bedroom curtains had been drawn.

The back door opened and Huwie crawled out followed by Mummy with a plate. She walked down the garden to the foot of the tree.

'Grizzle, Vassily, provisions,' she called, 'you'll have to come down Griz.'

I moved the wood and swung down the ladder. 'It's no good

calling *Vassily* like that, he's stone deaf,' I said, taking the plate of cakes.

'I know,' she said, 'but it seems only polite.'

'Is Hazel having any?'

'Later.'

'What's Daddy doing to her?'

'Really! Nothing.' She pretended to laugh, 'Just having a word.' She looked away and I knew that she had no more idea than I had. We both watched Huwie who had pulled himself to his feet and stood wobbling, looking at the ground as if daring himself to take a step. Then he plumped down on to his nappied bottom and sucked his big toe instead. I laughed.

'He'll be walking soon,' Mummy said, 'then just wait!' She spoke with a sort of proud exasperation. She picked Huwie up. 'Come in when you want a drink.' She closed the back door behind her.

I climbed up the ladder one-handed, balancing the plate on my other hand. There were four slices of strawberry jam Swiss roll and two butterfly cakes with little jelly lemons stuck in the buttercream. I didn't bother to pull the ladder back up.

Puddle-duck took a butterfly cake. He pulled off the lemon and ate that first, then the crumbly sponge butterfly wings, then he scooped the buttercream out and sucked it noisily off his finger. I ate mine properly to show him how. But he was looking past me at my formicary.

'Ants,' I said, and wiggled my fingers about. 'Want to look?'

I knelt down and lifted the lid from the tank. There weren't many ants out and you couldn't see much. I prodded the nest with my finger and at once it was crawling with them. The longer you looked, the more you saw. 'Watch,' I said. I dropped a jammy corner of Swiss roll on to the ramp. At first nothing happened and Puddle-duck started to fidget; then news spread and first one or two and then many ants scurried towards the cake, swarming over it until it made your eyes go funny. Puddle-duck gave a loud excited laugh.

I looked out of the window to see if Hazel was out yet, but could see nothing. The bedroom curtains were still closed and Mummy had shut the door to keep Huwie in.

'Look!' Puddle-duck shouted.

The ants had started dismantling the cake, lugging ragged boulders of crumbs down to the nest. Puddle-duck was jumping around so excitedly I thought he'd knock the tank over. He shrieked and a warm bit of his spit landed on my cheek, I scrubbed it off with my fist. It was only spit but it felt like acid. I put the lid back on the formicary.

'Down,' I said. I climbed down first and waited at the bottom for Puddle-duck who clung weedily to the rungs of the swaying ladder, cake crumbs stuck in the corners of his mouth.

We went into the kitchen. Mummy was washing up and Huwie was sitting in his high-chair cramming fistfuls of cake into his mouth. He looked like a little chick with his fluffy hair standing on end. His cheeks were rough and scarlet from teething. Puddle-duck went to stand by Huwie, gently stroking his hair.

'What's his name?' he asked, pointing at Huwie and brushing his forehead.

'Huw,' Mummy wiped her hands on a tea-towel and put her face close to Puddle-duck's. 'Huw,' she said closing her lips around the word as if she was going to kiss him.

'Who,' Puddle-duck tried.

Mummy smiled and shook her head. She said it again, this time emphasising the two sounds, 'He-oo,' and this time Puddle-duck got it right and Huwie crowed and waggled his cakey fingers.

'Would you like to hold him?' Mummy asked, gesturing first to Huw and then to Puddle-duck. Puddle-duck did his face-splitting grin and sat down in readiness. Mummy pulled Huw out of his high-chair and put him on Puddle-duck's lap.

He held Huwie very stiffly round the middle as if he was
a parcel. Huwie looked so much brighter than Puddle-duck
and his head seemed almost as big with its fat red cheeks.
Mummy poured two mugs of milk. I took another piece
of the Swiss roll. It was filled with home-made strawberry
jam that looked disgusting, brown and lumpy and nothing
like shop jam – but tasted good. I didn't want to look at
Huwie on Puddle-duck's lap. It made me go all squirmy
inside. I'd had more than enough of Puddle-duck for one
day – or for ever. I wanted him to go home now. I'd been
nice to him and now I wanted to be alone to read, or to
do anything. I wanted to go back into the tree-house by
myself and pull up the ladder and read my comic or watch
the ants.

Daddy came into the kitchen then. 'Tea?' he said.

'Kettle's there,' Mummy said, keeping her eyes averted. This
is how they argued, not in shouts but by hardly speaking,
by not looking at each other, by the grate of frost in every
interaction.

'What happened?' I asked Hazel later. Puddle-duck had finally
gone home and we were watching 'Doctor Who'. She was lying
full length on the leather sofa and I didn't dare ask her to move
up which left me with the scratchy armchair or the floor. I'd
chosen the floor.

'About what?' she said.

'You know, Daddy.'

'Nothing.'

'Something must have.'

'He just told me off.'

'Is that *all*.'

She glared at me. I saw that she was flushed and her eyes
looked puffy, as if she'd been crying. Although she drove me
so mad with her smug friends and her smug hair I didn't like
to think that she'd been crying. But Daddy never told us off.
He never got involved.

'It wasn't my fault,' I said.

'Don't have Puddle-duck round again.'

'It wasn't me. It was Mummy. She asked him, not me.'

'Don't have him round here again.'

'Who says?'

'Just don't.' Hazel could make her voice go very quiet and cold like pebbles dropping down a well.

'How can I stop him?'

Hazel frowned at the television. 'Make him not want to come,' she said.

'Oh *yes*. How am I supposed to do that?'

'*I* don't know. Hurt him. Or frighten him.'

'Hurt him. But how?'

'Easy peasy Japanesy,' she said, looking away.

'If it's so easy peasy tell me how.'

'Don't be pathetic,' she said. 'Just do it.'

That night, Daddy had one of his dreams. The scream ripped my sleep open and left me trembling. Hazel burrowed her head under the pillow and pretended to be asleep. I lay wide awake, my thumb in my mouth, my heart hammering so hard it hurt. I could hear more sounds, something like a man crying. But it could have been wind and rain moaning round the roof. I could hear Mummy padding about, a sigh as she went past our door, her feet on the stairs, the bathroom taps running, the toilet flushing, doors clicking, and, finally, quiet again. I lay at the edge of my bunk, leaning out a bit so I could see the red glow of the night-light in the corner, all patchy where Hazel had stuck bubble-gum stickers over the spots, and thought about what she'd said. Hurt him or frighten him. How could I? I couldn't. Hurt Puddle-duck? I could not do it. But although I never could, the thought stirred inside me. Deep down in my stomach I felt a sort of tightness, a sort of excitement but very dull and muffled. Because you don't

57

deliberately hurt or frighten people, that is what I'd been brought up to believe and the belief had soaked right through me. Was part of me. Hurt Puddle-duck? I could not do it.

8

The bridge is blown up. I knew, of course, that it would be, because I've seen it before. Good. Is that the right response? What a bloody stupid film. Anything to do with my father? It is only a story. But did he help build a bridge like that? Not like Alec Guinness at all, don't know where I got that idea from, more like Jack Hawkins, black hair when he was young, a widow's peak, thick-set. But not much like Jack Hawkins either. Why should he look like anyone?

I switch the television off and rewind the video, listening to the whirring that grows in volume like an aircraft preparing for take-off, then a click and quiet. The quiet is a relief.

I could take it that Daddy wants me to look at the papers. That's why he appeared, that's why he rested his hand in the place where they are. I could take that as my excuse to pry. Pry! How Foxy would scoff. It wouldn't be prying. If Daddy was really here that *could* have been what he was indicating. If he really was here. The idea makes me go cold again. I don't believe in ghosts. But there was *something* and it did not come from me. I did not summon Daddy up. I wasn't even thinking about him. I never would have thought to summon up that smell, his spicy, pipe smoke smell. Not a ghost because I do *not* believe in ghosts. But maybe a good-bye visit.

I could have said *I love you.*

It was my chance.

I could ring my mother and tell her I'm going to open the envelope. But it's half-past two. I cannot ring her now. What if she is sleeping? And she'd only say, 'Whatever you like.' Or pretend not to know what I mean, *what envelope?* She doesn't want anything to do with waking the sleeping dogs. If I took the envelope, unopened, with me tomorrow and suggested that we look inside together, she would not want to. What's inside might upset her and then she would blame me. It might make her angry, it might cause a rift between us just when we should be drawing close.

I open the Atlas again. South-East Asia. Burma. On the map it looks quite innocuous. Area: 261,789 square miles; Population: 20,500,000; Capital: Rangoon. Geographical facts. The shape of it, a frill at the bottom that is the Mouths of the Irrawaddy. I strain my eyes to find the River Kwai, I cannot find it in Burma or in Thailand. It is not there, or if it is, it's too insignificant to mark. Scale: 1 inch to 158 miles. Think what life is taking place within each flat square inch – the loving and the fighting; the birthing and the dying; the screams of birds. All those beating hearts. Staring at the grid of fine black squares that mesh the page I feel quite dizzy at the concentration of life they represent.

The tape on the flap of the envelope has gone brittle with age. It is hardly stuck down, easy to remove. But the flap is stuck fast, old glue, old spit, it will not come up. I slit it with the cheese knife, stupidly, in a rush now, and cut my thumb.

He does not want me to open it. Funny if it was nothing but bills or . . . old love letters . . . or money? I stop. Money? Some sort of crime, hence the secrecy?

Blood is running down my thumb, not a bad cut, a little flap beside my nail. My imagination is running away with me. What do I think he is, was? A great train robber? The sort of cut that stings and catches. I lick away the blood and suck my thumb. The memory of comfort conjured up by the sensation is acute, the ball of my thumb, nestling in the ridged hollow behind my upper teeth. The rhythmic suck comes automatically back though

TEASE

I haven't done it for – twenty years? My mother never minded me sucking my thumb. My father wouldn't have noticed, but my Swedish grandfather would scold, tell my mother to smother it in mustard, warn that I'd ruin my teeth. But my teeth are perfectly fine. Nice teeth. Straight. Nicer than Hazel's actually. Oh get to the point, Zelda. The taste of blood. Get on with it.

I slip my hand into the manila envelope and pull out a letter and a further envelope, foolscap but folded round its smaller wad of contents. I put this aside and with my thumb back in my mouth, I read the letter:

Dear Ralph,

You will no doubt have me down as an abject coward when you have read this. You have my absolute permission to think ill of me, to think what you like.

I have done wrong by you 3 times. You entrusted me with a parcel of papers when I was moved from Kanburi to Tarsao thinking they would be safer with me since the Japs were turning the camp over. When we met in London that once in 1948 you expected me to hand over the diaries. I told you that they'd been found and confiscated by guards at Tarsao. I lied. It turns out, Ralph, to be as hard to confess this by letter, and, I hope, from beyond the grave as it were, as it would have been to do so to your face.

Bear in mind I was utterly demoralized and degraded. Literally demoralized. Suffering from dysentery on top of Malaria I was very far gone. The fact is I was so humiliated by the filth of my body that I used every possible means to clean myself up. I know you will understand at least that much, that you experienced illness of at least the same degree. I used much of your diary as lavatory paper, Ralph. I have no excuse. It was a diabolical thing to do when you had trusted it to my safe keeping. I thought I would not survive, possibly you would not survive, and thus it would be of no significance.

I am sorry. Would that I had had more self-control. That was my first wrong.

The second was in my lie to you: that the papers had been found and confiscated, a plausible fabrication, so much so that I almost became convinced of it myself.

The third and greatest wrong, and one that I could put right, even now but out of cowardice I will not, is of not confessing to you face to face, not giving you these remaining scraps. Even as a mature man, a man of God, I cannot face this test. It is my greatest failure of nerve. I have done wrong by myself in this, Ralph. For I have been unable to seek your forgiveness and will die, still with my guilt weighing me down.

My memory of you is of a brave man. I know how you suffered in your soul over the Vince business. I wish it had been possible to talk and to pray with you. I do pray that you found peace with yourself. I do not think you did wrong.

I pray you will find it in your heart to forgive me.

Yours sincerely,

Benjamin Priest

I fold the thin blue paper and put it down on top of the envelope. I walk about the room. My back aches, I've been sitting cramped forward with my shoulders hunched. I need someone to rub my shoulders, Foxy with her fierce fingers, probing so deep it hurts as it helps. It is all so horrible I want to laugh. My father's diary used as lavatory paper. So mundanely tragic. This man, this Reverend Priest suffering a lifetime of guilt for *that*. I am almost glad Daddy will never know. Would *he* have laughed? He would have forgotten about the diaries, I'm sure. This farcical confession would only bring it all back. Bring what back? The Vince business? What's that? His dreams? I do not think they ever went away, not for more than a few weeks at a time. What was it that was in his dreams?

I am glad not to have to show him the letter.

Now the Reverend Priest can never be forgiven.

Would Daddy have forgiven him?

How can I know? I do not, did not know him. And he: did he know me?

He knew the woman who visited, in disguise. I never wore my own sort of clothes home. Normally I dress in period gear from the shop. Right now, I favour 40s' stuff – fifty years celebrated in Second Hand Rose. My favourite dress is a navy-and-white rayon knee-length number with a belted waist and white buttons down the bodice. I wear it with fake pearl beads and Cuban heels and my hair sausage-rolled round my head. I like the way people stare: older women stop me sometimes to tell me how I take them back.

But for going home I've always chosen something classy but nondescript. You could not read *me* by my clothes. Well-cut slacks, lambswool sweaters in navy or camel, tidy silver studs in my ears, hair dried smooth as it will go. Lipstick, just a dab of pink. It is not just for appearances or to fool them. It is not *just* a masquerade. Those sensible clothes make me sensible. Make me the sort of daughter I think they would like me to be. Of course, I should not be running a shop. I should be a solicitor, like Hazel, or a teacher, at least. Mummy sees me here when she visits, she knows more, sees more, in any case, I think, could see through me. Though she doesn't say much her eyes are very piercing. But Daddy: all Daddy knows is what he sees. Saw.

I did so want him to be pleased with me. I nearly married once. Daddy would have approved if I had married Guy. He was the right sort of man: an architect, well spoken, quite – but not too – handsome.

I thought I was in love with him. The love blossomed up in my heart whenever we sat, together with my parents, round the table and Daddy laughed at one of Guy's jokes, or Guy leant respectfully forward to listen to Daddy's advice. I felt approved of, grown-up, included. But when we were alone . . . At first it was good. We bought a flat in Highbury. Guy had the roof converted to a garden with a sun-lounge and Astro-turf where we could sunbathe naked, visible only to helicopters and low-flying planes. But I grew bored with Guy. I knew it when I found myself obsessively inviting people round to dinner or organising outings. The prospect of a weekend at home with only the two of us appalled me. 'We're never alone,' he'd complain, and when I caught myself mentally adding, 'Thank God', I knew it was over.

I could never have taken Foxy home to sit at the table with Daddy. I have never loved a person like I love Foxy. It is so intense . . . I don't think I would wish to love like this again.

If Foxy was gearing up to finish with me tonight then I have had a reprieve. Poor Daddy. One effect of his . . . he could not have foreseen. If she was going to finish with me then she still will. I must not be complacent. As if I ever could where she is concerned. She will have to wait now. How long . . . weeks? months? till after Christmas? till I am 'over it' whenever that might be?

Over it? I don't think I have started it yet. He is not really dead to me yet. And until then, how can I grieve?

When I have a nightmare Foxy holds me and soothes me, her voice gentle in my hair. She holds me until the fear has begun to subside, until I feel too hot and then, although I still want to be held, I move away to my side of the bed. In the worst nightmares I kill people. I do it carelessly, without thinking much about it and then I realise. Often the person I kill is a child. Sometimes I carry the dead child with me for a time, even dressing it, bathing it, tucking it into bed, until I realise that it is dead, that I killed it, and that is when I wake with the fist-in-my-throat attempt to scream.

Although Foxy is so lovely in the night about my nightmares, she does not want to hear about them in the morning. She'll listen if I insist on telling her, but when I start trying to work out the meanings she gets snappy. Dreams mean nothing, she says, it's just waste electricity crackling about in your brain.

So now Connie and I swap dreams over our morning coffee. I recounted to her one of the child-killing dreams. I said: 'It is a warning, I must not have a child.' But no. She said that the child represented an aspect of myself. 'What aspect?' I asked. She pinched her cigarette-holder between her lips and leafed through her dream book. 'A part of your psyche you have discarded or should discard,' she said, which gave me something to think about.

*

One night, after one of Daddy's dreams, I got up. Hazel was at a pyjama party at Bridget's house so I was sleeping in her bunk which she hated me to do. 'You make it smell,' she always said, if she realised, but I did *not* and I never ate biscuits in her bed so there were no crumbs for her to complain about. I preferred the top bunk anyway, but I liked to sleep in Hazel's bed when she wasn't there. I don't know why. The scream was not so loud from the bottom bunk but it woke me all the same and for a second I could not think where I was, could not think what the dark thing looming above me – the top bunk – was. The scream yanked me from a deep sleep into a sweaty trembling wakefulness. Because I was alone I got out of the bed. I went and stood by the night-light. I picked one of Hazel's stickers from a white spot. Quietly, I opened the door and peered out on to the landing. I could hear Daddy's voice. He wasn't screaming now, he was making a high, soft, keening noise. I could hardly believe it was his voice – but there was no one else whose voice it could have been. The noise fluctuated, as if he was rocking back and forth. I was shivering and had a feeling like acid eating up my stomach. I had to go to the toilet. I crept out on to the landing and across to the bathroom. In the mirror I looked very white and old. Mummy came in. 'What are you doing?' she said. She sounded very angry. 'Back to bed.' 'I need a pee,' I said. 'Bed.' She wet a flannel under the cold tap and wrung it out hard so that her knuckles stood out. 'Bed, I said.' She picked up a towel and pointed towards my bedroom. She had big brown semicircles under her eyes like bruised smiles.

I went back to my room and stood by the door. I could not believe that she could do that. Make me go back to bed when I needed the toilet. It wasn't fair. It wasn't right. It would be all her fault if I wet the bed. But I could not get back into bed. I felt swollen to twice my size with indignation, but filled too with a sickly excitement. I looked out of the door again, but at that moment Daddy lurched out on to the landing. He was wearing only pyjama trousers tied with a white cord, but the fly was gaping open and I saw, for the first and only time, his penis, like a big squashy purple acorn. I shrank back into the room and leaned against the door. His face had been purple too, and wet, his brown eyes without spectacles wild and wide like a madman's. He had not seen me. I could hear him in the bathroom being sick, then Mummy's voice again and water running.

I crept back into Hazel's bed. I could not get the sight or the sound of him out of my head. I lay with my thumb in my mouth waiting for everything to settle again so that I could go and pee. I noticed pencil marks on the wall beside Hazel's pillow. I squinted closer: it was a list of dates written in tiny writing, faintly in pencil, stretching back over the past two years. I didn't understand what they were for, completely random dates, except two were the same, two December 24ths, but all the others were random, about seven or eight a year.

I heard Mummy go downstairs. I knew she would be fetching the whisky for Daddy. Maybe to help him get back to sleep. Nothing could help *me*. I got out of bed and put on the big light – at least I could do that with Hazel away. But I missed her being there, her breathing, her cross presence in the bunk below me to keep me still.

'You're not allowed to write on the walls,' I said to her during an argument.

'I haven't.'

'Have.'

'Haven't.'

'What about by your bed?'

'You've been in it again, haven't you, when I was at Bridget's. I knew you had. It stinks.'

'Doesn't.'

'I hate you. I wish I had my own room. When I'm twelve I'm *making* Mummy let me have my own room where you won't be allowed in, ever.'

'I'm telling about you writing on the wall.'

'Don't care.'

'Am.'

'*Tell tale tit, your mother can't knit, your father can't walk without a walking stick.*' She stuck her fingers in her ears.

'They're your mother and father too.' She was humming, a high-pitched sound, pretending she couldn't hear. 'If you tell me why you wrote those dates I won't tell,' I shouted in a voice she must have heard. But she stamped out of the bedroom and slammed the door.

Later, I heard her in the kitchen talking to Mummy. '*When* can I have my own room? We've got lots of rooms. Why can't I now?'

'When we get round to decorating.'

'I hate Grizzle.'

'No you don't.'

'I do.' She went out to the tree-house then. I watched her flounce down the lawn and up the ladder, then the ladder jerking violently up through the trap-door. I thought of telling Mummy about the writing on the wall, but I didn't. I lay down on Hazel's bed instead and ran my finger over the pencilled dates.

9

The night is deep. Three o'clock is the deepest time. Night-time is like a lake that must be swum, a vast, deep, black lake. For the first few hours there's still the light behind you from the shore you've left, drifting music or voices perhaps, still the comfort of other presences. And later towards dawn, there's the sense of a community ahead, lights flicking on, radios, early buses trundling along the shore. But in between there is the cold swallowing dark in which you can be lost, in which either shore is too hopelessly far behind, too far ahead. It is no wonder that people die most often, in the small mean hours, the lost hours of the night.

My toes are cold. I sit on the floor in front of the gas-fire hugging my legs, feeling the satin of my white pyjamas warming, reflecting orange back at the flames. On the video, the dots between the 3 and 03 flash on and off, on and off. There is no ticking. I would like a ticking clock, a clock with a pendulum that swings, one that you wind up with a key. A chiming clock. A chiming clock would be a friend in the night.

I should go to bed, snuggle in with Foxy. The fat envelope is on the table. I could wake Foxy, she might not mind. She might get up and we could open the envelope together and know whatever there is to know.

This is a special night. This is the night following the day on which my father died. This night will never come again.

I *will* not sleep. I will keep vigil on this night. Keep watch. But for what? It was yesterday he died. And since he died how many others – in this country, in this continent, in this world – how many others have died after him? And how many have been born? How many conceived? All the stopping and starting of souls.

The telephone. It makes me jump. It cannot ring at this time of night. Swiftly I cross the room and pick it up with a hand that is slippery with sweat.

'Grizzle?' It is Hazel, her voice thick with tears. 'I can't sleep, thinking. I knew *you* would be awake.' She sobs into the phone. Answering tears come to my eyes. I don't know what to say. 'I keep thinking of him . . . doing it . . .' she sniffs and gulps out the words, 'Whatever was in his head?'

'I haven't even thought of that,' I say. The telephone is wet as if her tears are running from it, welling out of the regular pepper-pot pattern of holes. 'I've been thinking more about the past.'

'Why do you have to say *commit* suicide? It's always commit isn't it? Commit suicide, you can't say suicide without saying commit. I said it to Colin, Daddy's committed suicide . . .', she wails as she hears herself say it. I can feel her grief in the room with me summoning mine. 'He did love us, didn't he?' she pleads.

'I don't know,' I say. 'Haze, I don't know.'

'I thought he was here,' she says.

'What? Me too.'

'He was in the room . . . I sort of sensed him, of course Colin says I'm projecting but *I* know. Do you know what I said, Grizzle? I said, "I love you."'

'I couldn't say that.'

'And then he was gone.'

'I couldn't say it.'

'Of course Colin doesn't believe me.'

'I've been thinking about the tree-house.'

'But then he didn't see.'

'And Puddle-duck.'

'Poor Mummy.'

'And how he used to scream at night.'

'Poor Mummy. *She* found him. Imagine *that* Grizzle, finding him like that.'

'How I could never sleep.'

'And poor us.' Her voice chokes up again. I hear her blow her nose. 'What are we going to do without him?'

We cry on the phone for a minute or two. No words, just sobs and gulps travelling the wires between York and Durham. I hear Colin in the background urging Hazel back to bed. I sniff hard. This can't go on all night. 'I'm glad you rang,' I say.

'I feel so alone.'

'You've got Colin.'

'Yes but . . .'

'I know.'

'Is Sybil . . .?'

'She's being wonderful. But . . . I feel alone too.'

'See you tomorrow old bean.'

'Try and get some sleep.'

'Night-night Grizzle.'

I cry for a bit standing and then sitting. I wipe my nose on my pyjama sleeve. I am glad she rang. Even though our childhood was one long competition, one long fight, Hazel is still my sister. We share something no one else can share, something that cannot be said, that we cannot say, an understanding of what was in and what was *not* in our lives . . . of what was underlying but . . . Oh it is not explicable. It is frustrating. You cannot know what you never had. Oh shut-up! I had a happy childhood. What the hell am I whining on about?

And there is another feeling in me that I can hardly believe and will not credit. A little wormy feeling of jealousy that he visited her too, that I wasn't singled out. How can I be so . . . *ghastly*? I will not feel it. But if I am feeling that it must mean I believe he

70

really did visit us, after his death. That there is something, some sort of existence after death. Must it? No, no, no . . . hang on a minute . . . Or?

Hazel knows about Puddle-duck too, what we did. *I*. What *I* did.

I pour another glass of wine. It tastes delicious: red velvet against the salt taste of my tears. On the envelope is a smear of blood from my cut thumb. The cut has sealed itself down now like the envelope flap: a narrow red V. I open the inner envelope at last, and, my fingers only trembling the slightest bit, pull out a wad of thin papers and with them a smell of age and grime. The small rectangles are covered in writing, unbelievably minute writing, fuzzy graphite, too smudged and small to read. It must be possible. Not all rectangles, many of the papers are lacy at the edges with holes as if something has been eating them. They make my hands feel soiled. I spread them out on the carpet in front of the fire, grubby, soft, yellowish, like pieces of old skin all mottled with the bruisy indistinct writing. But it *is* Daddy's writing. At the edge of one piece I make out a few words *until the night falls*. The writing slopes like his, the 'g' has his characteristic loop that I used to try and copy when I first did joined-up writing. I lean forward, squinting at the impossibly tiny marks. Daddy wrote this, prisoner Daddy, stranger, young man – younger than I am now – unmarried Daddy. I get up and switch on the big light.

I run my finger-tips over the pages, straining my eyes until I find a page where I can make out a few sentences:

under a couple of foot wading from bed to latrine, little point, waste sloshing about under beds . . . alive . . . mosquitoes breeding even in our hut.

In the kitchen drawer is a magnifying-glass, I don't know where from – not something I've had a use for before. I go and fetch it, pausing for a moment outside the bedroom door.

I can hear Foxy's sleep; not that she's snoring, there's just the thick sound of silent contentment.

> *three small bowls of rice today with something green, sea-weed Mac suggested, tasteless. 14 hours bamboo cutting. Hands in shreds. A stomach cramp, stopped, hands on knees waiting for cramp to pass, kicked in back of knee by guard just above worst ulcer . . . pain like nothing I . . . so fell beat with stick till I . . . Vince gave me a smoke. His obstinate cheerfulness an ins* (piration?)

I lift my head. Through the round smeary glass the pencilled words are furry round the edges. I breathe on the glass and polish it with the hem of my pyjama top. I flinch at the first word:

> *suicide today, Dutch . . . poor bugger need hardly have troubled. Elephant to shift bamboo clumps . . . incredible force and kindness and yet starved and beaten . . . cholera again . . . moved . . . will not be fed . . . in gut and reeling . . . came round in hospital hut . . . amoebic dysentery . . . by door. At least still*

Each word is an effort to read because of its indistinctness and because of the odd sensation of reading this diary, these words of my father, words he never said I could read; that he might object to me reading: words that he may have forgotten – of reading myself into his nightmare. I take another gulp of wine that is thick in my throat. I will be ill if I don't stop drinking. I should sleep. Even an hour's sleep . . .

> *Rain like . . . inches flooding down . . . the river bed filling a rage of yellow . . . Vince . . . a living skeleton but still smiling . . . just a kid . . . losing teeth . . . bringing me a smoke and half a lime . . . ulcer to the bone . . . look of my own bone which is yellowish, to touch it, warm . . . dressed with a kind of leaf*

recommended by Chinese women . . . five funerals today . . .
elephant . . . the look of . . . in its eyes . . .

My eyes ache. Several pages are completely indecipherable, full
of holes and darkly stained, spindly lines and traces of squashed
ant or mosquito. Fragments of the paper coming away on my
fingers like the soft scales of a moth. The egg-shaped hollows
in Daddy's legs where I put my childish finger. Daddy's finger
touching his own bone. I hold the papers up to the light but for
pages it is too far gone to read. Then pages from another time.
Earlier? Because the margins of the paper have gone, there are
no dates, there is no order to it.

Read 'The Happy Highwayman' by Leslie Charteris. Excellent
vocal concert outside canteen. Jap idea, camp commandant
recently said . . . those who want to be fit are fit whatever
the food, those who want to . . . and so forth. Something in it.
Tin with remaining Black Horse cigarettes stolen. What rage.
To find I could kill . . .

Chosen for party up river tomorrow, beyond Tarsao . . .
rumoured to be more primitive conditions but can hardly
believe . . . walk of twelve hours lost two . . . ulcer spots starting
in four . . . to blast rock for siding . . . just at point of despair
when dragonfly like green mercury in a thick shaft of sun

Tomorrow will be a long day. A funny expression, it will be a
day of average length but much will be in it: travel and grief and
. . . what is Mummy doing now? Is she sleeping? The doctor
will have prescribed her something to help her sleep for a night
or two. She will be all right. Soft in a grey blankety sleep, just
now she will know nothing.

could be in hell . . . but discipline . . . Vince . . . if a fly has
landed on it throw it away be you starving . . . if a man is fit
enough to dodge a blow he's fit enough for work . . . mist wreaths

amongst the feathery bamboo . . . calls of frogs . . . the damp in my broken . . . all the time it rains the ground mud with inches of water on top . . . railway extends beyond Kinsayok they say . . . rumoured that allied bombers . . . Bartlett's funeral . . . fizz of flies . . . game with Aussie, Vince, word associations . . . 11 more cholera deaths men falling like

I have tried sleeping pills, of course I have tried. At university and again with Guy. 'You have to sleep, baby,' he said. Sometimes he would stroke my forehead, the hair back from my eyes to soothe me. He did take care of me. He will be married now to someone else, taking care of someone else. They will have babies. The children will have an architect-designed Wendy house in the garden – or perhaps a tree-house. Once, on holiday in Norfolk, we drove within ten miles of Little Dealing and I persuaded him to take a detour to look at 'The Nook'. I wanted to show him the tree-house. We rang on the bell but there was no one at home. Feeling like burglars, we let ourselves in through the side gate. squeezed past the dustbins and into the back garden. While I reeled in a blast of nostalgia he studied the construction of the tree-house. 'Amazing thing,' he said, 'exploiting the potential of the tree's structural qualities . . . can you see how incredible . . . the walls built to incorporate the movement of the tree even in a gale.'

Sometimes I do miss him. Not *him* but the life I could have had with him. Wife and mother. Mother. Where are the babies I could have had?

all day long the thin men file past . . . there is a walk a stiff stumble . . . I find my own limbs falling into it . . . to latrine . . . Vince with incredible kindness . . . decent and . . . headache pulse of just under . . .

Only these snatches picked out from the papers, nothing much else legible. Only snatches from his experience, from his head, writing it then as if to *me now here* although there was no me then: the process of communication so strange. Him sitting as he wrote – on a bunk? on the ground? writing by daylight or firelight or what? Writing with a blunt stub of pencil, the paper resting on his knee or a book? And writing to an unknown woman, to his daughter, Zelda. And Zelda reading, in the small hours of the morning following his death. His suicide.

> *little difference between those dying of dysentery and avitaminosis in here and those dying of starvation and over-work out there . . . the songs of birds, plangent*

Plangent is not a word I ever heard him use. It is not his sort of word, it is a poet's word and his use of it plucks at me inside like fingers on a harp. I could still have them. Babies. I could have three or four. Me? A mother? Ha!

Sleeping pills did make me sleep but it was dirty sleep, not clean. It did not do the job of real sleep which is like a tide that cleans the shore, smooths down the footprints, the scuffles in the sand, leaves it fresh with maybe a frill of flotsam, seaweed, beached dreams. Drugged sleep is only stagnant. You wake the same with a dry mouth, you mutter and stumble through the day. I would not take sleeping drugs again. Brandy helps sometimes. Sex does, straight after, almost unaware, soft and languid I can slip down – before I catch myself – into the sweet net of it and sometimes, just occasionally, I am cradled all night.

> *a roaring rush uprooting the bushes, rolling boulders with deep intermittent rumbles . . . all manner of . . . from latrines . . . rice ration cut . . . burning oil on water . . . and quinine . . . no mail for three months . . . Mother and home*

Daddy's mother died when I was ten. We used to visit her in Colchester and I was always car-sick. She loved my mother more than her own son I think. They used to drink sherry and get red-faced in the kitchen, sending out blasts of laughter while everyone was waiting for lunch. When Huw was born she came to stay at 'The Nook'. I brushed her stiff laquered hair for her and did it in a fancy style. I liked her tiny shoes and her powder-compact with a crinolined lady on the lid and a powdery circle of mirror inside. The powder puff was flesh coloured and grubby at the edges. Its lady-like smell made me sneeze. Her funeral was my first. She died of a stroke. No suffering, my parents said, it's what she would have wanted, I thought that was a lie. She didn't want to die. She was in the middle of knitting a cardigan for me.

I felt sorry for Huw, squirming in his shawl at the funeral in a cold church because she was his only granny and he was too small ever to know her. Mummy's parents had both died before I was born. She was a late bloom, she said, a surprise, born when her mother was forty-six and her father fifty-eight, their only child. I thought of the photograph of her with her long white plaits. 'They didn't know what to do with me,' she said sometimes and I would think of her on the lawn meeting my father, think of him untangling her kite strings. Before. Before the war. Before he wrote the diary. Only fragments now. Holes right through the last few pages, eaten right through so that there are only the odd words edging the holes.

Could not walk . . . skeleton carried up 45 degree . . . blastings . . . never a complain . . . every sinew . . .

Belly and . . . blown . . . on top of dysen . . . . . . carried back on stretch . . . still no complaint but he is fin . . . an see it in his ey . . . at night the cry of a wild cr . . . the dark like a knife and then he begged . . . my last . . . my last streng . . . Bleak Mid Win . . . food . . . cannot . . . my own hands . . . heart . . . black

I feel sick from the wine and from crouching forward to read. The gas-fire is scorching my side.

*Vince . . . wooden cross . . . en by ants, . . . imm . . . ately, such
greed seething . . . m the jungle . . . to sa . . . . . . im from agony
. . . the wrong thin . . . . . . he right thing . . . three amputations
. . . do not care now if I d . . . benign tertian mala . . . and lost
track . . . cannot hear, quinine . . . bubble it is . . . htening . . .
tapioca but*

And on the last page only one word legible: *Vince.*

I walk about the flat, past Foxy's study, up the stairs, past the
bedroom door behind which Foxy sleeps, into the bathroom.
There I am in the mirror but I am almost surprised to see myself
reflected back. It is as if I am not really here. My mind is struggling
in a jungle with my young father, struggling to digest him and
the fragments of his words. He was between about twenty and
twenty-three when he wrote the diary, years my junior. I touch
the skin under my eyes where the years are starting to show.

I cannot match what is written with what I know of him. How
can it be true? All the death, the filth, the disease, the pain, my
Daddy's bone open to the air, somebody kicking him when he
was down and in agony? And whatever else he suffered. How
can that be true of the man behind the newspaper, the man with
the golf-clubs? I wash the gritty sensation of the old papers from
my hands and brush my teeth, fiercely, to get rid of the bluish
wine stain. I scrub until the froth I spit is flecked with blood but
in the mirror my lips are still blue. I reach for a lipstick – Foxy's
– and fill them in cherry red. Bright lips in the small hours. Last
time I put lipstick on I didn't know that he was dead.

Sitting on the edge of the bath I clip my toe-nails. I rarely
remember to cut them and Foxy complains when I scratch her
in bed. They are painted maroon, but sluttishly chipped, and
there's a pink crescent at the base of each where the nail has
grown. The dark slivers lie on the bathroom tiles like some sort
of bugs. Daddy detested insects, it comes back to me suddenly
how much he loathed them. We abandoned a camping trip in
Scotland once because of the mosquitoes that whined around

the tents, the swarm of flying ants that settled on the canvas so that we could see the dark moving clusters of them as the sun shone hotly through the orange walls. We went to a guest-house instead which suited Hazel, Huw and me because there was a big colour television – but annoyed my mother who loved camping. She had bought a new Calor-gas stove especially for the trip.

In that respect, Daddy was a coward. If there was a wasp in the room, or a spider in the bath, he would ask Mummy to remove it, or if she was out, one of us. I asked Mummy why he was so scared. 'It's not rational,' she'd say, a touch of disdain in her voice.

I don't like flies, ordinary black house-flies. I don't like the querulous noise they make, or what they do. They inject saliva into the surface of food to predigest it and then suck it up through their proboscis. I cannot eat anything that a fly has been on. If a pair of flies reproduced and all their grubs survived to adulthood and bred, it would only take a year for there to be a ball of maggots bigger than the earth itself. But I don't mind spiders. I quite like snails. When I was a child, ants and beetles were my favourite things.

When I was very young, before we lived at 'The Nook', I started a beetle collection – dead beetles. Only sometimes it was hard to tell whether they were dead or alive. There are hundreds of species of beetle. I liked ladybirds, but my favourites were stag beetles with their bright black armour and antlers; smart insects, special and shiny as party shoes. I found a dead one and put it in a match-box with a picture of edelweiss on the top. I found another one floating in the water-butt and because I had no more match-boxes, put it in with the first one. They were identical, just like a pair of new patent-leather shoes, snug in their box. I covered them in a piece of white tissue, slid the box shut – and forgot them. Some time later, it could have been weeks, I opened the box to find that one of the shoes had come alive and eaten most of the other. There were frail bits of antler and leg and empty wings gone dull like scabs. The other one looked dead too. I tipped it out in a bush in case it *still* wasn't dead and threw the match-box in the dustbin. My feet were cold like a dead person's and my tongue was too heavy in my mouth to tell anyone the terrible thing I had done. But in the night sometimes when I couldn't sleep I couldn't help thinking of what had been happening in the match-box on the window-sill while I slept or read or played. The terrible thing that had happened, the beetle waking up to find itself imprisoned with a corpse and the hunger that had turned it cannibal before it died.

How *can* I reconcile the ordinary everyday grumpy man, living an ordinary everyday life, with the man in the diary? I did not know that man. I did not know that he'd had malaria and dysentery and maybe even cholera: that he'd had huge ulcers on his legs; that he'd been beaten; or that his closest friend had died, when he sat at the table with his newspaper, when he hammered the Tabasco bottle with his fist till the fiery droplets splattered his food. I did not know that about him. It is too difficult to assimilate.

Ah, but the dreams.

I look at the pages again. I've grown used to the scale of the writing now, can read a few scraps more. Often there is that name: *Vince*. Who is, was, this bloody Vince? A friend who was injured and died and for whom Daddy felt responsible? I don't know what to do now with what I know. I feel I have gulped down a great uncomfortable meal, full of hard corners and edges, a meal I cannot throw up but will never digest.

I settle back on the futon, wishing I had never opened the envelope, wishing I had thrown it in the bin.

10

One Saturday, after a riding lesson with Elaine, I came home to find Puddle-duck sitting drawing at the kitchen table. My mother was leaning over the manuscript of a story she was working on, crossing out and squiggling with a red Biro. They looked very companionable and I felt that I was intruding, barging in on their busyness, all sweaty and smelling of horses.

'What's *he* doing here?'

'Griselda, don't be so rude. Do you think "The Custodian of Pleasure" is a good title? Or too . . . highbrow?'

'Don't ask me.' I threw my riding-hat on a chair and got myself a drink of orange squash. 'Hello,' I said to Puddle-duck who was smiling at me.

'Vassily's mother's had to go out,' Mummy explained, 'and I said that of course we'd be glad to have him here. He's staying the night.'

I choked on my squash. 'Mummy! Where will he sleep?'

'Well, Hazel's staying at Bridget's and . . .'

'She's *always* staying at Bridget's!' I slammed my glass down on the table. 'Hazel would *die* if he slept in her bed. And anyway I'm not . . .'

'All right, but it means clearing out the spare room.'

'I'll help.'

'It needs doing anyway – Hazel's having it after her birthday.'

'Oh.'

'High time you had your own rooms.'

'Yes.'

'It's not as if we're short of rooms . . . it's just . . .'

I knew what she meant. There were two rooms that were unused except to store junk, as well as a long dim attic room, but in them all the plaster was falling off the walls and the wiring was ancient. It would take some work to make them comfortable and Mummy was always too busy with Huw and her writing to get round to it. Hazel had bought her an ugly pink blob of plastic for her birthday with A Round Tooit written on it for a joke.

It should have been what I wanted, to have my own room. None of my school-friends had to share with their sisters but . . . but in the night I liked to hear her breathing; I liked to feel the bunks shift as she turned over – even if it did make her furious when I did the same. It was too babyish to admit, but I didn't want to sleep alone.

'What's for tea?'

'Daddy's bringing fish and chips home after golf. What have you drawn, Vassily?' Mummy leant over his shoulder. 'Oh! That's beautiful. Look Grizzle.' He had sketched a tree with a swing. It was much better than anything I could ever have done. It looked like our apple tree and our swing only seen from above. As I watched, with a deft little flick, he put a bird in the tree.

'Is it our swing?' Mummy touched him on the shoulder, pointed to her chest and then to the garden. She was catching on fast to a way of speaking in signs. Puddle-duck nodded and beamed. 'Can I keep it?' Mummy asked. He nodded again. I had never seen him look so happy. At school he was bad at everything and shrunken into himself, but in our kitchen, watching my mother Sellotape his drawing to a cupboard door, I could almost *see* him swell with pride. And something stirred inside me, something like wet dark wings unfurling in my chest, something I didn't want to know.

Huw started to wail from his bedroom and Mummy tutted, paper-clipped her pages together and went to get him up. I took a biscuit from the tin and wandered out into the garden. Puddle-duck followed me.

'Where's your mum?' I asked.

He pointed down the garden to the windows of their flat.

'At home?'

He nodded.

'So why are you here?' But he just beamed at me. I went down the garden and sat on the swing. The sun was warm and shone on the wasp-eaten windfalls in the long grass. I sniffed my hands that smelt gorgeously of pony and leather. I took hold of the greasy, fibrous ropes. At least Hazel wasn't there to be angry that Puddle-duck *was* there. *Not* my fault but she would still have blamed me. I swung for a bit, the branch squeaking above me. 'One day that branch'll give,' Mummy was always warning, 'don't go too high, just in case.' An apple thudded into the grass.

Puddle-duck went to the bottom of the tree-house ladder and looked hopefully up. I pretended not to see. I didn't want to be in the tree-house with him again and I certainly didn't want him in it alone. He put one foot on the bottom rung of the ladder, and looked for my reaction. His legs were very thin and his grey socks wrinkled round his ankles. One plimsoll had a little hole in the toe.

'Would you like a swing?' I got off and offered it to him. He settled himself on the seat. I waited but he just sat there, dangling. '*Go on*,' I shouted. He gripped the rope tightly as if he thought he might fall off and swayed his body about. I realised he didn't know how to swing. I could not believe it. *Ten* and he couldn't swing! Behind him I pushed. I pushed his thin ribby back and then, as he went higher, the edge of the wooden seat. The branch shrieked and bounced as the swing flew through the air, leaves, twigs and apples pattered and thumped all around him. I closed my eyes and saw him flying off the swing and through the air, flying, flying away. He was making strange high sounds I couldn't understand, a sort of rhythmic yelping. I couldn't tell if it was joy or fear or what. I kept pushing and he kept yelping until my arms grew tired and then I got fed up and stopped. As the motion grew gradually gentler, Puddle-duck lay right back on the swing, his hair falling away from his face, his legs stuck straight out in front. His face had gone dreamy as if he was in a trance.

Mummy came down the garden carrying a crumpled red-faced Huw. 'That's right,' she said, with an approving smile. 'You play with Vassily. Only do go easy on that swing.'

'Vassily says his mum's *there*,' I said. But Mummy only shook her head. She squatted down and chose an apple for Huw to gnaw on.

'When's tea?'

'Well Daddy said six, but my guess is it'll be nearer seven.'

'Can we go for a walk?'

She frowned. 'Don't see why not. But don't go far – and don't be long.'

We went out by the side gate. Puddle-duck followed behind me like a little dog. I led him round the corner to the big house, part of which was his flat. I pointed to the door. 'Can we go in?' I asked. I thought that if Wanda was there I could leave Vassily behind, tell Mummy it was a mistake, then I could go home by myself, spend the afternoon reading my *Bunty* in the tree-house alone and enjoy the luxury of shop fish and chips without him spoiling it.

Puddle-duck looked nervous, but he nodded and we went up the path. The front door was enormous, twice as wide as our front door. The floor inside was covered in lino, orange flowers inside brown squares. I'd never seen lino on *stairs* before. There was a smell of not especially nice cooking. On the window-sill was a dead spider-plant in a pot and a pile of unopened mail overflowed the bottom step. We went up the stairs, Vassily in front now, his plimsolls smack, smacking on the lino. The landing was carpeted and cleaner. There were two doors. Puddle-duck approached the farthest one, outside which was a doormat on which the word WELCOME was picked out in red bristles. I'd never been to a flat before. Everyone else I knew lived in a whole house. To my surprise, Puddle-duck took a key out of his pocket and fitted it into the lock. I didn't have a key of my own, it had never occurred to me that I might need one.

The flat smelled of Wanda's weird perfume and incense and bacon. The carpet in the hall was deep and white. I'd never seen a *white* carpet. On the walls were pictures made of silver and gold string wound round nails: a bridge, a church, a windmill. We went into the kitchen. A mobile with brass bells hung over the table – the cloth was an Indian bedspread, covered in crumbs and blobs of jam that blended in with the pattern. Three white wormy bacon rinds lay on the draining-board amongst the cups and plates.

Puddle-duck opened a cupboard and produced a packet of chocolate finger biscuits, the sort of thing we only had at parties, an unopened packet, and he ripped it open, as if it was nothing, and offered me one. I put it in my mouth like a cigar, sucking the chocolate off the end. I thought he must be showing off, that he would get into trouble for opening a new packet without permission.

We walked past a closed door. I got the sense that Wanda was there, behind that door having a rest probably. Puddle-duck led me into the sitting-room. It seemed strange to have a sitting-room upstairs with the tops of trees outside the window and the telephone wires wobbling with birds, so close. The room was messy but not dirty. There were ornamental frogs everywhere, funny ones and life-like ones in every shade of green – wood and china, plastic and stone. There was a long-haired white cat asleep on a cushion on the white plastic sofa. I stroked it and it opened one gooseberry green eye and purred. In front of the fire was an orange sheepskin rug. It was a surprisingly nice room because of the light and the waving leaves outside, and because

everything was new. I don't know why I was surprised. I must
have expected squalor. On the walls were some of Vassily's
drawings, trees and swings, horses in a field, lots of pictures of
houses – our tree-house. None of the pictures had any figures
in them and I was relieved that at least he couldn't draw *people*.
I could hear a bit of noise from Wanda's bedroom. She must be
getting up. I thought we should go.

'Will she be cross?' I asked Puddle-duck pointing to the door
of Wanda's room as we stepped out of the sitting-room. I felt
quite scared, like a burglar or a snoop – although I don't know
why, it was Puddle-duck's home, after all.

He didn't answer. He led me into his room instead and stood
looking proudly around. It was a tiny room, a room cut in half,
with a very big window. It was like a toy-shop. The shelves
were piled high with toys, new things still in their boxes: an
Etcha-Sketch which is something I wanted, a Spirograph, puzzles
and painting-by-numbers sets, carpentry tools, a chemistry set,
board-games, Meccano, binoculars, racing cars, Dinky toys and
hundreds of soft toys: teddy-bears, lions, seals, bunny-rabbits
and a gigantic white polar bear that slumped in a corner, big
as an arm-chair.

I couldn't believe Puddle-duck had all these things. I had
thought of him as poor, with his scruffy clothes and plimsolls.
Hazel and I had *nothing* compared with all this. But I noticed
there were no books, that's another thing that made this flat
so different from our house where there were shelves of books
everywhere. Except that on the floor by his bed was a baby's
board book, the sort of thing that Huw chewed on. It was very
old, the corners all soft, bits of the paper pictures worn off the
grey board. It was open at the picture of a swing in a tree,
very different from ours. I went and looked out of the window,
straight down through the branches and into the tree-house.
Twigs from our tree scrabbled against his window. I could
see the branch on which we sat, the glint from the glass of
my formicary, even one of Hazel's ballet pictures on the wall.

And I could see the whole of our garden too, the tree with the swing that looked, from here, exactly like Puddle-duck's drawing, the kitchen door, and Mummy standing outside. As I watched she reached her hands up over her head and bent down to touch her toes. I turned away. It wasn't right that he should be able to see down on our garden so well, to see even into our tree-house. A private place.

He pulled at my sleeve and picked up the book. He started again making the noises he'd been making on the swing and now I recognised them as the words of the poem in the book. It was Robert Louis Stevenson's poem, 'The Swing'. *How do you like to go up in a swing, up in the air so blue? Oh, I do think it's the pleasantest thing, ever a child can do!* He said it quite well. If you knew what he was saying you could recognise it. I had *A Child's Garden of Verses* at home. Once it was my favourite book. I felt a tiny sensation inside, like a finger nudging my heart. I made my lips curve into a smile.

Then I heard a man's voice and jumped. For a moment I'd forgotten we were sneaking and should have been quiet. I flinched and put my finger to my lips. Puddle-duck pushed his door to just as Wanda and the man who belonged to the voice came out into the hall. They were laughing in a silly way. The man called her Hotpants and then he left. I was glad Puddle-duck couldn't hear, or couldn't know I heard. I'd have died if anyone heard anyone call my mother *that*. I stood still, my hands screwed into fists, flinching, waiting for her to come and discover us – but she did not come in. Instead she went into the bathroom – that was made out of the other half of Puddle-duck's room – and started running a bath. She couldn't have heard us then, she couldn't know we were there, even though Puddle-duck had said his poem quite loudly. I wondered if she was a bit deaf too. She went out and back into her bedroom and then the bathroom door shut and I relaxed. Through the heavy fall of water I could hear her singing as she took of her clothes. She had a sweet little-girly voice. I looked at Puddle-duck but his face was bland. So strange that he couldn't hear what I was hearing. I wanted to go.

I pointed to the door. He nodded. The taps were turned off and I heard Wanda climbing into the bath, a shifting of water, a luxurious sigh, the squeak of her bottom on the bottom of the bath. She resumed her singing as we crept through the hall and out. Puddle-duck locked the door and then tried it, like an adult, to make sure it was locked. Why Wanda would want to be locked inside her own flat, I couldn't imagine. We never locked *our* house if anyone was in.

After tea, which was spoiled for me by the sight of Puddle-duck's hearing-aids on the side-board and all the tortuous attempts at conversation, we played Cluedo. It was not like Daddy to play games. He usually went off into his study and smoked, or sat in front of the television glowering at anyone who spoke. He liked watching news programmes and anything with Nana Mouskouri in it – also Morecambe and Wise at which he laughed and thumped the arms of his chair. Mummy preferred natural history programmes, but Daddy left the room or retreated behind a shuddering newspaper at the first sign of any mating.

Mummy and Daddy sat on the sofa and Puddle-duck and I on cushions on the floor, the Cluedo board on the coffee table between us. Everything looked shabby after the brightness of Wanda's flat. It would have been cosy if the fourth person had been anyone but Puddle-duck. He didn't know how to play it, of course, although he had a set in his room. Why have it since he'd obviously never played it? I didn't feel like playing. Normally when I play a game I couldn't care less who wins – but I wanted to be sure Puddle-duck didn't. My heart was actually thudding with anticipation when I thought I knew the identity of the murderer. But I was wrong. Mummy won, so that was all right. Miss Brown did it with the candlestick in the library. When he left the room to go to the toilet, I told Mummy that Wanda had been at home all afternoon.

'How do you know?'

'Pud – Vassily said, and anyway, I just know.'

'It's no concern of yours, Griselda,' Daddy said. I folded the board and slid all the pieces, the cards, dice and all the deadly little weapons into the box. My bottom lip fattened and tried to curl out like it did when I wanted to cry. I hated the way Daddy's voice went all thin and tinny when he was cross with me, his mouth crinkling as if someone had pulled tight a drawstring in his lips. He looked at me as if I was stupid, or as if I'd done something really wrong when all I was doing was telling the truth.

The only good thing about having Puddle-duck to stay rather than anyone else was that he wouldn't hear if Daddy had a dream. I never had a friend to stay because of that, because I couldn't bear the thought that anyone else might hear his scream or know about the dark paddings about, the water running, the horrible soothingness of my mother's voice in the night. Secret noises that nobody else should have to hear.

Hazel risked it. Bridget had slept on a camp-bed in our room more than once – or she supposedly slept on the camp-bed. Actually she and Hazel squeezed into Hazel's bed together. I hated it when Bridget stayed the night because they didn't want me there. 'You have to include Griselda,' Mummy told them but naturally they didn't. They snuggled under the covers, giggling and whispering, ignoring every single word I said.

'She's like a baby,' Hazel told Bridget. 'She has to get up for a wee-wee twice a night.'

'Jeez,' Bridget said. 'You have to learn to control your bladder.'

'It's for your own good,' Hazel explained once, as, after a flurry of whispering, they unhooked the ladder and slid it under Hazel's bunk. So I lay awake, even until after their scuffling and giggling had stopped, too embarrassed to jump down, afraid that I would wet the bed and that my pee would drip through the mattress on to Hazel and Bridget below.

In the morning I walked Puddle-duck home. It was Mummy's idea. She put his pyjamas and toothbrush in a carrier bag and helped him strap his hearing-aids on. She even combed his hair that was so greasy the comb-marks stayed in. It was half-past ten when we went round. We had had bacon and scrambled eggs and I had looked at the Giles cartoon in the *Sunday Express* like I did every Sunday. It was mid-morning in our house but in Wanda's flat it was the crack of dawn. Puddle-duck shouted 'Hello' very loudly as we came in, but it was all dark and quiet. Eventually I heard a moan from behind Wanda's door. 'Hello,' I called brightly, 'I've just walked back with Vassily.'

The door opened and Wanda came out. She was wearing a green nylon baby-doll nightie, very short and completely transparent and her hair was a massive tangle. 'What time do you call this?' she said.

I looked at my watch. 'Twenty to eleven.'

'Oh. Oh well.' She gave a rueful smile and went into the kitchen. I could see everything, all her bottom, even a little mole in the middle of one buttock. She put the kettle on, stretched and yawned. She smelled like a mouse cage and under her arms were ovals of coarse black stubble.

'Coffee?' she offered.

'No thanks.'

'Has he been good? Come here, little spook, did you miss me?' She pulled him against her so that his face was only a film of green nylon away from her breasts and squeezed him energetically.

'He's been very good,' I said. I was wondering if she'd heard us the day before, but she showed no sign.

'I'm no good till I've had my fix,' she said, stumbling over to fill the kettle and unscrew a jar of Nescafé. She licked her finger, dipped it in the jar and licked off the granules. She spooned some more into a jar and yawned again. Vassily wandered off.

'We played Cluedo,' I said, just for something to say.

'Yeah?'

'Well ... Bye.' There was too much flesh and human smell in Wanda's kitchen for me. It made me blush, thinking of Puddle-duck so close to an as good as naked woman – even if it was his mother. I'd seen Mummy naked, drying herself after a bath or swimming, she was very open in that way, a way that Daddy frowned upon and called 'Scandinavian' as if that was a swear word. But Mummy's body was shivery and neat and matter-of-fact. Somehow Wanda's body, the bosoms, the bottom, the dark place under the rounded curve of her belly, made me think of Daddy running through the hall all wild and exposed. The thought of all the hairy, shadowy, purply, secret places, adult pulpiness and smells, made me feel hot and sick. I went home and straight up the ladder to the tree-house where I watched my neat and tidy ants.

11

Past four o'clock. Past the deepest hours of the night. Approaching the time when I will take Foxy her cup of tea. Assam with a drip of milk and one teaspoonful of sugar – to start her up as she says. Like Wanda with her Nescafé fix. And she will stretch and yawn and I will breathe in *her* adorable blend of sleepy and intimate smells. *Approaching* that time. I will wake her at seven – no six-thirty. I will cook breakfast for her, her favourite breakfast: fried mushrooms on toast with lemon juice and black pepper sprinkled on top. I will spoil her because she will be spoiling me, driving me all the way to my parents' house when I could perfectly well drive myself. When we get there she won't stay, not for more than a cup of tea. She will not wish to intrude on our family at such a time. I can just see, just hear, her saying it. How well I know her. And I will want to shout, *But you are my family*. If she was a man she would be, if we were married she would be. She would be my next-of-kin in the eyes of the law. Our eyes don't count in this.

I clear away the glasses and plates. Quarter of a bottle of wine left. I retrieve the cork from under the table and force it back into the neck of the bottle. A sign that it is really morning – I will drink no more wine, my body has crossed the divide between late and early, greets the idea of alcohol with revulsion now, craves coffee instead. The kitchen floor gleams. That's something good I've done tonight.

And I've learned some things about my father. The sitting-room feels too hot and stuffy. I gather up all the scraps of paper, all those tiny words. I carry them into the kitchen where the light is brighter, a horrible fluorescent tube that flickers and stutters for about five minutes when you switch it on so we leave it on all night. We're always saying we'll fix it but we never do. Never have, yet.

> *4.43 Planes overhead invisible ... est canopy ... big jobs, multi-eng ... gue of lice ... splits ... ter filth ... but ... Vin ... ch ... ter*

Oh it is useless. What can I make of it but splintered suffering? Suffering he wanted to forget. Why do it? Maybe my mother is right. Why rake over dying coals? Why waken the sleeping dogs? Why ransack the cupboards for skeletons? But ... Vince mentioned again. Obviously a great friend. I think about my father's friends that I met. Those he played golf with; those he played bridge with; people from work; people who came to dinner; people whose loud voices and cigarette smoke drifted up the stairs; people who patted our heads, mine and Hazel's, and said, 'Aren't they different, Ralph. Chalk and cheese.'

> *detachment of Aust ... and wash and ... and teak I ... orchids ... ible variety ... ugly chocolate brown ... purple ... fleshy and a mass of mauve ...*

I can't look at this any more. He should have had it back. *He* should have had the choice. The dead man, the Reverend Priest, should have sent it back to him. I feel a spurt of anger that he lied to my father. Anger with his widow for sending what was left of the diary to Mummy instead of directly to him. Anger with Mummy for sending them to me instead of giving them to him. For not respecting Daddy enough to allow him to make his own choice. They were *his* memories, nobody else's. And, inevitably, anger with myself for not taking action sooner, for putting it off until it was too late. Now he can never forgive his cowardly friend. Would he have forgiven, laughed it off, the disgusting fate of most of his diary? Would he have understood? I don't know. I did not know him well enough to possibly know. What was in his head when he died? Why choose yesterday instead of today, tomorrow, this time next year? I wonder if these scraps, these scrubby bits of paper would have helped, would have saved him? When he stood on the chair, or the step-ladder, whatever he stood on, when he slipped his head through the noose – how did he know how to make a noose? *I* wouldn't know how. When he kicked away the chair, when he felt the rope jerk and clench his throat, heard the clatter of the fallen chair, felt the pressure . . . what . . .?

No. I cannot. No. What shall I do? What shall I do?

My Daddy.

I need . . . I cannot . . . I must calm down. Must breathe. The kitchen floor is cool and clean beneath my feet. My feet are white, my nails are cut. The knees of my pyjamas are bagged. What will I wear tomorrow? Black? I often wear black anyway. There used to be rules, precise periods of mourning: two and a half years for a parent, three months for an aunt. Each period had its own uniform. Black crêpe and bombazine for deepest mourning, shading through heliotrope or grey for half-mourning. Black silk ribbons threaded through the hems of the drawers and petticoats of Victorian women. I bought a job lot once. Long white drawers with black ribbons. They sold well. Mourning drawers. I should have kept a pair back. It's so free now. You can wear what the hell you like, yellow to a funeral, black to a wedding. Who will give a damn?

A tiny fragment drifts to the floor. There is no breeze. No movement. But it seems to pick itself up and flutter to the floor. Almost as if it has been selected by invisible fingers. Goose-pimples rise on my arms as I bend down for it. It is the scrappiest little bit of paper, eaten by ants or something until it is nothing but grubby lace. I strain my eyes but there is no message there for me. I thought maybe . . . I cannot pick out a single whole word. Is that it then finally? No message.

I hope Mummy is asleep, and Hazel and Huw, though it makes me lonely to hope that. It's as if they are on the other side. As if I am dead and they are alive or the other way round. But not forever. One day forever, but not yet. I hear the sound of an engine outside, a car starting up and my heart lifts. Someone is up and awake and off to work. Outside the window, the street is dark, the street-lamps flick on as I look, dull red brightening to orange. The glass is cold and soothing to my brow. At the door I put on a pair of wellingtons, Foxy's, too big for my cold bare feet, gritty inside. I open the door and go down the concrete steps on to the front path, in time to see the car disappear round the corner. I listen to the sound die away. There are lots of sounds – more weighty vehicles, juggernauts, on the distant motorway, the thin dreamy wail of a child. Several lights on in the flats opposite. Daft to imagine myself alone. I should get a computer and hitch myself up to the Internet – then I could connect with people in another time-zone, or form an insomniacs club in this one. Perhaps there is already one in existence, a network of bleary-eyed folk, having virtual sex, virtual relationships, living virtual lives all through the lonely night.

A cat slinks up to me, its eyes collecting and refracting what little light there is into crazed gold. It rubs against my boots. I pick it up and snuggle my face in its cold fur but it struggles and I put it down. It stands for a moment beside me, its tail held very high. It reminds me of myself. It wants to be close but not to be held. I feel trapped with arms around me for more than a moment. Even *Foxy's* arms. I cannot stay in them for long without feeling breathless. I try to remember my father's arms around me. I don't think they ever were though surely he must have held me as a baby. Sometimes there was the bristly whisky-scented brush of a kiss on the cheek, whisky-scented because he would have been drinking if he was moved to kiss me. And now his lips, his mouth, is dead. Bristles keep on growing after death and finger and toe-nails. My toe-nails are clipped, gathered and put in the bin. Dead bits of me. I want to wake Foxy. I can't be alone any more. I'm frightened. It is homing in on me, settling like a swarm, not just the fact of Daddy's death but the fact of death, of mortality. Mine.

I must stop thinking.

Foxy.

It is cold out here with a clean lemon line of dawn just starting to edge the roofs. The sky is punctured by a single star.

In bed. She grumbles a bit in her sleep when my cold feet brush against her, my cold knees nudging into the heat of the back of hers. I should not, I should leave her but my cold hands are desperate for her warmth. My face presses against her back, I move my hand on to her belly that has slid sideways with the gravity of sleep. I feel goose-pimples spread on her skin as my chill affects her, as I steal her warmth. I slide my hand up to her breast and feel the nipple pucker. I push my body closer. If I was a man I would enter her like this. How it must feel for a cold and lonely man to bury himself in a woman. Just now I can feel the weakness of a man, his penis tensed and shuddering, yearning towards completeness. I slide my hand between her legs. She is awake now. Not that she has given a sign, but the quality of her awareness has changed the minute tensions in her body. Her breathing is deeper. Her body grows hotter, she pushes her back against me, her bottom, and her heat floods me. Her live heat.

But one day she will be dead.

I cannot do it, touch her any more.

This is the morning after the day my father died.

One day the hand that absorbs her humidity will be only bones, she will be bones. I take my hand away and she gives a disgruntled sigh.

Foxy – Sybil to me then – came into Second Hand Rose to buy a hat for somebody's wedding. It was years since I'd graduated and I was surprised she remembered me. We couldn't find a hat to do her justice, but she tried on a lace blouse, stepped out of the changing-room to ask my opinion. The old-gold lace lit up her hair and skin, clung to and sculpted the shape of her breasts, the narrow curve of her waist so that I could hardly speak. She bought the blouse and returned next day to suggest a drink. I could only say, yes, but I was confused, quite terrified of her in a way. Did she mean *just* a drink? I thought she was amazing, so elegant, so bright. The welter of words that can trip off her tongue when she gets going, that spill from between her bright and smudgy lips. The slim elegance of her hands and feet, that make me feel peasant-like beside her. We shared a bottle of wine in a wine bar that's gone now, knocked down to make way for a car-park. We shared a pizza, discovering a mutual passion for anchovies. All evening I was anxious and tantalised. I had never been with a woman before. Was this simply friendship or was it a prelude to something more? Surely the warm lingering looks she gave me; surely the way she touched my arm, my knee, my thigh; surely the husky intimate note in her laugh promised something more than simple friendship? But I did not know, did not want to make a fool of myself by misjudging her, misreading, in my usual clumsy way, the situation. All my lovers had been male. I'd never even considered sex with a woman. But this woman . . . And in the end when we kissed the taste of anchovies was strong in our mouths, the taste of anchovies and lipstick.

I kiss the back of her neck and her hair tickles my lips. *Foxy, please don't leave me.*

'Zelda?' A question in her voice.

'Sorry.'

'Let me hold you.'

'No . . . I'm getting up again. Sorry, sorry.' She turns and I edge away from her heat, from her arms.

She sighs. 'What time is it?'

'Nearly five.'

'No sleep? You must sleep, pumpkin, just a little.'

'I can't.'

She puts her hand on my arm. 'You're trembling.' I let her hold me for a moment, then I pull away.

'What have you been doing all night?'

'Looking at my father's . . . looking at some papers.'

'What?' Suddenly she is alert.

'Bits of a diary, from Burma . . . or Thailand.'

'From the war? You never . . .'

'I wanted to wait till I saw him, but . . .' and I start to cry. Not as if I'm crying. It's as if I'm a conduit for someone else's gulps, someone else's hot salt tears. She plucks tissues from a box by the bed and wipes my eyes.

'Oh Zel . . .'

I take a deep breath. 'I'm all right.'

'I'll go and make some tea. Or coffee?'

'I didn't mean to wake you.'

'Well, whatever, I'm awake now. We'll have some tea. It's morning.'

I feel her get out of bed, the mattress springs up. I pull her warm pillow down to fill the space she's left. Through my eyelashes I watch her putting on her dressing-gown, lifting her hair over the collar, tying the silky belt around her waist. She feels under the bed with her feet for her slippers. 'Close your eyes,' she says. She leans over and puts a cool finger-tip on each of my swollen eyelids. 'I'll bring you some tea in a minute.'

She goes out. My eyes won't open, it's as if she's sealed them shut.

It's morning she said.

The relief swallows me up.

And when I wake it's light.

Foxy draws the curtains, sunshine floods across the bed. I squint against it. I'm stranded for a beat, don't remember a thing. A blessed beat of peace. I've slept, it's morning, Foxy's here with a tray of toast and coffee. Cutting through the aroma of coffee, a cusp of orange, the scent of marmalade. A smile rises to meet the day, I feel rich, I have slept. And then it slams back. The weight of yesterday. My father is dead. And Foxy, this Foxy, with her hair swept up now, her silk shirt and her jeans, this lover of mine is going to leave me.

'What time is it?'

'Eight.'

'Eight!' I struggle to a sitting position.

'You were sleeping so soundly . . . you needed it. I left you *this* long.'

'Yes.' There is a cold, skinned-over cup of tea beside the bed. She picks it up. 'See. Eat your breakfast now and I'll run you a bath.'

I cannot let her leave the room until I know the worst. If I'm going to be dumped I want the pain of it now. I want all the pain to come together.

'Foxy . . .'

'Mmmm? Must put some water in the radiator, check the oil.'

'Last night?'

'Yep?' She smooths her hair back, dips to look at herself in the dressing-table mirror.

'Before . . . before you spoke to my mum . . .'

'Mmmm?' She turns.

'Were you . . . were you going to end it?'

She pauses. It's no good, she doesn't answer fast enough.

'Don't worry.' I force coffee past the lump in my throat.

'No,' she says, but it is too late. She studies my face for a moment and sits down on the edge of the bed. 'No . . . I did want to talk but . . .'

'Let's talk then.' My voice has gone very odd. It sounds hollow and echoey as if it is issuing from a cave.

'Zelda, darling, not now.'

'Why? Nothing's changed since last night has it?'

'Yes. You know it has.' She fiddles with the silver filigree slide that holds her hair. I gave her that slide. She takes off her glasses and smiles at me. It seems to be a genuine smile. There are small red dents on each side of the bridge of her nose. 'Things *have* changed. Something like a death . . . it *does* change things.'

'But not how you *feel*.'

'Yes, how you feel.'

'No.' I swallow some more coffee.

'Yes.' She rubs her hand against my duvet-muffled thigh. 'It's not static, Zelda, a relationship, *you* know that. It's not the same two days in a row. I did want to talk to you yesterday, it's true. But not to *finish* us, just to talk . . .'

'About what then?'

'But *this* has superseded *that*.'

'What?'

She shrugs. 'Look, we can talk on the journey if you want. I must get the car ready.'

'I'm giving you a chance,' I say. I feel very detached as if I'm not speaking or even thinking these words, but these are the words that come. 'I'm giving you a chance to finish it now if you want to. I can drive myself to Norfolk. You can pack up and leave before I get back.'

'But I don't *want* to leave.' She knits her fingers together as if she is quite upset. 'I want to go through this with you. I want to . . . well *support* you, I suppose.'

'And then?'

'And then I might get struck by lightning, hit by a bus. *You* might fall madly in love with a Sumo wrestler.' Unwillingly I smile. 'Who the hell knows?'

'I s'pose.' I pick up a slice of toast, it looks enormous. I nibble a corner. The marmalade is warm and sticky.

'I'll go and check the car and run your bath.' She straightens herself up, smooths her hair, replaces her glasses. The moment has gone. She never said the word 'love'. She touches me on the hair with her lips before she goes out. Along with the marmalade I taste a bitter edge of resentment. I am not begging her to stay. I would not beg her.

EASY PEASY

I have left all my lovers. I have never *been* left. Guy was devastated when I ended it. He sent letters, cards, tapes of songs that he considered significant, great stiff Cellophaned sprays of Interflora roses that had no scent. I had felt sad and powerful. I wouldn't let him see me. I thought I was being cruel to be kind, a clean break heals quickest, all that. And I'm sure he healed. If Foxy wants to finish it I want it to be quick and clean, I don't want her drawing it out, deceiving me about her wishes. I don't want her lying beside me dreaming about the time when I'll be gone.

12

Daddy heard me refer to Vassily as Puddle-duck. It was at Sunday lunchtime. I was talking to Hazel, not to him. I thought he was listening to my mother.

'What did you say?'

'I said,' I looked at Hazel for support but she was busy cutting up her meat, 'I said I hope Vassily isn't coming round.' In each of the lenses of my father's glasses I could see a reflection of the spiky cactus between the curtains on the window-sill. But I could not see his eyes.

He drew in a deep breath. 'First of all,' he said, 'that poor child is very welcome in this house. And secondly, what did I hear you call him?'

'Vassily.' He tapped his index finger briskly on the table and waited.

'Puddle-duck,' I mumbled after a long moment. 'Everyone calls him that. It's his nickname.'

'Well you don't,' he said. 'Do you understand?'

'He doesn't mind.'

'Understand?'

'Yes.'

He turned his attention to Hazel. 'Nor you.'

'No, Daddy.'

'I don't think there's any harm . . .' Mummy began, but his look stopped her.

'Cut up,' cried Huw. He was two now and no longer fitted his high-chair so he sat at the table, balanced precariously on cushions. He clattered his fork on his plate.

I shushed him before Daddy could get any more annoyed, and cut his Yorkshire pudding into tiny gravy-soaked squares.

When we'd finished lunch, Daddy said, 'Now I'm going to call round and see if Vassily would like to come and play. Objections, Astrid?'

She shook her head but pressed her lips together till they went white. Hazel gave me a filthy look as if this was *my* doing. After we'd helped with the washing-up we climbed up into the tree-house.

'It's not my fault,' I said, before she could start. She sat down on the branch-seat and gave a long theatrical sigh.

'I won't call him Puddle-duck then,' I said. 'I'll call him Dog-belly.'

She giggled. 'Grizzle!'

'Well that's what he's got. All those teats, like a dog. Disgusting.'

'They can't really be teats, not like ours.'

'They are.'

'They're probably chicken-pox scars.'

'You didn't see them.'

She pulled up her blouse and twisted round to see the little cluster of hollow pink scars on her side where she'd scratched her chicken-pox, much worse than mine, the year before.

'You know ages ago ...' I began, taking advantage of her reasonable mood, 'when you got in trouble – the first time Dog-belly ...,' I luxuriated in the word, enjoying the prickle of spite it gave me.

'The first time Dog-belly what?'

'Came round.'

She didn't answer.

'What *did* Daddy do? When he punished you I mean?' I waited. I didn't expect her to answer. But she gave a puzzled frown that made her look more like Mummy than ever. 'Nothing,' she said. 'He didn't really do anything. He didn't touch me. He just made me feel awful, like . . . rubbish . . . like nothing.'

'Oh.' I didn't probe. I didn't think that sounded too bad as a punishment, though there was a deep hurt scrape in her voice as she said it.

'Anyway, *I'm* not playing with him,' she said, flipping back into her usual self. 'And he's not coming near me. I've got homework.'

Hazel had just started at grammar school. She had her own bedroom now and I was still not used to it. Sometimes I slept in the bottom bunk though I didn't like that empty bed above me; sometimes I slept in the top bunk but then I missed Hazel below. I asked Mummy if I could have an ordinary bed instead but she said it was useful to keep the bunk-beds for when I had a friend to stay. What about Elaine? Why didn't I invite Elaine to sleep the night?

Because I was afraid that Daddy would have a dream, that's why. I didn't want Elaine to hear him cry out or see him running wildly down the landing. I didn't want her to know that about my family. I couldn't understand how *Mummy* could not mind.

We watched Daddy come through the side gate, hand in hand with Puddle-duck. 'Have fun with Dog-belly.' Hazel slipped elegantly through the trap-door and down the ladder. Now that she was at grammar school she always had the excuse of homework and could get out of anything. She left the house half-an-hour before me each morning to catch the bus, leaving me to dodge Puddle-duck alone. I watched her swing down the garden towards the house. She was wearing a kilt and green knee-socks.

'Hello Vassily,' she said loud enough for me to hear. 'Grizzle's in the tree-house, Daddy.'

'Griselda!'

I hugged my knees to my chest and groaned.

'Griselda, your friend is here.'

'OK.'

I watched my ants as I waited to feel the tug on the ladder that would signal Puddle-duck's approach. One ant, at the bottom of the ramp by a crystallising drop of sugar solution, was damaged. It looked as if it had been trodden on, one side of its body all squashed. But how could that have happened in the safe little plastic world? As I watched, another ant came up the ramp, examined the wounded creature, fed from the sugar and then began to drag its fellow along. The squashed ant struggled, its legs waving feebly. I wonder if ants have voices? I wonder if there were minute wiry cries of pain too fine for me to hear? The second ant dragged the invalid half-way up the ramp. I was touched. I thought that maybe there was an ant hospital somewhere in the labyrinth of flaking tunnels. But instead the injured ant was lugged to the edge of the ramp and pushed over. It clung for a moment and then dropped lightly to the bottom of the tank. And I noticed something I hadn't seen before. A litter of dead and brittle ants on the bottom, amongst the scattered dirt.

Puddle-duck still had not arrived. I looked out of the window to see Daddy pushing him on the swing, pushing from the front, showing him how to bend and straighten his legs to work the swing himself.

'I do think it's the pleasantest thing, ever a child can do,' I muttered. I felt like calling out: *I thought Dog-belly had come to play with me, not you*, but that was stupid because *I* didn't want to play with him, and the longer Daddy did the less I would have to. But I still didn't like to see Daddy playing with him. I put the trap-door down to shut them out.

It started happening nearly every Sunday afternoon after that. As soon as lunch was over, Daddy would go out. Sometimes he'd be gone an hour or more and then return with Puddle-duck, sometimes he'd leave him to me to play with when I was there – I tried to be at Elaine's on Sundays whenever I could but they were always going off for outings in their bubble-car and all my other friends lived too far away. I began to dread Sundays.

One Sunday when I did manage to escape, Hazel got stuck with him. When I returned she was very quiet. 'You must not let this happen,' she said.

'I know, but . . .'

'Remember what I said you must do?'

I remembered.

We always called him Dog-belly between ourselves, nobody else knew that name. It was our secret. At school he was still Puddle-duck and at home, to Mummy or Daddy or Wanda, Vassily.

'It's a funny name, *Vassily*,' I said to Mummy. She was blowing eggs for us to paint for Christmas tree decorations. She paused. A long trail of clear slime dangled from the tiny hole.

'Polish,' she said, 'like Pudilchuck.' She gave another blow, her face growing pink, and the slime turned yellow. 'We'll have omelette tonight.'

'But he's not Polish. And Wanda's not Polish, is she? She talks funny though doesn't she?'

'That's just her accent – Ipswich I think. And his father was Polish. He went off before Vassily was born. Not a word since.'

'Why did Wanda call him Vassily, then?' I asked. 'Why not a proper name like John?'

'It is a proper name. Don't be so small minded.' She gave a final blow and emptied the shell. 'There.' She handed the shell to me. I cupped it in my hand, so light and white as the moon. Then she mused, 'Maybe that was the father's name. Maybe she loved him.'

'She's got another boyfriend now,' I said.

'Has she? Yes, well . . .' She picked up another egg and a long pearl-headed hat-pin to pierce it. The hat-pin had been her mother's. It made me wince to imagine pinning a hat to your head with such a thing.

'Why does Daddy like him so much?'

She forced the pin through the shell too hard and cracked

it. 'Damn. Oh I don't know, Grizzle, questions, questions, questions. Maybe it's because he's got no father of his own.'

'What about *us*?' I said.

'What *about* you?' She picked up another egg and frowned. 'You're all right.'

In the spring, my father and Dog-belly started to make a pond. It was halfway down the garden in a corner of the lawn under the flowering cherry. They dug the hole together. Dog-belly was pathetic, no help at all. Daddy even had to show him how to use the spade. Sometimes I sat in the tree-house hugging my knees and watching them. I hadn't been invited to help, and nor had Hazel. She said she didn't care. She didn't want to be grubbing out in the dirt. She was always out with Bridget or her new grammar-school friends, or doing homework. I hardly saw her properly any more now that I was alone at night.

'I'm not sure about a pond,' Mummy said one night. We were watching a programme about penguins. Hazel and I giggled as a whole smart-suited bevy of them waddled and slithered down an icy slope and belly-flopped into the sea. 'Adult male Emperor penguins can be more than a metre high,' the narrator said. We couldn't believe it, bigger than Huw, up to my chest. They looked so tiny on the television, as if you could sit one on your hand.

'Half dug now,' Daddy said. Only *half*, I thought. Already it was enormous.

'I'm worried that Huw will tumble in.' Mummy glared at him. 'Really Ralph, I do think we might have discussed it.'

Hazel and I exchanged glances. There was a rare steely edge in Mummy's voice.

'It'll be an asset,' he said.

'But dangerous. My idea is, since you've started it, that we fill it with sand. It can be Huwie's sand-pit till he's older. Then you can have your pond.'

'You're being ridiculous.'

'Well, I want a fence round it then, a barrier of some sort. Otherwise I'll never be able to let Huw out of my sight.'

'Astrid. It's an ornamental garden pond. It's not Lake Windermere for Christ's sake.'

'You can drown in an inch.'

'I've had enough of this.' He got up and slammed out of the room. Mummy sat very still staring at the screen. The newspaper that had slid off his lap rustled on the floor. The penguins launched themselves up out of the water, landing on their bellies on the ice but we didn't laugh. The front door banged.

'What's up with *him*?' Hazel said. Mummy didn't answer, she was staring at the carpet, twisting a strand of hair tightly round her finger. Huw began to fret from his bedroom and she went upstairs to see to him. 'Steptoe and Son' came on and we watched that. Mummy cheered up and made us some popcorn that exploded in the kitchen like a volley of machine-gun fire and filled the house with a golden smell.

That night Hazel was friendly. She came into my room and sat on the bottom bunk. 'I like my new room,' she said, 'but I do sometimes feel lonely at night.' 'So do I,' I said. I could never have admitted that if she hadn't said it first. 'Good-night old bean,' she said as she went out. 'Good-night old bean,' I replied. That was what we always said when we were friends. We hadn't said it for a long time. Sometimes I thought I'd do anything to be Hazel's friend. 'Make him not want to come,' she'd said. 'Frighten him, or hurt him.' That was a year ago and I had done nothing. There was nothing I could do.

I had worked out how to spell Dog-belly with my fingers. If the subject of the boy or the pond came up at table during breakfast or dinner I would spell that name under the table over and over until I felt better. He wasn't in my class any more. We were in the top class at junior school and had been streamed. I was in the top stream, and he, to my surprise, was not in the bottom. He had learned to read and was climbing. He was in the middle.

I'd made up a rhyme that I would say to myself when I was

skipping, or when I was running along in the morning, trying to avoid him on the way to school: *Dog-belly, Puddle-duck, Puddle-belly, Dog's muck*. I ignored him at school and he stopped smiling at me which should have been better. But it irritated me. It was as if we had made an agreement to keep our friendship secret, when there *was* no friendship. Only the awkward Sunday afternoons.

They lined the deep oval kidney-shaped hole with white sand, patting it into the sides, throwing out any sharp stones. I watched them from the tree-house, Daddy's big hands showing Dog-belly's small ones how to smooth the sand. I wanted to help. It looked like fun making the raw ugly hole look so pure and pretty, like the inside of a shell. When I'd said to Mummy before that I wanted to help she just said, 'Help then.' I objected that he'd never asked me. She said that he didn't need to ask me and, naturally, he'd be delighted if I helped. I thought she was wrong. For some reason he didn't want me to help, or Hazel – not that she cared. He only wanted Dog-belly. But sitting up there in the tree, one sunny spring afternoon watching them with the silvery sand, I decided to see if Mummy was right. I climbed down the ladder. I didn't say anything. I just picked a handful of sand from the plastic sack and started patting it against the earthy side of the hole. It felt cool and made a solid noise as if I was patting the flank of a horse. Dog-belly smiled at me. He, at least, seemed pleased that I was helping. Daddy ignored me at first and then looked up and said, 'No, not like that.'

'Like what?'

'Look, you're knocking earth from the top on to the sand.'

'Sorry.'

'You're breaking up the edge with your shoe. Move.'

'There's not room over that side for me.'

'Careful, you'll ruin it.'

I stood back and watched them. There were grains of sand under my nails. I stood there for a few moments waiting for Daddy to say something else. Dog-belly kept looking up, grinning his yellow grin, but Daddy kept his head down.

'That's right,' he said to Dog-belly, his voice a hundred times more gentle than when he spoke to me. I went into the kitchen to wash the sand off my hands. Mummy was sitting at the table picking bits off the joint to chew and reading the newspaper while Huw took all the pots and pans out of the cupboard under the sink.

'What's up?' she said.

'Why does Daddy like Vassily better than me?' I asked.

'You dope.' She laughed. 'Course he doesn't.'

'He acts like he does.'

'Well . . .' She shrugged. 'Daddy is . . . complicated. I don't know. He's not harming you, is he Grizzle? And he's happy.'

'Happy?'

'Well . . .'

Huw started crashing saucepan lids together and I went back out to the tree-house and shut myself in.

When Daddy finally took Dog-belly home, he didn't come back for ages. We'd had our Sunday night baths and washed our hair and were sitting by the fire while it dried and still he wasn't back.

'Where *is* Daddy?' Hazel asked.

'Gone for a walk, I expect,' Mummy said, 'bending over that blasted pond all day, he'll need to stretch his legs.'

Dog-belly had left his cardigan at our house. On Monday evening Mummy sent me round to Wanda's with it.

'Oh *Mum* . . .' I objected.

'Or you could take it round in the morning, walk to school with him.'

'I'll do it now.'

Wanda seemed delighted to see me. 'Come on in and have a drink,' she said. 'Daft little spook, he'll forget his head next.'

She led me into the sitting-room. The curtains were drawn,

the lamps were lit, the television was on with no sound and a record was playing. 'Pink Floyd,' she said. 'Like it?'

Vassily, wearing a dressing-gown, was curled up in the arm-chair with the cat, watching a film and sipping Coca-Cola. The television, unlike ours, was colour. An incense stick stuck in a plant pot had left a worm of ash on the table. There were magazines strewn everywhere, recipes, knitting patterns, beauty tips. Wanda was dressed in a long red crushed-velvet dressing-gown, tatty but luxurious looking. Her eyes were smoky and huge.

'Having a night off,' she said. 'Do join us.'

'Off what?' I asked but she didn't hear.

I hadn't meant to stay or even step inside. But it was very cosy in the room and Vassily had hardly even looked at me. He was engrossed in some Carry On film. Without the sound on, it was as if the characters were under water, a tank full of bright silly fish opening and closing their silent mouths to the rather odd music.

'Bacardi and coke?' Wanda waved the bottle at me. I was flattered. The only alcohol I'd had before was a thimbleful of ginger wine at Christmas. That was something I liked about Wanda – she didn't treat me like a child. I was disappointed with the drink, it tasted just like ordinary coke. But still, coke was a treat in itself. Mummy wouldn't buy it, but Wanda actually got it from the milkman on Saturdays along with her milk.

'How's your love life?' she asked, curling up on the sofa with her feet tucked underneath her. The sofa made puffy, squelchy sounds as she snuggled her body down.

I laughed. 'How's yours?' I replied, very cheeky. Where her dressing-gown fell open I could see the skin on the inside of her knee, very white skin, a little rough. She made a funny face and I laughed again. I took another gulp of my drink. I was surprised at the way laughs kept fizzing up inside me like the Coca-Cola bubbles in my glass. She had a silver ring on every finger. She saw me looking and took one off. It was a puzzle ring. She undid

110

it so that it was just a loose jumble of uneven loops and fidgeted it back together. She had quite thick fingers and chewed nails. 'Can I have a go?' I asked. She handed it to me and topped up our drinks. I looked over at Vassily who was still absorbed by the television, a full glass clasped between his hands. I hoped there was no Bacardi in his coke.

'TV addict,' Wanda said quite proudly, following my glance. 'Though that's a wonder he makes anything of it.' She pulled the lobe of her ear. I could smell her patchouli oil and the clashing muskiness from the joss-stick. My teeth felt dry and tacky from the drink.

'German measles,' Wanda said.

'What?'

'Got it when I was carrying . . .' she nodded at Vassily.

'Oh . . . and did that make him . . .?' I fiddled with the ring, but I couldn't make the pieces fit together.

'Could have been worse, that sometimes make them blind and all.' I tried to imagine being deaf and blind. There was a film about Helen Keller I'd seen on the television. I couldn't think how, if you couldn't see or hear, you could do anything. How you would even know that you were there. I took another swig of my drink. The idea made me dizzy.

'Vassily gets on very well, considering,' I said.

'Well he's doing speech therapy and that,' she said. 'Poor little spook.' She sighed. I thought the name suited him – Spook – little spindly ghosty boy. 'He's no oil painting, is he?' she continued. 'But you should of seen his dad.' She rolled her eyes and held her breath while I imagined a hero. 'At least I assume that was his dad.' She laughed again. 'Your dad now he's a . . .'

'A what?'

'He's a nice dad. He's nice to my Vass.'

'Yes.'

She took the ring and showed me how to do the puzzle. 'And your mum, she's nice too. A nice family.' There was something a little grudging in her tone. I could see the deep and downy crease between her breasts. I knew what the word sexy meant. I burped and blushed.

She laughed. 'Better out than in.'

'I ought to go and do my homework.'

'What a good girl.' Wanda's voice was wistful now. I finished my drink. The record ended, the arm of the record-player swept across and clicked. The room suddenly seemed very quiet.

'Let's have another go first.' I took the ring back and shook it apart. This time I did it.

'Keep it,' she said.

'Really?'

'If that fits you.' It was too loose even for my middle finger but I didn't say. I wanted to keep it.

'You're quite pretty,' Wanda said, pulling her head back and surveying me critically.

'I'm *not*.'

'Give you a few years.'

'It's Hazel who's pretty,' I said, willing her to disagree.

'Horses for courses,' she said. 'Got ten minutes?'

'S'pose so.'

'Come here then.' She took me through into her bedroom. It was extremely untidy, the bed all rumpled and strewn with more magazines, clothes all over the floor, and soft toys. A black furry gorilla lolled on her pillows.

'There's a lot of toys in this house,' I said. Standing up I felt most peculiar, very squat as if there wasn't much space between my great big head and feet.

'We like toys, me and Vass,' she said. 'We go up town Saturdays, shopping. That's our treat. Look . . .' She picked up a wind-up monkey, swept a litter of envelopes, tissues and lipsticks off her dressing-table, wound the key and set the toy down. It loped along for a few steps, then suddenly turned a somersault on its fists, landed back on its feet and walked right off the edge of the dressing-table on to the floor where it buzzed helplessly, its legs scissoring in the air. She shrieked with laughter and flopped on to the bed. 'Int that a scream?' I smiled and sat down beside her wondering what on earth it must be like to have such a childish mother.

'Right then,' she said. She narrowed her eyes at me and picked up a hairbrush and a comb. She crawled behind me on the bed and knelt so that I could see our two faces in the mirror. She lifted strands of my hair up and started to comb them backwards from the tips to the scalp. 'Back-combing,' she explained. My hair swelled as she worked through it into a voluminous brown fuzz. I spent many hours a week trying to calm my hair down into something as biddable as Hazel's, ironing it, even sleeping in a Balaclava helmet, and here was Wanda trying to make it worse. Under the bare backs of my thighs I could feel crumbs on the nylon sheet. The green nightie was a bright puff on the floor. 'There . . . what do you think?'

I turned my head from side to side. 'Not sure,' I said.

'You want to get a bit of henna on that,' she said. 'You'd look fantastic. Now eyes.' She crawled off the bed and rummaged through a dressing-table drawer. 'Kohl,' she said. She sucked a little brush into a moist point and dabbed it on a block of black stuff. 'Keep still.' Her face was very close to mine. She had black marks from the brush on her lips. The rough tip of her tongue was nipped between her teeth as she painted tickly lines above my eyelashes and then on the lower rim of my eye. I felt the brush slip and slide on my eyeball. 'Oops! All right?' I nodded. My nostrils were full of the scent of her breath and her skin. 'I'd of loved a girl,' she sighed, as she finished. 'Not that I don't love Vass, of course. But I *would've* liked a daughter.'

I felt almost jealous of the daughter she didn't have.

'There, what do you reckon?'

My eyes looked smoky and mysterious. Like something out of a Turkish delight advertisement. 'Fabulous,' I said. Although I wasn't sure.

'Told you you were pretty, didn't I?' She looked proud. 'Getting tits too.' She touched my chest where small lumpy swellings were starting under my nipples. I jerked away from her hand. I hadn't realised they showed. I was terrified of getting breasts at all, and particularly of getting them before Hazel who would never forgive me.

'Better go,' I said. My chest smarted from the sudden casual touch of her hand. I hurried home, clumsy and nauseous from the drink.

'Good God,' Hazel said when she saw me. She was weighing out butter and flour for tomorrow's domestic science lesson.

'Wanda did it,' I said. 'What do you think?' I put my hand up to the warm fuzz of my hair. I could see my white face reflected in the dark glass of the kitchen window.

She pulled a face.

'And she gave me this,' I said, twisting the ring round my finger. She pretended she was too busy watching the needle flicker on the scales to look.

Mummy came in. 'Oh there you are. I was about to send out a search party.'

I touched my hair again. 'Like it?'

'Well, it's certainly different.'

'It's back-combed with kohl on my eyes.'

'Coal?' Hazel said.

'Kohl.'

'Anyway, it's bedtime. Are you all right? You look a bit flushed.'

'Fine,' I said. But when I went upstairs I was sick.

Next morning Dog-belly was waiting for me outside. I had what I suppose was a hangover and was too dopey to dodge him. I didn't want to walk with him. Just because I liked his mother didn't mean I had to like him. His hair looked clean for once. He had had it cut and his hearing-aids seemed to stick out further than ever on either side of his narrow yellow face.

'Hello,' he said, careful and loud.

'Hi.' I went to walk past him.

'Griselda!' By some bad luck my mother had happened to step outside at that moment with the milk bottles. When she called I thought I must have forgotten something.

'What?'

'Walk with Vassily, won't you?' There was a slight warning inflection in her voice.

'OK.' I walked along in silence. He said one or two things, even touched my arm in a friendly way to try and spell something to me, but I didn't look. I felt as if a balloon was inside me wanting to burst, my dislike for him was so strong: dislike, resentment and I don't know what else. I wished I need never see him again. Hazel's words came back to me once more, her cool precise voice, the way she'd said it as if it was obvious what I had to do. Hurt him. OK. Hurt him. But how?

13

'Your bath's ready.' Foxy comes in, her glasses steamy. 'Oh Zelda, you've let your coffee get cold now!'

'Been dozing.'

'Well, that's good, but come on, up.'

'Bossy cow.'

She smiles, stretches out her hands and pulls me from the warmth.

The bath is deep and almost too hot and she has poured some of my lime bath soak into it. I twist and pin up my hair and slide down into the water. Less than twelve hours ago I lay in this bath, ignorant, innocent, of my father's death. The morning sun streams dazzlingly through the bathroom window, curdling in the steam. Foxy perches on the edge of the bath.

'More coffee?'

I shake my head. The water is tight, hot, comforting. Somehow I goose-pimple for a moment against the heat of it; minuscule bubbles, fine as dust, rising from the down on my arms and belly.

'I've been looking though your father's papers.'

'Oh?' I close my eyes.

'Do you mind?'

I don't answer. Of course she would look at them. I left them on the kitchen table where she could not fail to see. And being Foxy, it would be impossible for her not to

116

read them. So I can't, I shouldn't, mind. But still, I find that I do.

'Course not.'

'Sure?'

I smile up at her. 'There's not much you can make out, is there?'

She considers. 'Enough.'

'Enough for what?'

'Well . . .' she touches my shoulder with her cool index finger. She looks incongruously smart, here in the bathroom, hair done, lipstick on. She's taken off her fogged-up glasses. From this angle, below her, I can see the signs of age in her face. The skin is not so tight as it used to be, the pores lax. As she looks down there is a suggestion – just a suggestion – of looseness about her jaw-line and cheeks, a puckering on her throat.

'What do you think?' I ask.

'I think . . . well obviously he suffered. I think he was a very sensitive, a very intelligent, very . . . beautiful man. I'm sorry now I never met him.' I can tell from the considered and slightly artificial way she speaks that she has planned what to say.

'But *I* never knew him. Not *that* him.' I cannot keep the wail out of my voice. 'If *you* had met him you wouldn't have seen those things.'

She purses her lips and shrugs. 'Maybe.' She pauses. 'Or maybe familiarity breeds contempt?'

'That's not true, that's not fair.' I smash my hand down in the water and splash her immaculate blouse.

'Oi!' she moves away. 'All right. Sorry.'

The water laps against me, through the wet white skin of my left breast I can see the faint beat of my heart. 'I could have known him better,' I say.

'Maybe, but Zel, it was up to *him*.'

'I never asked him anything about . . . about his past. I never . . .'

'But *he* was *your* father.'

'. . . even looked at him properly, not for a long time, if ever, I never . . .'

'He was the adult. He should have set the agenda.'

'. . . even took him into account as a *man*, do you know what I mean? An individual, an individual with a separate . . .'

'There's no way you can blame . . .'

'. . . identity, personality. Separate from being my father, I mean . . . and even that . . .'

'Hey . . . Zelda . . . calm down.'

I give up, smile weakly, and slide further into the water so that it tickles the lobes of my ears. I shut my eyes against Foxy's concern. I can feel a laugh stuck in me like a bubble in a coiled-up hose-pipe, thinking of what she said. *He should have set the agenda.* That jargon. I can just imagine his face if I had said that to him. 'Father, it's up to you to set the agenda.' No. I can't imagine his face, I can't picture it at all. And I will never see it again.

'Sweet-pea?' The laugh crawls silently through the coils. Sweet-pea. A legume. Hazel and I called each other Old Bean. Another legume. Pulse. Nothing but a slight coincidence, not amusing. But coincidences are part of it. The texture of it. Of what? Life, experience. *It.* Coincidences, correspondences. Correspondences – letters, diaries. I correspond with you. Respond to me. Oh shut the hell up. I snap open my eyes.

'All right?' Her face is creased with concern.

'Oh Foxy.' I am exasperated.

'What?'

'Nothing.' How can I say, stop caring? I do want her to care but not like this. I don't want her concern, her kindness, certainly not her pity. I want her genuine passion, not her compassion. Genuine passion or nothing at all. But I can't say that because I *do* need her now.

'I've put the papers back in the envelope. Maybe you should take them with you?'

'Yes, no, maybe, I don't know.'

'Show them to your mother, Hazel, Huw?'

'Maybe.'

'Sit up,' she says, leaning over to squeeze a sponge in the water. 'I'll do your back. Then we really must hit the road.'

TICKLE

1

Screams in the sky, slits in the dark, streamers of shrieking light. A rocket plummets over the cliff edge and into the sea. In next door's garden the bonfire has relaxed down to a glow of embers; the children with their excited shrieks and scribbling sparklers gone to bed – and the last remains of the paper-faced man turned to cinders or blown away in ashy flakes. I press my forehead against the cold window and my breath mists the glass.

Mummy doesn't know them very well, next door. If they had known today was the day of Daddy's cremation, as Hazel indignantly pointed out, surely they would have had more tact than to burn their Guy just where we could see? But Mummy hadn't told them. The funeral was kept very low key, family only. Because of the inquest, result: death by suicide, as if we didn't know, as if we needed the stress of awaiting the verdict, the funeral was delayed for several weeks. Because Daddy took his own life, Mummy invited no one, wanted no party, wake, whatever you call it, wanted no funeral meats. I think that's why. And now it's over and done with and night has come, and as usual I am left awake. Mummy, Hazel, Colin and Huw all voted for an early night and left me to watch a late film and now, to drift about the house, to summon up the resolve to go to bed.

The crematorium was lined with brown veneer. The flowers weren't real, nor the arrangements inside, white blossoms of silk or polyester. Hazel clutched my hand as the coffin slid behind a Dralon drape and I had an urge to laugh, not that it was funny, but there seemed something absurd about the automatic swish of the curtain, the discreet swallowing of Daddy.

While we were inside there was a hard fleeting shower which had splashed the real flowers, the wreaths and sprays of white roses and carnations, the chrysanthemum golf-bag from the golf club, with mud. Because Mummy had invited nobody, I was startled when we got outside, blinking in the wet sunshine, to see Wanda.

'Have I missed it?' she said. 'Fucking taxi-driver . . . oh I am sorry.' Her face went scarlet and I thought she would weep with embarrassment. She threw her arms round Mummy, who stood stiffly allowing herself to be embraced but giving nothing back. Colin shuffled his feet, waiting for an introduction. Hazel took his arm, 'An old family, sort of, friend,' she whispered.

Wanda's hair is black, newly black. I wonder if she dyed it for the occasion? And she was wearing a black brocade coat. She's lost weight, I'm sure, and looked sallow – maybe black's just not her colour. If it wasn't for her earrings, a long silver cat dangling from one lobe, five graduated rings of silver in the other, she might have passed for conventional. She gave me a hug. 'Hello stranger,' she said into my ear. Her smell has changed: more musk than patchouli now.

'Well, what a surprise.' Mummy collected herself. 'We're not having a . . . a do,' she said, 'but if you'd like to come back for a cup of tea?'

'Gasping for one.'

'Come with us.' Huw beckoned and led the way to his car. It was nearly an hour's drive home. Mummy went with Hazel and Colin. The wet road glittered through the dusty windscreen and caused my eyes to water. I was upset, holding back my feelings, not just about Daddy but about Foxy too, gritting my teeth against them, forcing them down and out of the light of my consciousness. Because they . . . well they would wait.

Dustbins were being emptied on the outskirts of town. It seemed a terribly ordinary day. We got stuck behind a tractor and trailer and had to crawl for miles. A yellow sycamore leaf drifted on to the windscreen, the sky was blandly blue.

'Where are you living now?' I asked Wanda.

'Felixstowe, back to my roots.' She leant forward and waved her hand between us. 'Look.'

'Nice.'

There were two rings on her wedding finger.

'You're telling me. Engagement: zircon, my birthstone,' she waggled the finger so that the stone flashed, 'and wedding, white gold. Yes. I'm an honest woman – at last.'

Huw glanced down at her hand. 'Who's the lucky chap?'

I laughed. Huw has a lucky dip of such stock phrases, always at hand. I was surprised to be laughing on this day, checked myself.

'Stan,' Wanda said. 'Stan the man. Younger than me – but what's ten years? He make me . . . he make me happy.'

'I'm very glad.' I smiled over my shoulder at her. *Happy*. I thought, he makes her *happy*.

But her smile fell away, her face suddenly bleak. 'I can't believe he went and topped himself.'

I could sense Huw stiffening. We both looked straight out through the windscreen. We passed a couple of gaudy Lycra-clad cyclists hunched over their handle-bars.

'No,' I said.

'Still, I don't suppose it make much difference in the long run, how you go,' she tried, but her voice faltered, unconvinced.

'It'll all be the same in a hundred years, eh?' Huw squirted the windscreen washers and switched the squeaky wipers on to swoosh away the dust.

After a mile or two of awkward quiet Wanda began to talk, about Vassily, about his architectural firm, about his wife and daughter. I was glad my face was turned away. I could hardly believe what she was saying. That that boy, that dog-bellied spook, had become a success, made me tremble with shame at the way I had been. Never cruel before or since. That episode a shadow on my childhood. I did not know if she knew about my cruelty. I never knew if Vassily told on us. 'He's a born father,' she was saying, 'none of you . . .?'

'Not as yet.' Huw sounded very firm.

*

I sit at the desk in the room that Daddy called his study. I slide open the top drawer and take out the contents: a tobacco tin full of red, blue and yellow golf tees; a chrome lighter; a pad of blue Basildon Bond; a small electric screwdriver; a packet of wine-gums – and Daddy's best fountain-pen, a fat gold Parker 51. I put a wine-gum in my mouth, a long green one, CLARET it says on the top in raised letters. Claret? Green? My mouth floods with sticky childish juice. I take the top off the pen and hold it poised in my hand as if I'm going to write. It looks a very important pen, I used to think that, for writing important letters with, business things, things that required his stern cramped signature. Children weren't allowed to use it, you'll spoil the nib, he said. I try it. No ink. But there is a bottle of blue-black Quink by the blotter. I suck ink through the snout and inside the cavity, wipe the precious nib on the blotter making a sideways smudge amongst the mysterious blots and squiggles; numbers, names, the trying out of spelling – obssesion, obsession, ocassion, occassion, ocasion, occasion. It makes me smile, they are just the sort of words *I* can never remember how to spell. Daddy. I make a blot into a man, the profile of a man in a bowler hat.

I will write a letter, a letter to Foxy.

*

'That's obvious why you moved here,' Wanda said to Mummy when we were home. We were all standing in the sitting-room with cups of tea all gazing out of the bay window at the sea. 'What a view.'

126

'Yes, we bought it for the view.'

'Not the wisest decision,' Colin added, 'in terms of the coastal erosion.'

Hazel gave him a look.

Mummy took a sip of tea and sighed. 'Well, Ralph was set on it . . . a good price . . . and it's near the golf club.'

'Him and his golf!' Wanda gave a throaty laugh.

'Yes.' Mummy's voice tight. I had a sudden start, looking at Wanda, something occurring to me. Not Daddy and Wanda? Surely not. I tried to catch Hazel's eye but she was busy brushing something off Colin's shoulder.

I stepped back and sat on the arm of an armchair. Now I was the audience and they were the actors, but their backs were to me. The funeral tea. Widow, family and possible mistress sipping tea from china cups. Widow a head taller than mistress, elegant beside her daring.

No, it was not possible, surely. Daddy and Wanda. And yet, and yet . . . possibly it made a sort of sense? No. But not impossible . . .

'A little semi, not much but it's our own,' Wanda was saying, she glanced up at Huw who had put down his cup and was lighting a cigarette for himself. He saw her eyeing it and held out the packet. 'Thanks. Not what the doctor ordered, but still. How are you doing?'

'Can't complain,' he said. He held his cigarette between his finger and thumb just like Daddy had done. His profile was Daddy's too.

'He's going great guns,' Mummy said. 'Lots of auditions.'

'Ads mainly.'

'And Coriolanus, not like you to hide your light . . .' Hazel smoothed her hair.

'Well, as I said, can't complain.'

'And Vassily?' Mummy sat down in the armchair beside me. Her face, under its powder, was pale and sweating, not like Mummy, not like Mummy to look defeated.

Wanda began recounting Vassily's success story and I went out of the house and wandered away to the backs of the cliff-top shacks and caravans. They had a neglected tatty air and most of them had wildly optimistic 'For Sale' signs in the windows. A sign: DANGER: LARGE AREAS OF CLIFF CAN GIVE WAY WITHOUT WARNING was stuck to a gate-post. I went cautiously to the edge, the place where the last shack had tumbled, and looked down. A bit of drain-pipe still dangled from the cliff and on the beach there was some debris, part of a brick chimney stack. The sea swirled below me, a dark cloudy brown as it dissolved the cliff. I stepped back, suddenly dizzy.

Daddy and Wanda.

Yes. Like a new beam shone down the corridor of my past, fresh details were illuminated, fresh shadows cast.

Wanda here at the funeral. What else could it mean? Had Mummy invited her? Why would she? I walked past the shacks and down a sloping footpath to the beach. Not dressed for it, not planning for it. I went for a long walk, walked until the light was flat pewter on the sea and the shore darkening, walked with my hands in my pockets, the salt ruining my black suede shoes. As I walked, faster and faster, I let go of all my control. I let furious thoughts well up inside me. I shouted, raged at the sea-gulls and the greedy sea, dashed tears from my eyes, not tears for Daddy now, tears for myself, overwhelmed by the faithlessness of husbands and lovers, wrenched by the pain of betrayal. I walked until distant fireworks began to scratch the sky and the sea smell became tinged with woodsmoke. And when I returned, Wanda had gone.

2

If it had not been for my ants, I might have spent less time in the tree-house. Somehow, as a refuge, it was spoilt now that Dog-belly was always in and out of it.

One Sunday afternoon, from my bedroom window, I saw Daddy holding the ladder while Dog-belly climbed up and then, once the thin legs had disappeared inside, he began to climb up himself. A shout of protest stuck in my throat. I could not believe it. He had *never* been into the tree-house. Even Mummy did no more than occasionally pop her head through the trap-door to talk to us. It was *ours*. Hazel's and mine.

I thought it might collapse with the weight of Daddy, that the branches might break and the whole structure come crashing to the ground with a splintering of wood, smashing Daddy and Dog-belly's bones among the broken branches. My ants would be all right, they would survive the fall and be set free. I wished the tree-house *would* collapse then that would be an end of it. But Daddy only put his head through the trap-door and did not climb right in. He stood there on the ladder, wobbling a bit, like a headless man.

I heard Mummy's voice. She had gone outside and was laughing at something. My thumb went in my mouth, my teeth finding the comforting ridge of my knuckle. I watched as first Daddy, then Dog-belly came down the ladder. I was terrified that Daddy might have seen my ants.

'Daddy would never agree,' Mummy had warned when I asked if I could bring the formicary home from school. 'You know how he is about creepy-crawlies. You couldn't have it in the house.' I brought the ants home and kept them in the tree-house where he never went. I had been jubilant to have that teeming little world for my own. I admired the industrious creatures, their minute bulbousness and sheen. Although they were all separate they acted like one creature, many bodies with a single intention. Dropping a chicken's wish-bone in one day had resulted in an extraordinary tumult of activity – but not in chaos. The ants stripped the bones and stowed the meat as if they had been in training for that very event for all of their lives.

Hazel didn't mind having the ants in the tree-house as long as the tank stayed on my side, on my shelf. 'As long as you promise never to let them out,' she said.

'Course not.'

'They're like prisoners,' she mused, prodding with a lolly-stick and watching the creatures boiling over the surface of their nest.

'They're not prisoners,' I said, 'not at all. This is their whole world.'

She pulled a face as if I was mad.

At least they were safe in their tank, that's what I thought, safe from predators or the stamping feet of human beings.

Daddy didn't mention the ants. From the angle his head would have been at as he stood on the ladder, I realised with a rush of relief, the tank would have been behind him. He could not have seen it.

*

Dear Foxy,　　　　　　　　　　　　　　　　　　*5.11.90*

　　I'm going to stay a few more days. The funeral was all right.
I'm glad it's over. I'm glad you didn't come – but thanks for

offering. Colin is being his usual obnoxious self but he and Hazel are leaving tomorrow, and Huw too. I'll stay with Mummy for a few days because she might need me.

Also because I've done something I'm ashamed of, something that has upset me – my own fault. I read your diary. I didn't intend to, I was looking for some tampons, we'd run out in the bathroom, I thought you might have some, I looked in your bag. I saw your diary in there and I should not have looked. No excuse. So I know about Kris. I wish I didn't, I wish I hadn't read it. No, that's not quite true, I'm glad I know but I wish it wasn't true. Of course I was livid, that's why I left before you got home, I couldn't face you. Thinking back I realise you never lied, you just never told me quite the truth but I think that is as bad as lying. Driving down here I realised that if there was Kris there will have been others, because you don't make it sound that much of a big deal. I realise that if I hadn't shut the diary quickly, shoved it straight back in your bag and fled, if I'd read right back through the year I'd have found other names: Sally perhaps? You spent a lot of time with Sally, or Dana, or Jez?

To think how stupidly I trusted you. To think I missed you so much whenever you were away, the welcome I gave you on your returns, my mouth full of you when maybe the night before . . . oh I can't bear to think about it. I feel so stupid. At the moment I hate you.

I've put this to the back of my mind today, tried to think of Mummy first. An old family friend came, Wanda, I think I've told you about Wanda. And now I think . . . oh never mind. When I get back perhaps we could talk.

Yours, (yours? I don't think so)

Zelda.

*

Daddy and Dog-belly finished the pond. It was Easter Sunday. I thought that because it was Easter, Daddy might not ask him round, or that maybe Wanda would have taken him away for the weekend. But no, as soon as the table was cleared after lunch, there was his yellow face peering round the door. Hazel had gone out with some friends. I slunk outside and sat up in the tree-house with my Easter egg. I unwrapped the spotty blue-and-silver foil and wedged my thumb-nail in the crack to split the egg into halves. I held the two halves of egg over my mouth and nose to inhale the trapped breath of chocolate before it floated away. Then I broke off a fraction of shell, thicker at the edge, patterned like crazy-paving, and closed my eyes as I put it between my lips. My teeth sank into it. Nothing else has the texture of chocolate, soft and brittle at the same time. My mouth was filled with its sudden melting velvet.

But I was not happy. Daddy and Dog-belly were stretching a great sheet of green plastic over the hole. I watched from the little round window as they weighted it down with bricks around the edges so that it was pulled quite flat. Then Daddy fixed the hose to the tap in the garage and let Dog-belly direct the water into it. The water pooled on the taut sheet. As Dog-belly stood, a stupid grin on his face, holding the streaming hose out stiffly in front of him, Daddy crawled round on his hands and knees easing the bricks so that the plastic, bulging now with water, stretched to fit the contours of the hole. The water made a fatter, a deeper, a tumbling sound the more of it there was. I could smell the freshness of it, like the smell of rain. Mummy, carrying a struggling Huw on her hip, came out of the kitchen door to watch. She said nothing. 'Me swim,' Huw shouted, and Mummy glared at the back of Daddy's head.

When the pond was full it made a kidney shape, clean and glinting in the corner of the lawn. It reflected the clouds that moved across the sky. It reflected the frothy pink cherry blossom from the tree above it. A petal fluttered down and floated on its surface. Nature accepted it, this new pond, easy as that.

I had wanted to hold the hose-pipe. I had wanted the thrill of all that water pouring through my hands. I had wanted to help create the pond. But now it was finished and had nothing to do with me.

I realised that without thinking what I was doing I had eaten all of my chocolate egg. My stomach heaved with the queasy bulk of so much sweetness.

'Are you going to cover it, or build a barrier?' Mummy said. 'Otherwise how am I supposed to keep *him* out.' She hitched Huw further up her side.

But there was no reply.

You couldn't look out of the tree-house now without seeing, in one direction, the big glinting kidney of the pond, or in the other, Dog-belly's window and sometimes the small cheesy wedge of his face.

*

I fold my letter to Foxy in half, take out one of Daddy's pale blue envelopes, and slide it in. I lick the gum with the point of my tongue and stick down the flap. On the front I write her name, our address. Imagine it on the mat, the day after tomorrow; Foxy in her dressing-gown, shuffling to the door in her velvet mules. Imagine her putting the letter on the table while she pours her coffee, finds her reading-glasses, then sitting down, pushing her messy red-grey hair back from her face, slitting open the envelope, unfolding the pages of blue Basildon Bond, and reading. Imagine her reaction. *Shit*, she might say, maybe she'll sit with her head in her hands for a bit, then roll herself a skinny fag while she thinks. Maybe she will ring me here, maybe even turn up unexpectedly. Will she be contrite? Will she be angry, somehow deflect the blame all on to me for invading her privacy so that *I* end up apologising?

The pen has left a dark smudge of ink on my middle finger where it has been pressing. I open the envelope, pretending I'm Foxy and read the letter all unaware, as if, as she might, expecting a love letter. Then I tear it in half, in quarters, tear each quarter into tiny squares too small to read, confetti, too small to piece together and make sense of – as if anyone would bother – and throw it in the bin.

3

The morning after the pond was finished, Easter Monday, Daddy invited Hazel and me to go to the golf-course with him. On the golf-course was a big pond, full of weed and at that time of year, he assured us, frog-spawn and tadpoles.

'Is Vassily coming too?' I asked.

He shook his head. 'What do you say?'

'OK. Haze?'

'S'pose so.'

I felt grudgingly pleased. This was the exciting bit after all, putting life in the pond. Dog-belly might have helped to make the pond but *we* were doing the best bit, fetching the tadpoles, *us*, Daddy's actual children. Mummy smiled at me, as if to say, *There, you see* . . . I think she was relieved too that for once we were preferred.

'We'll have to do something to stop Huwie,' Mummy said. 'I can't open the back door without him making a bee-line . . .'

'All right, all right.' Daddy was wearing his green cable golfing sweater. He was pink and newly shaved and his hair glistened with some sort of cream or oil. 'Ten minutes then,' he said. Hazel and I went to dig out some old fishing-nets and plastic seaside buckets from the garage.

'We might get fish too,' I said.

'You have to *buy* fish from the pet shop.' Hazel's voice infused with scorn.

135

'We might catch one.'

'That would be stealing.'

'Why isn't catching tadpoles stealing then?'

'You're so thick,' she said.

I smarted. But I was determined not to fall out with Hazel. 'At least *he's* not coming,' I said.

Hazel and I got into the back of the car. There was a scratchy tartan blanket folded on the back seat. The inside of the car smelt coldly of petrol and sick because Hazel was usually sick in it on long journeys. 'Watch out for balls!' Mummy shouted as we drove off. We had sandwiches and apples in our pockets. We had to wedge the long bamboo handles of our fishing-nets diagonally across the car. It was a long drive to the golf-course on narrow winding roads and I was afraid Hazel would vomit and ruin everything. But she sat with her eyes fixed on the horizon, breathing deeply of the cold air that buffeted through the open window, sucking on barley sugars – and though she went a greenish white and wouldn't speak, she was not sick.

Daddy parked outside the club-house. We climbed out of the car into a salty whistle of wind.

'The pond's over there, see?' Daddy pointed away into the distance.

'Isn't that the sea?' Hazel said, leaning back against the car.

He laughed. 'Not that far . . . down by those bushes.' He smiled at us as he lifted his golf-bag out of the boot. I noticed that one of his clubs was wearing the embroidered felt cover I had made him for Christmas. I wanted to kiss him. It was good to be out with Daddy.

'Do your coat up,' he said. I fastened the wooden toggles of my duffel coat.

The golf-course straddled a road. 'Stay this side of the road,' Daddy instructed. 'The pond's by the ninth hole. I'll pick you up as I pass.'

'OK.'

He swung his golf-bag over his shoulder and set off for the club-house. 'Be good,' he said.

We ran over the short tussocky grass to the top of a rise. There was a faint wavering silver line in the distance that was the sea. Sea-gulls screeched. The wind blustered and moaned and my eyes streamed. My loose hair whipped about my face, my ears stung. I pulled up my hood and even buttoned the little tab that made my chin itch.

It was the first time that Hazel and I had been to this golf-course. From where we stood we could see it reaching down all around us: the greyish hairy grass; the flashes of violently yellow gorse; the sandy dips of the bunkers; the velvet putting-greens each with a frantic white flag on a rattling pole. We ran down the slope, our fishing-nets catching on the lumpy grass, screaming into the wind. I didn't think I would ever be able to stop running – the slope was steeper than it looked. It was funny, my legs going faster and faster like cartoon legs, my top half holding back, trying to stop. I tripped in the end, rolled on the grass unhurt, breathless. Hazel flopped down beside me. We lay on our backs, panting. The wind was not so fierce when we flattened ourselves down and there was even a faint warmth from the sun. We watched rags of clouds tearing and mending in the blue. I felt madly alive, my heart beating against the ground, my eyes smarting with brightness. It was so good to be out with Daddy for once, good to be with Hazel too, with no Bridget or Harriet or Susan or any of her other million friends.

We got up in the end and walked towards the pond. Hazel told me about a boy she liked at school. She was nearly thirteen and had a little spot beside her nose. She was about to start her periods she said. I asked her how she knew but she just smiled mysteriously. 'It's so *different* at secondary school.'

'What is?'

'Just everything. Your whole outlook changes. Junior school seems so utterly . . .'

'Utterly what?'

'Just utterly. You'll see.'

'Fore!' came a yell from somewhere and a golf ball zizzed past between our heads. It landed with a thwunk and a rattle in a clump of gorse.

'It could have killed us!' Indignantly I looked round for the culprit.

'*One* of us,' Hazel corrected.

A man came down the slope, followed by another. The first man was wearing a tweed jacket and his face was red and seamy under a long vertical streamer of white hair.

'Be off with you,' he said.

I wanted to laugh. 'You nearly hit us.'

'This is a golf-course young lady. Not a bally playground.'

'We're waiting for our father. He's playing golf,' Hazel did her sweetest smile.

'You'll get yourselves brained prancing about on the clearway.'

The other man caught up. He was fat and out of breath. 'See where my ball went?' he panted.

We shrugged. 'We're going to the pond,' I said. 'Do excuse us.'

'Bally cheek!'

When we were out of ear-shot we fell about laughing. 'Do excuse us,' Hazel parroted. 'Did you see his face? Bally cheek!' I lit up with pride. It was not often I impressed her.

'Let's get his ball,' I said.

The gorse bushes were dense and crammed with yellow coconut-smelling blossom. The shrubs were old and tall enough to have crawlable passages beneath them. I went in first and found a ball straight away – and then another and another.

'There's tons of them,' I shouted. Hazel came in too though usually she hated to get dirty. We wriggled on our bellies in the sand through increasingly low passages, meeting thorny dead-ends and scratching our hands as we extracted more and more lost balls. I saw one lodged in the bush above me. I put on my sheepskin mitten to get it down, closing my eyes against a rattling scatter of dead prickles. We found nine balls altogether. One or two of them were still white, still shiny and dimpled with tiny numbers and symbols printed on them, but most of them were old and discoloured to various degrees.

'We could give them to Dad,' Hazel suggested.

'The nice ones. Look at this.' A little piece of the outer skin of one ball had split and curled up. I forced my thumb-nail under it and peeled it back. It was very stiff and brittle. Bits kept flaking off between my fingers. Underneath, the ball was a mass of thread, densely wound together like a ball of wool. 'Look . . .' Fascinated, I finished peeling it, the sharp edges of the skin stabbing and jamming into the soft place under my nail. When I had finished it sat in the palm of my hand, a dull, heavy, yellowish ball.

'Can you unwind that stuff?' Hazel asked. Her face was very close to mine. I saw she still had a crumb of sleep in the corner of one eye.

I had to pick with my teeth at the rubbery surface to find an end. It tasted like rubber-bands, only stronger, and snapped off between my teeth. Eventually I found an end and began to pull it loose, it was stretchy, a sort of stringy rubbery stuff.

'Weird,' Hazel breathed. She began sorting through the other balls to find one to undo herself.

'I'd have thought they'd have been white right through,' I said. 'You know, like a boiled egg.'

'Without a yolk,' Hazel said. 'Me too.'

It seemed sort of cosy under the gorse bushes, out of the wind. We set about unpeeling the balls. The rubbery stuff came away easily after the first few strands broke off. In some places it was as if the strings had all melted together and whole lumps came away. It was very fine rubber, unevenly spun – and there was miles of it. It was fascinating to do, fascinating to turn the neat impacted ball into a great pile of looseness all tangled and chaotic.

'I'm addicted to it,' I said.

Hazel didn't answer, she was gnawing at one of the other balls trying to get her teeth into a crack.

'I wonder how you make them?' Imagining people, women probably, in white caps sitting at long benches winding and winding the mountains of stuff. It took ages to get to the middle. I thought that here would be a hard bit, like the seed in an aniseed ball. But when I got there, there was a hollow, sticky and milky as if it hadn't set properly. It smelt fiercely rubbery, like the smell when you undo an old hot-water bottle with its rubber all perished.

It seemed rude somehow, that the centre of a hard thing like a golf ball was all soft and gooey. Unformed. My fingers were all tacky and I felt cold and cramped all of a sudden, realising that gorse prickles had fallen down my neck. I crawled out and stood in the wind, stamping my feet to drive away the fizz of pins and needles, while I waited for Hazel.

We put the golf balls in our buckets and continued on our way to the pond, a big murky oval fringed with dark sand, like a miniature sea. There was a bicycle in it, one handle-bar and a bit of wheel projecting from the water.

'I can't see any weed or any frogs or anything,' Hazel complained. 'Daddy must be mad.'

'Stop calling people mad,' I said. I was disappointed that the pond wasn't brimming with life. I'd imagined bulrushes and dragon-flies, water-lilies, frogs on lily-pads and glamorous goldfishes, one of which, whatever Hazel said, I'd been determined to take home. 'We'll just have to search,' I said. 'There must be *something* living in it.'

I waded in first. I could feel the cold of the water through my wellington boots. The bottom was soft and yielding under my feet.

'Catch something then,' Hazel said. I took another step in. There was a hard thing under the sole of one boot, the muddy sand swirled up, thickening the water which lapped the top of my boot and I felt a cold trickle inside.

'Come on,' I looked over my shoulder at Hazel who was still at the edge, one fastidious foot poised above the surface. I thought I saw something dark moving through the cloudiness. I wanted to get out. The water was so cold I could hardly believe I had boots on at all, it fastened around my ankles, my calves, like iron. I don't know what the dark thing was, it seemed long and sinuous. I thought maybe an eel. I didn't want an eel in our pond, that wasn't the sort of thing at all. It made my stomach churn, the idea of an eel winding round my legs, sliding over the top of my wellington and down inside. I trawled my net through the water, collecting a clot of slimy green weed.

'Look.'

Hazel was standing in the water now, only a little way in, dipping her net.

'It's like snot,' she said, 'put it back.'

'More than you've got.'

'We don't want that sort of thing in our pond.'

'No.' I swept my net backwards through the water to free it of the weed. I kept it near the surface, careful not to catch anything big and dark. I took a step to the side and my net nudged something. I prodded. It was something solid, something that swayed when I nudged it, just a fraction. When I lifted my net it was full of the tiny wriggly squiggles of leeches. I shivered and pulled it back through the water to wash them out. I stepped away from the thing, whatever it was. The water reflected oily rainbows at me.

'I think it's all dead and stagnant,' I said.

'Look.' Hazel had scooped up another golf ball, vivid green with slime. 'I bet there's millions in here.'

'I don't think there's anything we want though, do you?' My feet were beginning to ache with the cold. I could not get the feeling of that heavy nudge out of my hand. I wanted to get out but I didn't want to give up before Hazel. I took another step to the side. A sea-gull swooped low and cried as if it was lost. The sandy bottom seemed suddenly to give way and water cascaded into my boot. I tried to scream, panic gripped my throat, tried to turn, found my foot stuck, pulled madly to free it, lost my balance, fell.

Fell right under the filthy pond water. My mouth was open and my eyes. I saw one khaki dull underwater moment, only one underwater moment, a split second – but when I wrenched my head back above the surface, the brightness was blinding. I struggled up, and waded from the pond, water streaming from me. Hazel was standing on the edge, her hands in front of her mouth giving short sharp screams – I noticed she hadn't done anything to help me. In my mouth was the oily vegetable taste of the pond.

'Grizzle! Now what?' Hazel wailed.

'Thanks for saving me!' I turned away from her. I didn't know what to do. My hair, my duffel coat, everything was sodden. I'd lost one boot. I stood there dripping and began to cry. I spat and spat to try and get rid of the taste. My net floated out of reach in the middle of the pond. Somewhere underneath the water was my boot. I started to shiver violently. My tears were the only hot thing about me.

*

Dear Foxy,   *6 (just) Nov.*

I wish you had come to the funeral with me, it was very nice of you to offer. I'm missing you dreadfully. The funeral was all right – well what you'd expect, quiet, sad. At least it's all over now and we can carry on with our lives. Mummy doesn't seem too bad but I'm going to stay a few days to keep her company.

I don't know why but I've been having the most terrible dreams, maybe some sort of insecurity brought on by the funeral, or just being away from you, I don't know. Last night particularly, I had the most terrible dream about you and Kris. You two were in bed together and I was watching though you couldn't see me so I was powerless to do anything about it I just had to watch. Why should I dream such a thing? It's never even occurred to me that you and Kris might be more to each other than . . . well than meets the eye. Don't worry. I'm not accusing you of anything! I do trust you. But dreams are so strange, aren't they?

Can't wait to see you.

With all my love and more.

Zelda.

I slide this in an envelope. Send her on a guilt trip with no return. A shiver of satisfaction, yes, make her squirm. I'll take her back a present. I'll cook something marvellous, I'll be so good in bed she will be amazed. Buy champagne?

4

'We'll have to find Daddy,' Hazel said, calming down. 'He'll be livid.'

'We don't know where he is,' I tried to say but my teeth were chattering. My clothes felt heavy as if they were trying to pull me back down and into the water. The wind on my face was like icy breath.

The man we had seen before came hurrying down the slope towards us. 'Good Lord, girls.'

'We need to find Daddy,' Hazel said.

'Evidently. When did he tee off?'

'What?'

'What's his name?'

'Mr Dawkins. Ralph.'

'Ah . . .' he seemed to soften. He put up his hand to flatten his flying hair. 'You're *Ralph's* girls.' He looked at us with more interest.

I gave a hysterical shudder and a sob. I was starting to feel very strange, not cold any more, actually quite warm as if my clothes were soaked with water that was hot instead of icy cold.

'Well come along. We'd better get you up to the club-house before you die of bally pneumonia.' He began walking upwards. I could hardly walk. I limped along, one foot squelching water in its boot, the other had gone practically dead in its sock that was slimy and green. I couldn't stop crying in a silly snivelling way.

'I didn't *need* to save you,' Hazel hissed. 'I knew you wouldn't *drown*. It wasn't very deep.'

I didn't answer. I spat again to try to get rid of the awful taste that seemed wound round my tongue like weed. My nose was running but there was nothing to wipe it on but my soaking duffel coat sleeve.

'But anyway I'm sorry,' she said quickly, staring straight ahead and not at me.

'All right,' I managed to sniff.

'I bet your sandwich is ruined,' she said. She looked at my pocket and I felt the muscles in my stiff face bunch as if I wanted to laugh.

'See you've found yourself a ball or two.' The man had stopped to wait for us and was eyeing Hazel's bucket. 'Let me take your net.' He stuck it in his golf-bag.

'Would you like one?' Hazel held out the bucket to him as if it was a plate of biscuits.

'Don't mind if I do.' He selected the nicest, whitest ball from the top and strode on ahead, whistling through his teeth.

In the club-house I had to take off my clothes and put on a man's shirt, sweater and woolly socks. My clothes, stuck to my skin as if they had become part of me, were difficult to peel off. My clammy skin was very pink in some places and white in others, as if I'd been slapped all over. I was changing in a little cupboard, with Hazel waiting outside. The shirt came down to my knees. The cotton felt soft and dry and comforting against my fishy cold skin. But I felt stupid dressed like that, especially when the man made us sit in the bar to wait while someone found Daddy. He gave me a glass of brandy to warm myself up, which was awful.

'Ugh, you've got all *stuff* in your hair.' Hazel was jealous because she'd only got fizzy lemonade. The men in the room all made a fuss of me. I might have enjoyed it if I hadn't been so worried about Daddy. He came in after a while.

'Can't I leave you for five minutes?' he said, which was hardly fair because it had been an hour at least. Someone said what fine looking girls we were, and Daddy looked pleased and bought himself and the man who'd helped us a whisky. 'Chalk and cheese,' someone said, as usual. Daddy didn't seem very angry – he didn't speak in the car but that wasn't unusual. We had to stop for Hazel to be sick and he smiled at me while we were waiting. 'Warming up?' he asked. He drove off again as soon as we were home to finish his round of golf.

Mummy ran me a hot bath and helped wash the slime out of my hair. While I was getting dry, she looked at me thoughtfully. 'You're growing up,' she said and I pulled the towel round my body. I think that's the last time she ever saw me naked.

Although I wasn't ill, Mummy made me get into bed with a hot-water bottle. She brought me a mug of tomato soup, bright orange and speckled, and a pile of old comics to flick through. Once I'd finished the soup, I lay down and dozed, happy for once, special, fussed over, safe in my warm bed, listening to the everyday sounds: Hazel practising her recorder, Huwie's little feet thudding about, Mummy's voice.

Our pond stayed empty for the week. The following Saturday when Elaine and I got back from our riding lesson, Mummy was out in the garden, kneeling by a mountain of rough grey rocks. Huwie was lying on his tummy by the pond snatching up fistfuls of frogs' spawn and laughing as they squirted out between his fingers.

'Frogs' spawn?' I said. I went to look closer and saw a big clot of it at one side, some of the tadpoles already fidgeting inside their jelly balls. And there were two tangerine fish swimming under the weed, calm and smug as if they'd been there for years.

'They're pretty,' Elaine said leaning over.

'Where did they come from?'

'Mr Rutterford donated the weed and the frogs' spawn,' Mummy said. Mr Rutterford was the barman at the golf-club, who, on learning the cause of my accident, had offered Daddy some stuff from his pond. From her voice I could tell she was keeping something back. 'And he took Vassily to the pet shop since you and Hazel were both out,' she said. Elaine snorted. Suddenly I felt ill, the weedy feeling was in my throat as if I was going to choke on something.

'He would have taken you if you'd been here,' Mummy gave me a cautious look but I couldn't say anything in front of Elaine. I'd stopped telling even her about all the time Vassily spent at our house, it was too embarrassing. And Mummy was different about Dog-belly lately, not quite so quick to defend Daddy's odd friendship, not quite so keen to have Dog-belly round. Once I heard her say, 'You can have too much of a good thing, Ralph', and another time, 'Doesn't his mother have any time for him?' But I didn't hear Daddy reply.

'Anyway, what are you doing?' Elaine asked.

'Dry-stone walling,' Mummy said. 'I'm going to build a wall around the pond to stop *somebody* tumbling in.' She nodded towards Huwie. 'And I've always wanted to try this – want to help?'

Elaine pulled a face at me and shook her head. 'We're busy,' I said. 'What will Daddy say about the wall?'

She picked up a big flat stone and considered. 'Look at the lichen,' she said, 'isn't it pretty?'

Elaine and I went into the kitchen to make milk-shakes.

'A small fence would surely have sufficed,' was all that he did say. It was tea-time and we were eating one of Mummy's inventions, a pork and stuffing pizza. We waited for more but he just pursed his lips and reached for the Tabasco.

*

Dear Foxy,   *middle of the fucking night*

I know you have been having an affair with Kris. Or is affair too grand a word? I know you have had sex with Kris. It doesn't matter how I know, don't ask. Maybe some of your friends aren't so loyal as you think. I can't believe you could have cheated on me like this while I'm having such a bad time. I thought you loved me, only last week you did say you loved me and then you went off and slept with her. You fucking bitch.

I screw this up so hard I twist my knuckles. I screw up the last letter too, screw and rip. I take all the screwed and torn up paper into the kitchen, open the bin and find an empty tomato tin, stuff it all inside, then throw the tin back in the bin.

Oh, but I am a selfish cow. Tonight of all nights all I can think about is myself and that fucking bitch and what she does behind my back. I go upstairs, pee, wash.

As I pass the room where Hazel and Colin are sleeping I am startled to hear a groan of pleasure from Colin. I thought they'd be asleep. Or maybe it was a sleepy sigh. No it was the sound of Colin coming inside my sister on the very night of my father's funeral. I feel sick thinking of his red face, his . . . well I don't like to think. I'm surprised at Hazel, doing it tonight of all nights. Shocked.

Oh Zelda, go to bed.

*

The following day when I got home from school, Wanda was in the kitchen with Mummy. She wasn't having a cup of tea or even sitting down, I thought that was strange, Mummy always made people cups of tea. There was a sort of crackly feeling in the air.

'Of course he can stay,' Mummy was saying.

'Who?' I asked, knowing perfectly well.

Wanda smiled at me. 'Hello stranger,' she said. I smiled back. I couldn't help liking her. She had done her hair ginger now and was wearing a green embroidered velvet coat that came right down to her sandals. The patchouli oil was particularly strong, but I had started to like it – except on Dog-belly.

148

'Vassily's staying the night,' Mummy said, 'Wanda's busy.' I could see she was annoyed.

'Oh?'

'Yes, that int half a nuisance but . . . well . . .'

'It's perfectly all right,' Mummy said, 'just drop off his things before you go.'

'Better run,' Wanda said heading for the door. 'Bye-bye,' she shouted, waving to Vassily, who, I now saw, was on the swing. She blew him a kiss. 'You ought to come round for a drink again,' she said to me, 'that was fun last time, wasn't it?'

'Yes.'

'Bye Astrid, thanks,' she said, as she left.

Mummy slammed something into the sink.

'What's up?' I asked.

'Nothing at all,' she said, and with a bit of an effort, smiled. Then, 'How would you feel about moving house?'

'Why?' I sat down, quite shocked. We had moved several times when I was smaller but we'd been at 'The Nook' longer than we'd been anywhere and it felt like home.

'Daddy's going for promotion again.'

'But why?'

'That's the way of the world,' she said in a funny voice, 'onward and upward. And . . .' she looked around the kitchen, her eyes coming to rest on Vassily's reading book lying on the table, 'perhaps a change would do us all good.'

*

'Foxy, I know about Kris.'

Pause. Foxy wary. 'What about Kris?'

'I know that you slept with her.'

Another pause. A decision. 'What on earth makes you think that?'

'I don't think it, I know it.'

'Well you're wrong.'

'No I'm not. Don't lie any more Foxy, it only makes it worse.'

No, no. Just, 'Don't lie. It doesn't work.'
Foxy disconcerted. Myself under control, voice a little husky maybe.

No, start again.

Direct and unexpected, coming in upon her working, standing beside her at her desk.
'Foxy, since we've been together have you been to bed with anyone else?'
'Zelda! What a question!' She stands, a kiss, a nuzzle, her scent in my nose, the softness of her hair, maybe her lips on my ear. I disengage myself, gentle but firm.
'Well?'

But what if she said: 'Yes. So?' What if she chose to be belligerent rather than contrite? What if she's been wanting to tell me, relieved that I've finally given her the opportunity? What if she said, 'Yes, I'm in love with Kris and . . .' No she wouldn't say that, but what if she said, 'I want to leave you. You are too clingy, too possessive, jealous, you cramp my style.' No she wouldn't be so crass. Foxy would be kinder than that.

But why, *why*, when I gave her the chance to finish it, why didn't she?

The bed is narrow, the night-light is on, Mummy has kept it through all her moves, red toadstool with its white glowing spots, Hazel's bubble-gum stickers peeling up at the edges.
If I'm going to confront Foxy then I have to have a strategy ready to counter any possible approach she might take.
Maybe she wrote about Kris in her diary hoping that I *would*

see, expecting me to read it. Maybe she hid all the tampons knowing I'd look in her bag and see the diary . . .

For Christ's sake, Zelda, get a grip.

5

I took an apple and went upstairs to change. I didn't want to move, and change schools and have to find a new best friend. Elaine was the best friend I'd ever had, I knew I'd never find anyone else like her. I looked out of my window at the garden. There was blossom on the fruit trees and the grass around them was a juicy green. Vassily, swinging weakly to-and-fro, rocked the apple tree a little, making the blossom shudder.

At least he wasn't in the tree-house. I didn't think I wanted us to move and leave the tree-house behind but it suddenly looked ugly to me, a big lump in the branches of the tree with its front window like a round and empty eye staring. And the pond looked stupid with a wall all around it and a piece of corrugated iron propped in the gap for a gate, as if it was in prison. It wasn't my pond at all, it was Daddy and Dog-belly's. If we moved away there would be an end to all that.

Before Daddy had taken Dog-belly to get the goldfish, I had started just, *just*, not to like him but not to mind him quite so much. He had learned to read very well. He had a good joke book that he'd bring round. He'd point to a joke and I'd read it and – sometimes – laugh. I even did finger spelling with him sometimes. I tried to feel sorry for him – deaf, ugly, fatherless. But that didn't help. Pitying him made me dislike him more. It was as if he was small and skinny and deaf on purpose. And Daddy liked him more than he liked me. The feelings that gave me were dirty like rubbish in the pit of my belly, or the sediment left in my head after a bad dream. It was as if I had a goblin's face printed on my heart, ugly, far uglier than Dog-belly's, that was transfigured with hate whenever he was near. If he had been big and strong I do not think I would have felt like that. But he was weak. He was grateful for any kindness shown him – even if it was fake.

I was upset that Mummy seemed upset. Now that she'd shown that she minded Dog-belly, it seemed that we were being drawn into sides: Mummy, Hazel and I against Daddy and Dog-belly. Us against them. If it hadn't been for Dog-belly, everything would have been all right. Maybe we wouldn't have to move house. Not fair to blame *that* on him. But still.

I went out into the garden. I couldn't see Dog-belly at first. I found him inside the wall, crouching by the pond, watching the goldfish gliding under the green weeds. I stood above him looking down at the thinness of the back of his neck and the roughness of his splayed knees where they poked out of his shorts; seeing the green of the flowering cherry reflected in the water; seeing the pale smudge of his face and my own, indistinct, looming above it. He saw it too and turned, grinning up at me. I bent over the pond beside him. A water snail was sliding upside down on the skin of the water's surface like a grey tongue. A pond-skater dented the silky surface with its pin-prick feet.

It's only an ornamental pond, I thought, thinking of the real, natural pond on the golf-course; feeling a bristle of cold travel all up my spine; swallowing against the memory of a taste; a sensation as of weed caught round my tongue; squeezing my fist shut against the sensation of something heavy under the water, something that will just sway when you prod it.

'Grizzle.' Mummy's voice behind me made me jump. 'I've made you some sandwiches.' She held out the plate, thick white bread filled with brown jam, and some biscuits.

'Thanks.'

She smiled warmly at Dog-belly. It was not *his* fault, I could see her thinking that, poor little brat. He pointed to a cluster of tadpoles nuzzling the edge of the pond.

'Tadpoles,' he said. It sounded like 'towels', but Mummy said, 'Yes, Vassily, good', and bent over beside him to look.

When Mummy had gone back inside, I led the way up into the tree-house. Dog-belly seemed very happy. I had no plans to do anything. Why did I take him up into the tree-house when I hated him so much? Something seductive about such a strong pure feeling? I don't know.

Dog-belly sat on the branch. I offered him a sandwich. He munched it noisily. I had no appetite for mine.

'Knock, knock,' he said, miming a knock as he did so. His speech *was* much better than it had been.

'Who's there?'

'Lettuce.'

'What?'

'Lettuce.'

'What?'

I knew what he was saying. It was quite clear and any way I knew the joke. If I'd said 'Lettuce who?' he'd have squawked, 'Lettuce in and you'll see!' and laughed his squeaky laugh, his teeth all pointed and yellow. But I wouldn't play. 'Pardon?' I said. He gave up, chewed the crust of his sandwich, looking down and stirring his toe around on the floor. The face on my heart contracted with spite and it hurt. I wanted to say, 'Lettuce who?' then but it was too late.

Hazel's voice floated up, 'Grizzle?'

'Yes?'

'Is *he* with you?'

'Yes.' The house bounced slightly as she climbed the ladder.

'Let's have a biscuit.' Her neat blonde head emerged through the trap-door. 'Hello.' She smiled brilliantly at Dog-belly and hoisted herself in.

'What do you want?' I asked.

'Oh sorry, do you want to be alone?' She made a stupid moony face.

'Shut-up cretin.'

'Grizzle!' She giggled, shocked.

The biscuits were lemon puffs. She took one and so did I and held out the plate to Dog-belly. Flakes of shiny pastry sprinkled down all our fronts, even Hazel's. She brushed them off. Leaning back so that Dog-belly couldn't see her face, she mouthed, 'I want to see his nipples.'

'Hazel!' I started to laugh. Dog-belly, seeing me laugh, joined in.

'How?' I said.

'Peasy, watch.' She pulled up her blouse and vest. Her skin was very white in the underwater leaf-light of the tree, and laced with pale green veins. Her nipples were small pink ovals, risen just a little, just like mine. She took Dog-belly's hand. 'Touch,' she said. Now *I* was shocked. She held his grubby hand against her luminous skin, his fingers stiff across her nipple.

'Now you,' she said, looking at me. I shook my head, my face burning. 'Go on.'

I wonder if there is anything I would not have done for Hazel.

'Go *on*,' she said. I shut my eyes as I lifted my clothes. 'Higher,' she insisted. I was afraid she'd think I was more developed than her and be angry but she said nothing and I felt the rough jab of Dog-belly's fingers as she pressed them against my chest. I had a sudden vision of his face pressed up against Wanda's filmy green night-dress, against her voluptuous breasts. I opened my eyes and saw his face all flushed, the eyes bright, like a keen, excited little animal. I pulled down my clothes.

'Your turn,' Hazel said to Dog-belly. He hesitated. 'Go *on*,' she prodded the front of his jumper. I was afraid for a moment that somehow I had been wrong, seen or remembered wrongly, that his chest would be perfectly normal. I flinched imagining Hazel's scorn.

'No,' Dog-belly said and folded his arms.

'Help me,' Hazel demanded. She got hold of his wrists and wrenched them apart. I looked towards the house. From the little window I could see Huw sitting on his new tricycle by the back door. 'Pull his jumper up . . .' I got hold of the edge of it, but he snatched his body away from us and the tree-house rocked. There was a moment of pause. I looked at Hazel. Hazel looked at Dog-belly.

'Go on then,' she said. She folded her arms, waiting. Dog-belly raised his chin and looked her in the eye. It wasn't embarrassment I saw on his face, or fear, it was a sort of defiance. He pulled off his jumper and folded it neatly on the branch beside him. He loosened the knot of his tie, slipped it over his head and hung it over his jumper. Then he slowly unbuttoned his shirt, almost, it seemed, teasingly, fumbling over each button. He wasn't wearing a vest. He pulled the shirt open and there, on his bony chest, where the ivory ribs showed through the skin, were the six nipples, just as I'd described, the usual two, two rather flatter halfway down his rib-cage, two colourless puckered circles of skin just above the waistband of his shorts. Hazel touched them one by one with her index finger. Dog-belly sat absolutely still. I couldn't read the expression on his face. A little pulse was beating fast just above his collar-bone.

'It's really interesting, isn't it?' Hazel said.

'Yes.'

'Touch.'

'No.'

'Let's tickle him then,' Hazel said. I didn't want to. I wanted to get out of the tree-house and go inside and watch television. I wanted to cuddle my fat little brother and blow a raspberry on his creamy neck. I didn't like the expression on my heart. I looked at Hazel and suddenly saw her as a bully. But I had to help her. We tickled him all over his neck and chest and he gave a sort of shrieking laugh. 'Let's take his shirt right off,' she said.

'No. Why?'

'Dunno, just let's.' Together we wrestled him out of the sleeves of his shirt. Then the game felt over. He sat on the branch, scrawny and pathetic, his skinny shoulders hunched, his hands pressed between his thighs.

'I know what would tickle him properly,' Hazel said, eyeing my formicary.

'No!' I didn't want my ants let out and Dog-belly looked so defeated. Different impulses were welling up inside me, scrambling to win. I felt dizzy. Hazel had her determined look. I seem to be saying it was all Hazel, that Hazel made me do it. But that is not true. There was something in myself that wanted to be urged. If Hazel remembers this, I am sure she remembers quite differently.

'Go on . . . it won't *hurt* him.' She met my eyes when she said the word *hurt*.

'*I don't know* . . .' He sat there, uselessly, not looking at us to read our lips, not even trying to put his clothes back on. It was as if he would let us do anything to him, as if he almost wanted us to. I thought of the smug goldfish in the pond that he had chosen. I thought of all the times I'd watched him helping Daddy with the pond and how he'd been no help at all, not half the help I would have been. How *useless*.

'It would be funny,' she urged.

'We'd have to tie him up,' I said.

'Go on then.'

The only thing to tie him with was his own tie.

'It would only be a sort of joke,' I said. We lay him down on his back on the branch and I crawled underneath and tied his wrists together. He just fitted nicely, his chest splayed right out so that you could see all the ribs and the delicate spaces in between. I thought of a chicken carcass picked clean after lunch.

'We could take his shorts off too,' Hazel said, touching the button at the waist.

'No,' I said, 'that would be too . . .'

She considered. 'OK.'

Why did Dog-belly let us do what we wanted? He could have fought. There was nothing to stop him, really, before we tied him up, just shrugging us off, climbing down the ladder and going to find Mummy. If he'd cried or fought back we wouldn't have done it: but he did nothing. He just let us tie him up and lay there looking at us expectantly. My heart hardened. All right then. He wanted this and he should have it.

There was jam on the plate from the sandwiches. 'Let's put jam on him,' I said, 'then the ants can eat it.' Was that really my suggestion or was it Hazel's? I was worried about my ants in this game, worried that they might get hurt or killed.

'Brainwave,' Hazel said. She opened up one of the remaining sandwiches and smeared jam on each of his nipples. His eyes were open very wide. They were light green flecked with brown. He looked at me with a sort of trust.

'Go on then,' Hazel urged. I lifted the top off the tank. I thought just a few ants wouldn't do him any harm. He would hardly feel them.

'You have to help me catch them afterwards,' I said. 'Promise.'

'Course.'

There were several ants on the ramp between the sugar bottle and the nest. I picked the ramp up, wiggling it free from the nest and collapsing a portion of the careful structure. 'Oh blow,' I said. I held the ramp up, there were maybe ten ants on it.

'Go on then.'

I held the ramp over Dog-belly's front and flicked the ants off with my nail. They looked bigger against his pale skin, brown-red, shiny. I knelt down close to watch a couple pausing on the soft-beating skin of the diaphragm. I felt sorry for them, snatched from one world without reason to another. One of them ran right round his waist, underneath him and disappeared, then several found the jam on one of his nipples, gathered round it like a cluster of hair.

'More,' Hazel said, 'that's not enough.'

Dog-belly was breathing hard but he did not say a word, he did not cry out. There was nothing to stop him crying out and then we would have stopped the game.

'Go on,' Hazel urged. I thought just a few more wouldn't make any difference. Hazel would not touch the ants herself, she made me do it. I put my jammy fingers into the formicary and ants crawled on to them, making tiny tickling paths up my wrist. I didn't want them up my arms, inside my sleeves. I shook and flicked them on to Dog-belly, more and more until he was swarming. His skin had puckered into goose-pimples. Kneeling close beside him, I could faintly smell Wanda's perfume and a sweaty boy smell like pencil shavings and mouse droppings. Yes, he *should* have cried out and then we would have stopped.

Ants were crawling up over his collar-bone on to his neck, stopping, waving their feelers, stopping as if to converse. So strange for them, my ants, in this new, pale, jammy country.

'His mouth,' Hazel said. 'Look he's got jam round his mouth.' She picked up a sandwich and smeared more jam around his lips and then, when he screwed up his eyes, she smeared jam over them too so that the lids and lashes were clotted.

Dog-belly's heart was beating so hard that I could see it behind his ribs like a fist beating to be freed. Each beat of my own heart was distinct and painful, like a high and tedious bell. Was it that he was stupid, or was it that he was brave?

The ants seemed to prefer his face. They swarmed up his neck and the mountain of his chin to find his mouth, leaving only a few stragglers on his chest; they gathered about his lips which were clamped shut and then about his eyes. And then he started to scream, a frightening sound like tearing tin. The ants were all on his eyelashes, feeding at his tear ducts where wet was starting to come out. He simply couldn't stand it. When he opened his mouth to scream they trickled in, so he shut it again, clamped his lips together, squashing my ants between them, spitting, spitting out bits of dead ant, screaming again, jerking and jerking his body about.

'Stop!' I shouted, but he just screamed and screamed, his body thumping against the branch as if he would break his back.

'Get them off him,' Hazel said, 'quick, shut him up.'

'I can't. You . . .' I tried to get the ants off him but the touch of my fingers on his face made it worse, the screaming was too loud, not like the screaming of a small boy, and the ants were falling into his open mouth.

'Stop!' I shouted loud as I could right into his face.

'Slap him,' Hazel cried. 'Do something!'

'You.'

'What the . . .' the voice, sudden, loud, shocking as a rifle shot in our playhouse. Daddy's head through the door. Dog-belly's screams and convulsions. The lenses of Daddy's glasses glinting like white metal, his wiry hair on end.

Disgrace.

An atmosphere in the house like lead.

Arguments behind closed doors.

The word torture.

Even Mummy too angry to speak directly to us.

We were forbidden to go out for a month. We were forbidden to go into the tree-house. Mummy would not look at us when we were in the room but a door, a wall, away from us we heard her voice defending. *Only a game. Children get up to all sorts. Games get out of hand. They didn't mean it.*

It was late spring now. The sun shone heartlessly. The tadpoles grew legs. We had got our wish. Vassily didn't come round again. Daddy and Mummy weren't speaking except to fight. No one was speaking to anyone except Hazel and me but even we . . . we couldn't meet each other's eyes.

It was an evil thing that we had done. That's what Mummy said. Daddy said nothing, not a word to either of us, not a word for weeks.

After the month was up, I went out to the tree-house with my comic. I still felt bruised inside as if something bad had happened to *me*. It was all right at school but home was painful. There was no need for them to hate us so much. We had done a bad thing. But we were sorry.

I saw Vassily at school sometimes but he kept his distance. Once he walked just ahead of me all the way home. I listened to the slap, slap of his feet and watched the way his hair grew a bit too long down the thin back of his neck. I was thinking of saying that I was sorry. I was thinking of telling him a joke. But then we were nearly home and it was too late.

When I went into the tree-house I found that my ants were dead. Beside the formicary was a carton of ant poison. The tank was knocked over and the floor of the tree-house was covered in white grains and the shrivelled flecks that were the bodies of the ants.

I never went in the tree-house again.

Two months later we moved.

LICK

1

Sitting by the fire in Wanda's house. An electric-bar burns above a mound of flickering plastic coals. The room is small but a mirror opposite the window doubles it. If the curtains were open and it was daylight, it would reflect the moving limbs of the lime tree on the path in front. But in the February night it frames only the darkly flowered curtains.

I can hear juggernauts on the main road, roaring towards the docks. Inside the room there is just the sound of the mock coals creaking as they warm. No television, no radio voice, no music. Upstairs, very faint, so faint it might only be the sounds in my own ears, I can hear Wanda's relaxation tape – waves breaking on a shore, gulls maybe, against a regular pulse of blood.

Wanda's husband is away, driving his lorry to Marseille. And I am in Felixstowe visiting Wanda who is very sick. Soon I will go upstairs and offer her herbal tea and, if she likes, my company.

When she told me that she lived in Felixstowe now, I thought of the sea, of course, the buffs and greys of shingle, the queue of ferries and container-ships that stretch, sometimes, out further than the eye can see. And if you walk from here for half-an-hour, that is what you get. This house though seems far from all that. A tiny semi in an awkward elbowing position dominated by the roar of the dual carriage-way. Sometimes the windows rattle in their panes and the darkness outside is rusted.

EASY PEASY

On the mantelpiece, among the candles, ornamental frogs and bottles of pills, is a wedding photograph in a heart-shaped frame: Wanda in white satin, heartbreakingly radiant with confetti caught in her candy-floss hair, and Stan – whom I have never met – low-browed and muscular in an ill-fitting suit. His smile is abashed but also curiously sweet. And another photograph: Vassily, little Vassily holding a white fluffy cat. It is almost funny like a cartoon from MAD: a cruel haircut, great hearing-aids clamped to the sides of his head, a snaggle toothed grin. Looking closer though, looking as an adult at a child, I catch my breath at the vulnerability of him, the frailness of his neck, the open expression in his eyes.

There is a photo of Vassily grown too, a graduation picture. You would never guess, never in a million years, that they could be the same person. In this second photo, Vassily in mortar-board and gown against a bold blue studio background, you can see only too blatantly how handsome he became.

I wonder what Foxy is doing.

Last night I walked out. I am not here visiting Wanda purely out of the goodness of my heart. I have been planning to visit – some time. That plan might have stayed unrealised if Foxy and I hadn't fought last night. If I hadn't been casting about for where I could go, where I could run to that wasn't home, that wasn't anywhere she could find me, wasn't anywhere where I would have to sit and listen for the telephone and know it wasn't ringing.

'I don't want to be faithful to you any more.'

'So it's finished?'

'Up to you.'

'What do you mean, you don't want to be faithful?'

'I mean . . . just that.'

'I know about Kris.'

'Oh.'

'So?'

'That was just . . . stupid.' She smiles at me – a little sheepish. Does she expect *me* to smile?

166

'Why?'

She closes her eyes for a moment, sighs. 'Does it matter now?'

She has not asked me how I know.

So if it is not Kris who is the danger, then . . .

The question hangs there between us, unasked but plainly in existence. *Who is she?* No. I do not want to know. A sensation in my gut like fingers slithering but if I know nothing definite they cannot get a hold. I will not ask her who it is.

'I've been feeling . . . I don't know . . . itchy, twitchy. You know? I love you and I like living with you. I will not leave you if you can stand it but knowing you, Zel . . . I don't think you could stand it.' The smile wry now. Loving?

I can't help it. 'Who is she?'

'No one, no one in particular.'

How can I believe her when her eyes won't meet mine? She is such a terrible liar it is almost endearing. *Almost.* Her glasses are pushed up into her hair, her lipstick is even more smudged than usual. Her hair is going grey, for Christ's sake. In some lights she looks old. I like it. It makes me safe that she looks so much older than me but that is crazy because I am not safe. I am anything but safe.

'Who said anything about a *she*?'

'Not a *man*?' For an instant surprise jams itself between myself and the pain.

'No, course not.' But you never know with her. She is maddening.

I flinched away from the hand reaching out to touch me and went to the window. Streets, houses, sky – across which an aeroplane makes a slow white scratch. Trying to breathe into the cramped space of my lungs, discovering my jaw was clenched, I experienced rage. A sudden flash of my fist in her face, smashing her perfect nose.

But no. Instead I went out walking. She didn't try to stop me. I walked until it grew dark. I sat in the Minster breathing the antique air, listening to the pure voices of boys rising and evaporating on the stone. I sat in a café and let a cup of tea grow cold. I walked home several times but never went in. I did not know what to say. Before I went back, I wanted to know what to say.

I walked back to the Minster and gazed up at the bulk of it crouching against the glassy blue of the sky. A beautiful night, I suppose, crisp, shrill stars, an edge of frost. Late, where did the time go? The night a speeded-up film, lights blinking on and off, traffic, ropes of light, shop fronts dimly illuminated. My feet hurt, my shoes not made for walking. I stopped and looked in a shoe shop. Saw some comfortable leather boots, thought, what if I take a stone and smash the window and take the boots and run? Why should I ever be caught? And walking on, painfully now, shoes tightening with every step – and the growing sensation of someone behind me. I remember noticing nobody until then, though people there must have been. But now, late, alone, a male, following. The fear almost a relief at first because it was something else. I walked fast, biting my lips against the pinch in my toes, I walked to Second Hand Rose. The security shutters were down, the lights out, but standing back I could see a leak of light from between the curtains that showed Connie was in her flat above the shop.

I rang the bell. No answer. Awareness of the figure behind me lurking made me prickle. A thought: if I was murdered now . . . how sorry she would be. I dared to look round but the figure had hidden himself. I rang and rang: the bell was loud up there. Connie would have to come down. I stood with my back against the door, breath shallow and panicky, scanning the street, my thumb pressed over my shoulder on the bell, a long far off fizz of sound. Eventually I heard the thud of energetic feet on stairs, the rattling of locks. The door spilled light and I shoved my way in and slammed the door behind me. My heart was beating fast and hard and blackness crowded in at the edges of my vision. I bent down, my hands on my knees, breathing deeply, staving off a faint.

'What's up?'

I looked up at the young stranger who had opened the door. He was regarding me oddly, there in the half-light among the racks of clothes.

'Thought I was being followed.'

'Want me to go and look?'

I shook my head. Maybe I'd imagined it, maybe not. It hardly mattered now that I was safe inside.

'I'm Zelda,' I said, straightening up.

'Yeah I know. Ian – I'm with . . .' he nodded at the door to the stairs. He was *very* young, hardly twenty by the look of him. His bare chest was smooth, and there was the glint of separate, soft gold whiskers curling on his chin – though not what you could call a beard.

'All right if I go up?' I was already moving towards the stairs.

Connie, at the top, was dressed in a long white Victorian nightgown. A stock nightgown.

'Zelda.' She was in the act of lighting a cigarette, squinting through the bluish smoke. I was looking at the nightgown that went so oddly with her skew-whiff orange bee-hive. It was the most decorous thing I'd ever seen her wear – except she had no right to be wearing it. For once I did not care.

'Can I sleep here?'

'Course. Have to be the sofa.' Her fag-holder pinched in the corner of her mouth, she started tipping clothes and papers on the floor. 'What's the problem?'

'Coffee?' Ian said. He had put a Greenpeace T-shirt on now and tied his hair back. I recognised him. He'd often been in the shop with his girlfriend choosing clothes and getting Connie to make sense of his pornographic dreams. I threw Connie a look but she refused to catch it. She fetched me a blanket.

'No thanks.' I sat down and pulled the tight shoes off my throbbing feet. 'You get back to bed.'

'Zelda . . .'

'Not now, Connie,' I snapped. I had to be alone, away from Foxy and alone. I wasn't in the mood for Connie and her peccadilloes.

'I'll say good-night then.' I watched a worm of soft ash slowly bend and fall from the tip of her cigarette on to the bodice of the nightgown.

'Yeah.'

The bedroom door closed behind them. I could hear muffled voices, and Connie's deep cough – but no sex, thank God. I could not have stood that.

I lay down and curled up under the smoky blanket. I closed my eyes and waited for my heart to slow. I experimented with a thought: why should I care if Foxy has other lovers? The cushion was scratchy under my cheek. I shifted. Outside I heard an ambulance siren in the distance. What if we both had other lovers?

I tried it but found anger rising and struggling in my chest. If you love someone with a passion then how can you share them? *I* cannot. I could not bear it. I could never switch off my imagination. How could I rest easy with Foxy in someone else's bed. But *she* could bear it, wanted it. What does that mean? That she is a better, a wiser, a more generous person than me? Or that she does not love me with a passion that corresponds to mine?

I wanted to run, to somewhere she doesn't know, where there was no possibility of contact. And then I thought of Wanda. I had received a postcard, sent via my mother, from Vassily, telling me how ill Wanda was now, how much she wanted to see me. I'd shoved it behind the clock, thinking feebly that I *should* visit but making no plans.

Curled foetally on Connie's sofa, I decided that to Wanda's was where I must run.

2

Dear Foxy,   *11th Feb. Wanda's house.*

OK then, you get your way, it's finished. When I leave Wanda's I'll go and stay with my mother or . . . I don't know. I will be away for a week. While I'm away I want you to move out.

I want no trace of you in that flat when I return.

The flat might be in your name but it's you who did this, ruined everything.

~~I'm going to~~ ~~I've been to~~ *I'm going to a solicitor who says*

Remembering all the good times we've had together, all the promises you've made, I've thought you made, though if I think about it I see how careful you were not *to make.*

There's a postcard from Kris hidden in the kitchen drawer, came when you were out couldn't bear to give it to you.

All my love (still) Kris.

Well I hope you're happy.

I don't care who you have any more, Kris, Dana, woman, man, donkey, banana I don't give a shit.

You are a fucking cow.

But I love you.

I hate you

Remember the time when you gave me that

*

The stairs creak. The carpet glistens nylon in the electric light. I turn the handle gently. I don't want to wake Wanda, if she's sleeping, but no, but she's sitting up in bed, painting her nails. The bed is strewn with grubby cotton-wool balls smeared with old brown varnish. The room reeks of acetone.

'False,' she says.

'What?' I put the mugs down on top of the pile of magazines on her bedside table.

'Nails. Fell out with the chemo. That's a *very* rare reaction.' She sounds proud. 'I've stuck them on but I want them *this* colour. Tango. You can't buy them this colour.'

I sit down on the edge of her bed. She paints a final nail, screws the lid back on the varnish bottle and splays out her orange spiked fingers.

'What d'you think?'

'Yes.'

'All those years, trying not to bite my nails, longing for talons. That's so easy with false.'

'Mmmm.'

Her rings are loose on her wedding finger.

'That was nice knowing you were downstairs while I was asleep.' The smile on her face which has grown so narrow reminds me of Vassily's. I have never seen a likeness before, because her face used to be round and there was all the hair. I hadn't quite been able to suppress a gasp when I'd seen her this time. She has no hair left at all. 'Half of it went,' she'd said, 'so I thought sod this and had the rest shaved. Stan did it.' Her scalp is very pink and fragile, the ridges of her skull showing through. Now I notice how small and delicate her ears are, each one pierced several times with silver studs and rings. Since I've been downstairs she's tied a paisley scarf round her head and put on some make-up.

'That smell won't do you any good,' I say. 'Shall I open the window?'

172

'If you like. I spilt a bit on the bed. I reckon you could get high on this.' She picks up her sheet and sniffs.

I force up the sash. The roar of the traffic and a cold blast of its fumes fills the room. I slam it down again.

'Don't mind the sound of the traffic,' she says, 'that make me think of Stan. He'll be back, tomorrow. Didn't want to go at all and leave me. But you know. Money and that.'

I hand her her tea.

'Camomile, thanks. You *are* good. That's funny you turning up like this, just when Stan's away, just when I can do with a bit of company.'

'It's been much too long.'

She nods.

'Anything to eat?' I say. I feel out of my depth with someone so ill, I don't know what to do.

She pulls a face. She looks very striking in her head-scarf, and, curiously, younger – or ageless rather. 'Can't fancy anything now. Talk to me instead.' She pats the bed beside her.

I'd arrived mid-afternoon. She'd been watching the television, I could see the screen flickering in a corner of a room, otherwise I might have assumed she was out, she took so long to come to the door. When she did I had to smother my alarm. It was a shock to see Wanda – who lived in my imagination in a cloud of variously coloured fuzzy hair – bald, her face devoid of make-up. I really did not recognise her for too long a moment. But her dressing-gown was velvet, like the one I remembered from twenty years before – though surely *not* the same one. That was the only Wanda-ish thing about her.

'Vassily said you'd come,' was what she said as she reached up to kiss me on the cheek. I am not tall but she reached up. I had not realised she was so small. Her body in my arms as I hugged her was soft and insubstantial. She had been very tired. 'I was just off to bed,' she said, 'but you'll stop, won't you?' She had gone upstairs and I'd gone for a walk through the town and

173

down the steep hill to the sea-front. I'd stood on the promenade, watching the grey gulls bob on the darkening sea, attempting to assimilate Wanda as she was with what she has become. I wanted not to be shocked, appear shocked, when I was with her. I wanted to look her in the eye. I wanted to help her and I wanted to know about her. I wanted to ask her about Daddy.

I bought bread, fruit, eggs and a bottle of wine, in case she was up to a drink. I certainly needed one.

Now her face against the pillows is bright, vivacious. The crimson of her lipstick reminds me of Foxy and I catch my breath.

'How's your love life?' she asks as if reading my mind.

I say nothing for a moment feeling the leaden weight of it in my chest. She leans forward, the question in her eyes, interest. I feel a corner lift, the possibility of a little lightness. Maybe I can talk to her.

'My lover is bored,' I say, flinching at the dull, doom-tolling timbre of the word. 'Yes, bored. Wants other . . . you know. Don't know what to do.'

'And do *you* still want him?'

'Yes, I . . . at least I think so. And it's *her*,' I add, daring. No idea what her reaction will be.

'Her? Well fancy that.' She leans back and narrows her eyes. 'Just fancy.'

I smile and the corners of my mouth lift the weight and do let in lightness.

'I used to wonder . . .' she said. 'I never had any experience of women, but . . . well you can't help wondering, can you?'

I find myself telling her all about Foxy. I never expected this. She listens very well, nodding, making all the right noises in all the right places. But what can she say? No good seeking an answer from her, from anywhere outside myself. The answer is in me somewhere and that is the only place it is. But the air of confidence is exhilarating and comforting at the same time. I finish talking and there is a long pause.

'I've been thinking about Ralph,' she says, sipping her tea, looking down, examining her bright nails.

'You and Daddy?' I hold my breath and look at her. A fleeting expression of tenderness on her face is my answer.

I had tried asking my mother. On Boxing Day – the last time we were together. Huw had bought her an enormous jigsaw, 5,000 pieces, nearly all leaves and sky. Together, we – Hazel, Colin, Huw, Mummy and myself – had started it, arguing as we always did over puzzles because everyone else likes to sort the edges out first and I prefer to start in the middle.

'Trust Grizzle to do it the hard way,' Hazel said, an edge in her voice, and we glared at each other. But that was the nearest we got to a row. Not bad for a family Christmas. The puzzle was started but the table had got knocked. Everyone else had gone for a walk. I'd stayed behind to help Mummy with the lunch. I was setting the table when I knocked it. 'Damn.' I knelt to pick up the pieces, she bent over beside me.

'Mummy?'

'Yes?'

'Daddy and Wanda . . .' A drop of temperature suddenly, but I persevered. Since the funeral it had been on my mind. 'Was there anything?'

'Let's get this picked up.'

My mother's carpet is green and brown, the jigsaw pieces camouflaged. I stretched out and ran my hand over the shadow under the table.

'I mean,' I insisted, my tongue stiff, 'I mean were they having an affair?'

'I wish we'd never started this.' Mummy stood up and examined the puzzle. 'All forest, millions of leaves. It'll never get done. Don't know what Huw was thinking about. Does he think I've nothing better to do?' I stood up and she looked at me. Her pale eyes flooded black with hurt. 'I know quite well what you mean.' Her hand went to the corner of her mouth. 'Does it never occur to you, Griselda, that there are some places where you simply cannot put your big feet?'

She went through into the kitchen. I opened my fist and let the jigsaw pieces fall on to the table. One I'd picked up happened to fit, an edge piece, gold-leaf fragment, the completion of a blade of grass. I followed Mummy through into the kitchen but she kept her back to me tipping pickles – red-cabbage, onions, beetroot – from jars into glass dishes so that the kitchen reeked of vinegar.

Now Wanda smiles at the question.

'You were more than . . . ordinary friends?'

She considers, picks up the paper tag on the tea-bag string and fiddles with it, folds the flaps back so that it resembles a white moth against the orange of her nails. 'Yes,' she says.

'You were . . .' Lovers I want to say, but can't bring myself to use that word in connection with Daddy. She leans over, flicks open the cassette player, turns over a tape, presses play. The sound of water trickling, then the trilling of a bird.

'I like this,' she says, 'that's so restful.'

We listen together. For some reason the carefully calculated relaxing sounds get on my nerves. Water over stones, wind in leaves, another blasted bird. I long for a shout or gun-shot. 'Don't worry,' I say.

She opens her eyes and shakes her head. 'That's just, I don't know . . . I don't know how much you know.'

I take a sip of my tea, cooling now. I can't stand camomile. I should have had a proper cup of tea. 'Not much,' I say, 'it only occurred to me at the funeral that you and Daddy . . .'

'Really?' she laughed, something of her old laugh there, a huskiness. 'But you knew I was on the game?'

I look into the clear piss-yellow of my tea. I put down the mug. 'No. No, I didn't know that.'

'Oh.'

'When you were living near us?'

176

LICK

'Yes.'

I remembered an afternoon in Wanda's house, Vassily and me creeping around, the bedroom door closed on Wanda when she was supposed to be out. A man calling her a silly name – Hotpants.

'Very high class,' she says, self-mockingly, 'very appointments only and regular clients and that. *And*', she clinks her nail on the rim of her mug, 'independent, what I earned, mate, I kept.'

The window rattles as a particularly heavy lorry passes. The house is on a sloping bend so that lorries grind their gears just as they pass. 'I don't know how you stand this,' I say.

She shrugs again. There's an awkward silence between us, leaves rustling, or maybe the beating of wings. I try to get my mind in focus. There is something dreamlike about this conversation. 'So ... so my father was a regular ... what would you say ... client?'

'In a way.'

'A *way*?'

'Not quite ...'

'What?' I feel like shaking her.

'Well, yes, all right then. He was a regular client.'

I shiver suddenly. The room is very cold. Wanda, snuggled up in bed with her dressing-gown on is all right. I am dressed in a flowered rayon dress and cardigan. Very 40s' today, very uptight and shocked.

'I don't understand,' I fight to keep my voice even. 'I mean ... what about Mummy?'

She snorts, amused. 'There usually is a mummy.'

'Did she know?'

'Why do you think you moved so sudden?'

'Daddy's job.'

'That wasn't far. He could have driven.'

'They wanted the sea ... a change ...' I tail off. It is no good trying to beat away the truth with questions. 'I'm cold,' I say instead.

'Look in the drawers in the spare room – some of Vassily's stuff, sweaters and that.' I get up, smooth my dress. 'You upset?'

'No . . . I don't know . . . maybe a bit, you know . . .' I wave my hand backwards and forwards. She starts to say something else but I am out of the door.

I sit on the edge of the bed in the spare room – the room I'm going to sleep in tonight, as if, *as if*, there was any possible chance of sleep tonight what with Foxy and Wanda and my dad all sexy and knowing and unfaithful chasing each other round and round in my stupid naive head. How have I gone through life so trusting and half blind?

From the chest-of-drawers I pull out a big Guernsey sweater and slip it over my dress and cardigan. I pause in front of the mirror and look at my pale and childish face. On top of the chest-of-drawers is a jumble of things: a shaving brush, a shoe-horn, a pile of magazines and a chocolate box with a picture of kittens on the lid. I tilt up the lid and peep in. Photographs, the top one of Vassily, older than when I knew him, twelve maybe, leggy and tanned, astride a bike. I let the lid fall and sit down again. The bed-cover is lilac candlewick. The room smells damp. I think of Wanda's bedroom in the flat, the fleshy scent of it, the crumbs on the rumpled sheets, large breasts under a film of green nylon. Daddy went there. Daddy knew that. Just a garden, a fence, a tree-house away from Mummy and from us.

I go and put my head round Wanda's door and look at her. Does she look guilty? 'Something to eat?' I say. She shakes her head. 'Go on. How about some scrambled eggs?'

She shrugs. 'If you're doing some.'

Why *should* she be guilty?

Downstairs, I turn up the thermostat and the pipes gurgle and shudder and the house settles around me. It is a freezing night. This house is not cosy, not like Wanda's flat was cosy. The same nail and silver string pictures are on the walls, the same ornamental frogs crouch on every available surface, but there is little else I recognise. The angles are all wrong, the furniture too big and bossy for the rooms. I look at the wedding photograph again, study Stan's face, a good-natured, uncomplicated expression. Was he a client too? Are all men?

On an impulse I ring my mother. It's a cruel impulse but one I cannot help. I'm like an electric wire waving free and dangerous with all this information. I need to be earthed. There is no Foxy for me to ring now, not for me. And if I did? What would she say? She would not be shocked at all, nor would she understand my shock. She would think I was being naive and hysterical which I am being, I know. The phone rings many times. I close my eyes and visualise it on the polished telephone table in my mother's hall, the square coloured note-pad beside it, the pen fastened to it with a silky red ribbon because otherwise she never can keep a pen by the phone. It rings and rings. I am about to put it down, then:

'Hello?'

'Mum, me.'

'Griselda? What a nice surprise. I was just thinking . . .'

'I'm at Wanda's.'

'What?'

'Wanda's, you know.'

'How is she?' Her voice a little cooler, no one's voice has such a variety of temperatures, edging towards the formal, the more foreign. I will not have that.

'Very ill. Cancer.'

An exclamation.

'Mummy, did you know she was a prostitute?' A long rush of silence. 'And that Daddy . . . Daddy went to her?'

I can feel the flinch of pain like a tug down the wire.

'Griselda, why are you doing this to me?' Her voice quite clear and puzzled. No answer. 'Why can't you leave things be? What's it got to do with you?'

'Nothing.'

Indeed, *why*? I am a wrecker of silences. I don't know why.

Mummy breathes in wearily.

'Sorry,' I say. 'I don't know. I suppose I'm tired. Sorry. Let's forget it.'

'No.'

'What?'

'Let's get this said then, if you want it said. Yes, Ralph and Wanda.'

'And you knew?'

'Not at first. It . . . *dawned* on me.'

'Did you try to stop it?'

The sound of air-brakes outside.

'It wasn't just . . . the physical,' she says.

'What . . .?'

'I think she really loved him and he . . .' Another silence, not silence, a throbbing sound that is the blood pulsing in my ear against the white plastic of the receiver. 'All right?' But answers breed questions. Now I want to know more. I can't ask. 'And now he's dead,' she says. Silence. 'My best to Wanda.'

'Yes.'

In the kitchen I break eggs into a glass bowl and beat them with milk. My right ear feels tender from the call I should not have made.

I must not think of phoning Foxy. She would be no comfort, she would be calm and rational, unphased, and wrong. And probably, anyway, she would be out. My love is not rational and it cannot share. I will not phone Foxy. All I have done by phoning Mummy is upset her again. Why do I do it? Ringing back to apologise would only make it worse.

I watch the eggs gradually curdling in the pan, scrape the wooden spoon across the bottom and round the sides, pulling the set bits into the centre, scrambling the eggs slowly.

3

Christmas Eve. I drove, alone, south and east and into the flat
light of Norfolk where the fields glinted wet between hedges,
and outside village pubs trees were strung with coloured bulbs.
On the radio, for the last hour, the Nine Lessons and Carols
from King's College. My lips mouthing the words and tears
periodically trembling my vision, I drove towards the first family
Christmas without my father. The others' cars were already
parked outside the house. It was four o'clock, the news came
on and I switched off the ignition. I wound down the window
to smell the mild, salt air and heard the sea sigh and suck like a
vast sleeper in a vast dream. I took out my lipstick and did my
lips shiny and scarlet like a Christmas bow. I printed a kiss on
a tissue from my handbag and got out of the car. I put off the
moment, stood staring across grass and past the perilous cliff
edge Shangri-La holiday shacks at the North Sea that looked
so utterly cold and brown. I gave myself a shake and unloaded
my presents from under the bonnet of my Beetle.

Halfway up the garden path my longing for Foxy to be with
me was strong enough to stop me in my tracks, a sudden blast
of yearning. I stood with my arms full of presents, the hard edge
of a box digging into my chest. She should have been with me
but she had gone to Cairo instead with a couple of friends. I
could have gone too. I wished, fiercely, that I had. The windows
were lit up yellow, the curtains not yet drawn. I could hear my

mother's neighbours' television and see it blinking through the window: some Christmas children's nonsense.

'I wish you'd come home with me for Christmas,' I'd said, but Foxy had shaken her head. 'No, it's family ... a special family time.' 'But you're my ...' I had objected and stopped. We had been through all that too many times before. Then she told me of her chance to visit Egypt. 'You could come too ... only you can't really let your mum down ...' Oh Foxy, sailing down the Nile with your red hair flowing around your shoulders. Oh transparent faithless Foxy.

I pulled myself together and entered the subdued festive spirit in my mother's house. Mistletoe hung in the hall, as always, and the tree in the alcove in the sitting-room winked its fruity lights. The mince-pies were fresh from the oven, there was a pyramid of tangerines, bowls of nuts in shells with the old useless lion-headed nutcrackers lying beside them, a box of dates like a barge. Just Christmas, the same as ever.

My parents used to argue about Christmas traditions, Swedish versus British, but years ago, when I was still a tiny child. British won – apart from the straw goat under the tree; apart from the plain lutfisk dinner on Christmas Eve, little relics of my mother's childhood. I'd wondered if without my father, my mother might have reverted to more Swedish traditions, half hoped for it all to be foreign and different so that my father's absence would not be so glaring; half feared the betrayal of it.

Mummy welcomed me with mulled wine. We all kissed under the mistletoe, I even kissed Colin. Everything was warm and bright and fragrant with Christmas. I started to relax. But before dinner I made a mistake. Again, the same mistake. I brought out the envelope and removed the diary pages.

'This is what was in the envelope – you know that you sent me ...' I kept my voice light. I held them out to Mummy but her hands stayed in her lap; she did not look up and meet my eyes. She pursed her lips. 'I thought it would be something of that sort.'

LICK

'What?' Hazel took them from me.

'Some bits of Daddy's prisoner-of-war diary.'

'I didn't know he was a prisoner-of-war.' Huw's voice indignant.

'You *must* have known that!' I could not believe it, but his eyes were wide, his astonishment genuine.

Hazel raised her eyebrows at him. 'Sometimes I think you come from a different planet.'

'Let's have a butcher's,' Colin leant forward.

'But they're not legible,' Hazel let him take them, wiped her fingers on her sleeves. I noticed that she was dressed almost the same as Mummy, both of them in stretch pastel slacks and sweaters, both sleek and slim and discreetly jewelled. I was wearing a green taffeta dress with a nipped-in waist that, at home, had seemed Christmassy and right. But now I just felt silly and overdressed.

'I could do with a drink,' Hazel nudged Colin.

'Good idea,' Mummy stood up. 'Dinner won't be long.'

'Lutfisk?' Hazel guessed. 'Remember how we used to hate it, Grizzle, and we always had to eat it on Christmas Eve?'

'Afraid so.'

'Colin's come to rather like it, haven't you darling?' Hazel put her hand on his knee. Even after five years' marriage she can't keep her hands off the man.

'Yes. Quite illegible,' he pronounced.

I will never understand what she sees in him, pompous little hamster of a man with his puffy moustache and plump pink cheeks.

'They're *not*,' I object. 'You can make bits out.'

Colin went to the sideboard for the sherry.

'Listen . . .' I read out a snatch: water, mosquitoes, disease. Subjects that sat uneasily among the trappings of festivity. My voice faltered. I was going too far.

'Please,' Mummy's voice, quiet, 'do you really think your father would want you raking all this up? Tonight of all nights?'

'But . . .' I stopped and put the papers down. Hazel pulled a face at me, Mummy went off into the kitchen closing the door behind her with a firm click.

'I've got several large sherries here,' Colin said, 'do I have any takers?'

'Sorry Griz, but I do think Mum's right.' Huw picked up the papers and slid them back into their envelope. Then he bent down and kissed me on top of my head.

'Fancy you not knowing he was a prisoner-of-war.' Hazel frowned at him.

I looked up, saw expressions pass like shadows across his face, ending with a grin, a shrug. Lucky, incurious, easy-going Huw. My baby brother. How he managed to grow up so uncomplicated in our family, I'll never know. I felt like a child in a roomful of adults. Stupid, gauche, incapable of judging a situation. Guilty of bad taste. I sipped my sherry and shut up.

Late in the evening. The turkey was stuffed and snuggled under bacon rashers in its tin. Scrabble finished – Mummy victorious as usual – we sat round the fire finishing our nightcaps. Snowballs, for Mummy, Hazel and me, something I would never dream of drinking in any other setting, on any other occasion, with any other people. There was even a glacé cherry stuck on a cocktail stick to fiddle with. In the absence of my father, Colin, a stickler for detail, had put himself in charge of drinks. My misjudgment had been glossed over. It was like any other Christmas Eve – with one omission.

Hazel finished her drink and yawned. 'I'm going up.'

'Wait,' Mummy said, 'one thing I want to do tomorrow, is go to church.'

I relaxed a bit, almost relieved that at last something was different. A little smear of red from the cherry floated on the surface of my drink.

'Church?' Huw said. 'What that grey thing with the pointy roof?'

'Huw!'

'Hey, Mummy's got religion!'

She laughed. 'Not at all. It's just . . .' She fingered the pearls around her throat. I noticed how old her neck was growing and that made me sad. She met my eyes and smiled. I felt forgiven. 'It's not that I've suddenly become a church-goer or anything . . . I just feel . . .'

'If you want to go to church then, of course, we'll all go.' Hazel looked at me.

'I know Ralph's not buried there or anything. It's got nothing to do with him, that church. I don't think he even went in it.' She was referring to the flint-walled village church.

'I walked round the graveyard with him once,' I remembered. 'There's all these grave-stones for sailors lost at sea – bodies never found.'

'So sad.' Mummy let go of her pearls. 'He didn't believe in anything of course, but . . .'

'Well, that's agreed then,' Colin said. 'Top up anyone?'

I shook my head.

'But somebody,' Mummy drained the last eggy dregs from her glass and looked at me, 'needs to stay and look after the lunch.'

'Bagsy me!' I shot my hand up like a child.

Hazel raised her eyes to heaven.

Bed-time on Christmas Eve. I stood by the window looking out between the curtains at the sea. The wind lugged bulky soot clouds across the sky, edging them with silver as they crossed the slice of moon. I opened the little top section of the window and the raw, foaming, gull-screaming breeze made me shiver. I left the window open, and the curtains, so that I could lie in bed and watch the changing sky. The bed was the bottom bunk from my childhood. I don't know what happened to the top one, where it got left behind. The mattress was thin and dipped in the middle. I had expected the bed to be cold but when I climbed in there was the lovely surprise of a hot-water bottle in a soft crocheted cover. The smell was of hot rubber and frowsty wool. I snuggled into the warm space and pushed the bottle down to my feet.

Thought, Foxy always has cold feet.

Switched off the light. The plug gone from the night-light. Could hardly trouble Mummy for a screwdriver and a plug. Not quite dark though, watery moonlight rippling on the floor and on my bed. Before I got in I stuffed the diary back in my suitcase. Lay wondering why I can't get it right. Foxy makes curiosity a virtue. My curiosity seems a vice. Practically a weapon. All I seem to be able to do with it is hurt people. But all I want is to *know*. I want to know about Vince. I'd pored over the diary mentions of him many times and speculated with Foxy. Obviously he was important to Daddy. I just wanted to know *why* exactly. What had happened to him – and why the dreams? I just wanted to know who my father was.

I tossed about in the bed, trying to get comfortable, to fit my adult body into the childish space. I was grateful for the narrowness of the bed – no emptiness beside me.

I never could get to sleep on Christmas Eve. Like children everywhere I lay for hours awake.

There was the waiting for Father Christmas.

But there was something else too.

A horrible thing that cast a pall over all our Christmases.

Every Christmas Eve, Daddy would dream. The worst of his nightmares would come. Deep tongueless screams that split the night and made my eyes stare and my heart hammer. One time when I had fallen asleep and was woken by the scream, I saw my stocking was already filled. It lay on the end of my bed, a heavy, bulky, bulging thing, like a chopped-off leg. Father Christmas had been before Daddy woke us with his dream. Woke me at least – Hazel made no sound or movement. I eased my legs down under the blankets and under the stocking and heard the rustle of the things stuffed in there. I smelled, very faintly, the scent of tangerine and chocolate but I did not reach for the stocking. Not daring to disturb Hazel, I lay still. I listened to the footsteps on the landing, the water running in the bathroom, Mummy's soothing voice.

And I did not believe in Father Christmas any more.

Lying in the old bottom bunk, remembering that, I remembered something else: the pencilled dates on the wall by Hazel's bed. The dates that had seemed random except for one date – December 24th. It seemed so obvious now that she *had* been awake too, she had heard Daddy and she had wondered. She too had tried to make sense, make a pattern of it. I had not been alone in that.

The curtains flapped damply against the open window; my breath was a ghost in the almost dark. I did drift off to sleep, a shallow sleep from which I woke quickly, oppressed by a realistic dream. For a moment I could not shake off the sensation that there was something above me – a top bunk with a girl inside it. And that the girl was me. It was the child Griselda, the guilty child and her guilt weighed heavy on me. More, was a part of me. I had to blink and blink away the top bunk, the sensation on my face like hairs hanging from a wire mesh above me. I had to stretch out my arm from beneath the blankets and fumble, sweatily, with the lamp switch to be certain that all that was above me was the ceiling. My heart was beating like it did on the night of Daddy's dreams. But there would be no more dreams. Not Daddy's. Only mine.

I saved Foxy's present until last. We sat around the fire on Christmas morning – although it was sunny and mild, too mild for a fire – sipping champagne and opening our presents. No one sat in Daddy's leather armchair, and it seemed to have a real presence that morning. The flames were pale, almost invisible in a shaft of sunlight that lit up a furry coating of soot in the chimney. I unwrapped layers of gold paper and bubble-wrap. Inside was an oval mirror on a china stand, a swivel mirror, magnifying glass on one side. The stand was encrusted with china roses.

'Isn't that exquisite!' Mummy exclaimed.

'Exquisite.' I gazed down at myself in the magnifying side. I could see all the pores of my skin open in the stuffiness of the room, the eyebrow filaments that needed plucking, a patch of dry skin, shadows under my eyes.

'That'll take some dusting,' Hazel remarked, running her finger-tip over the stiff petals. 'Antique?'

'No doubt.'

I put the mirror down beside the pile of books, chocolates and bath-oils that was my haul. Mummy looked at me quizzically, I took a swig of my drink to stop my bottom lip from turning down like that of an ungrateful child. Foxy should have given me something more . . . intimate. I don't know what I'd expected, what could possibly have been inside those elaborate wrappings to make me feel better.

Mummy gave me detailed instructions about the basting of the turkey, the timing of the vegetables, the steaming of the pudding. Her GP friend, John, appeared just before eleven o'clock to accompany them to church. And then suddenly the house was empty and quiet but for tiny rustlings as screwed up balls of wrapping paper loosened. I wandered outside. The church bell began to toll, a simple and regular clang that made brassy shivers in the air. I thought of that sound carrying over the water, how far would it travel? Who would be hearing it miles across the water? The sun was shining tenderly on the calm sea. It was almost warm.

I thought about Egypt where it might be dark. What time exactly? No idea. Foxy was not in my time any more. I'd sent her off with my present wrapped in the same gold paper, and inside the gold paper, folded in black tissue paper, was an orange silk kimono most exquisitely embroidered with fantastic birds: emerald, crimson, lapis lazuli. Bought months before, before the summer, when my father was still alive. As soon as I'd seen it at a sale in Leeds I'd thought of her, how she would look in it, how she would feel in the silk of it. I had wanted to give it to her straight away but been strict with myself, hidden it, saved it up. I wished I hadn't bothered.

Next door's children came whooping out of the house, new roller-skates, a kite to fly, though there was not a breath of wind. I wished them Happy Christmas and went back into the kitchen where the smell of turkey was beginning to seep round the edges of the oven door. I looked through the glass into the hot light space. The bacon fat had gone clear and beads of sweat stood out on the pimply white flesh. I lifted the lids of the saucepans where pale sprouts and carrot sticks floated and put them back. Too early. I looked at the clock and lit the gas under the pudding. It was a bought pudding. The first Christmas pudding my mother had ever bought. Another difference. A sudden memory: the smell, the steamy brown-stained pudding cloth; between my teeth, amongst the dense sweet fruits, the thin bite of lucky silver. And stirring the pudding way back in the autumn, making wishes. Fragments of childhood, muscling voraciously up inside me.

Too quiet. I switched the radio on, something old and funny: Kenneth Williams's sneery voice and a rattle of tin laughter. I almost wished I'd gone to church. I collected the glasses and ran hot water into the bowl, squirted in detergent and watched the bubbles mound. The doorbell rang, such a sudden loud blurt that I jumped.

On the doorstep was a tall man with thick brown hair.

It took me a moment.

'Happy Christmas.' The voice a bit too loud, careful, the emphasis slightly wrong, familiar. I looked up into his face and saw but couldn't quite believe. An interesting face, narrow cheeks, faintly bristled, a pointed chin.

'Vassily?'

'Aren't you going to ask me in?'

'Oh . . .' I stood back to let him step in, turned away for a moment to control my face, calm the sudden rainy patter of my heart. He was standing, quite unwittingly, under the

189

mistletoe. I couldn't speak. Nothing would occur to me, not even a greeting.

He watched my face intently, waiting for my words.

'This is a surprise.' I managed.

'Just passing.'

'Just passing? Here?'

He chuckled. 'Well, to stretch a point.'

'Does Mummy expect . . . I mean she never . . .'

He shook his head. 'No, my mother-in-law lives up the coast – we're there for the holiday. When I realised how close I thought . . . Thought I'd say hello to your mother but . . .' he looked towards the empty kitchen.

'Everyone's at church,' I said, my heart slowing, my composure recovering. 'Sorry, Vassily, drink? I haven't even said Happy Christmas.'

It was hard to look at him. So big now, inches taller than me, and good looking. But Dog-belly was there like a speck in my eye that I could not blink away. We went into the sitting-room. He stood looking out at the view while I poured him a glass of Scotch – Colin's Glenmorangie, a present from my mother.

'They look precarious.' He nodded at the holiday shacks.

'See that gap . . .' I pointed, 'that one had just gone last time I came.'

He nodded solemnly and we fell quiet for a moment.

Then he turned to me again. 'I was truly sorry to hear about your father,' he said.

'Yes.' The fire was getting low. I knelt and put on a log. It spat and steamed, too wet. A spray of applause from the radio in the kitchen filled an awkward gap. We stood amongst the screwed-up paper and the stacks of presents. I could think of nothing to say. I could not make small talk with this man, with the memory of that little boy intruding, with the sharp splinter of shame pricking away inside me. I poured a sherry I didn't remotely want, just for something to do.

'My mother is ill,' he said. 'Ovarian cancer.'

LICK

'Oh.' I sat down quickly on the sofa, my knees suddenly weak and rubbery. 'I'm sorry to hear that.'

'She'd like to see you.' He sounded as if he was surprised.

I nodded, not imagining then that I ever would see Wanda, supposing that I'd never see her again. I thought of asking him to sit down, but that would only prolong this awkward agony. I wanted him gone. He looked taller than ever now that I was seated. He was wearing a beautiful silver-grey moleskin jacket. His fingers were long and flexible, gold hairs on his wrists, a wedding ring.

'You've done well, I understand,' I said, appalled to hear myself.

He nodded, finished his drink, put down his glass as if suddenly impatient. 'Well, good to see you Griselda.'

'You're going already?' I stood up to urge him on his way. 'You could wait for the others . . .'

'No.' He went to the door and I followed him. 'Must get back, just nipped out for a breath of air. Lunch, you know, the family . . .' I should have asked him about his child, I thought, I should have asked him about his wife. 'Say hello to Astrid,' he said, 'and Happy Christmas.'

'Yes.' I stood at the door and watched him go. He waved his arm, got into the pale Saab parked behind my Beetle. I listened until the sound of his engine had died away and went back into the kitchen. The pudding was fidgeting and bumping in its pan. I turned down the gas.

191

4

In someone else's kitchen, I lose my self-confidence. Whether to put the eggs on the toast or serve them separately? Whether to add pepper or leave that to Wanda? I don't know. The eggs are growing cool before I decide to pile them in a white china bowl and cut the toast into fingers. I choose her a fennel tea-bag for a change.

Wanda smiles as I push the door open with my elbow and manoeuvre my way in with her tray. 'I would have got up if you'd yelled.'

'Sorry. Would you rather . . .?' I step back towards the door.

'No, that'd be stone cold by the time I got down.' She pats her lap and I put the tray on it.

I hear a key in the lock downstairs. Before she can say it I know whose key it is. Hasn't he already travelled into my mind this evening?

My immediate thought: what a fright I must look, what a cheek to be wearing his sweater over my clothes. My hand goes to my hair.

'Now you'll have company while I eat my tea.' Such love in her voice, such expectation on her face as she watches the door.

His footsteps on the stairs, the bigness of him in the room, a charcoal grey overcoat. Cashmere, I suspect, a smell of night.

'Mum,' he stoops and kisses her. 'Griselda.' He nods at me, no smile, I am not liked. Why should I be?

'Sorry,' I say, 'I just came to . . .'

'No need to apologise. Mum wanted to see you. Glad you've come.' A slight lifting of the corners of his mouth.

'A new face.' Wanda does smile at me. 'Not new, but . . .' She has not touched the food.

'Do eat up,' I urge. She takes a tiny scrap of scrambled egg and lifts it slowly to her mouth. She parts her lips. I can feel just how enormous the morsel of egg seems, how Herculean the effort of putting it into her mouth. But she does so. She closes her lips and tries to smile with it inside her, the cool, damp scrap that she must swallow, that her throat rebels against swallowing.

'Shall we leave you alone?' I ask.

She nods. Her eyes are very shiny. I see a rising in her throat as if she wants to retch.

'Mum?' Vassily reaches out to touch her but she waves him away. I notice again the loose rings on her fingers, the way the stone in her engagement ring has slipped round out of sight. I remember the puzzle ring she gave me that I kept for years but have no more, the too-big feel of it on my middle finger.

Vassily and I go downstairs. He takes off his coat and slings it over the back of a chair. He sighs. 'She hardly eats a thing.' I want to smooth the coat and stroke it. How can he be so casual with anything so beautiful? All his clothes are beautiful. Some might say that he was.

Oh Foxy, Foxy, Foxy.

'Your sweater,' I say, looking down at myself, 'your mum said . . .' But he is indifferent. A lorry roars past. He goes to the window, looks out, turns and stands with his back to it, looking too big, out of kilter with the scale of the room. He is as ill at ease as I am. 'I was going to stay the night . . . but . . .' I sit down on the sofa, smooth my skirt over my knees. 'But now you're here and I've seen Wanda maybe I'll . . .'

He watches me speak, then, 'No, don't go. Don't disappoint her.'

'Vassily?'

He waits for my question.

'She's . . . dying isn't she?'

He pauses. He runs a hand down his throat, I fancy I hear the faint rasp of bristles, or maybe I imagine the feel of them. I watch the movement in his throat as he swallows. 'Yes.'

'But she was alone!'

He shakes his head. 'She won't *have* anyone to stay . . . Stan's here mostly. A Macmillan nurse comes every week and the district nurse most days. If Stan's away I try and come. She doesn't want to be a burden, she says. I *know*,' he finishes defensively, reading, wrongly, criticism into my look, 'I *know* it's not ideal but . . .' He spreads his hands.

'She doesn't seem too . . . down,' I say.

'She's amazing, Mum.'

'How long?'

He looks away. I don't know if he heard the question, if he saw my lips. There is a pause that is too long. Another lorry grinds its gears and roars. I can smell exhaust fumes.

'I don't know how she stands that . . .' I say and flinch, realising that, probably, he can't hear.

'It's surprising what you can stand,' he says, and I don't know what he means, what he's thinking of or remembering. Or whether he means anything at all.

'I'll find a guest-house,' I say, 'something on the front maybe. Where I can hear the sea.' Shit. I've done it again. What is the matter with me? 'I'll come back tomorrow. There's not room for both of us.'

'This house not big enough for the two of us?' He surprises me. I blush, a hot and childish buzz of blood in my cheeks. 'My mother will be hurt if you don't stay. And . . .' he hesitates.

'What?'

'Drink?' He reaches for his brief-case, opens it and brings out some groceries and a bottle of Famous Grouse.

'Colin was most annoyed that I opened his Glenmorangie . . .
at Christmas.'

'Colin?'

'Hazel's . . .'

'Aaah.'

'Va-ass.' Wanda's voice, panicky from upstairs.

I indicate the ceiling: 'Your mum . . .'

Vassily smashes down the bottle and takes the stairs two or
three at a time. Again, such love. I hear their voices, his feet
above me, water running in the bathroom. I shiver; despite the
heating, the fire, it is still cold. I switch the second bar of the fire
on, catch my reflection in the mirror: a mess. I roll my fat cool
curls round my fingers, take lipstick from my bag and re-do my
lips. Wish I hadn't, in the bleak electric light it looks too harsh,
the edges hard.

I don't want to be here, on a cold February night in a small
house with a dying woman and with a man I hardly know. But
who knows the worst of me. It was only a game. Children get
up to all sorts. They don't know what they do. I scrub the
lipstick off on a tissue and pinch my cheeks for colour.

Vassily comes down and into the kitchen. I go through. He's
brought the tray down, the food is almost untouched. The silly
yellow egg congealed in its bowl.

'She's had her pain-killers,' he says. 'She'll sleep now.'

I watch him tip the egg, a solid heavy shape, into the bin then
pause, his foot on the pedal, the plate of toast poised above it.
'Unless you want this?'

'No.'

Is he serious? How can I eat the food she could not eat,
old toast gone cold and stiff? Although I am hungry. Maybe
he reads my mind.

'I'm going to make myself some grub.' He slits open the
Cellophane of a packet of pasta shells. 'Want some?'

'Well . . . yes.' Unwilling to accept, unwilling to stay. I want
to go out and walk on the sea-front, fill my lungs with cold

clean air that has come straight from the sea, unbreathed, salty air. Wanda's house smells ... not unpleasant exactly, except for the traffic fumes but there is a sort of dampish sweetish ill smell. What happened to the joss-sticks? I am uneasy with Vassily, awkward and ashamed. And I want Foxy. I would put up with anything, I think now, anything if I could be with her, now, at home, her arms around me. I want Foxy.

No, you can't.

'Pour a couple of whiskies will you?'

I take two glasses from the draining-board and splosh in the whisky, too much I expect, I never know how much is right. I take a gulp and feel it in my head before it even touches my stomach. Because I am empty and not just empty of food.

I sit by the fire with my drink, watching the bulb flickering behind the dusty plastic coals. I touch them and they are hardly warm. For decoration only, created to give the illusion of warmth. The heat comes from the coiled orange bars above. I can hear Vassily in the kitchen, clattering about as he cooks, the little grunts and sighs he doesn't know he's making. He did that as a child, made noises when he bent over his books at school, when he did anything that required concentration. The sudden sizzle of onion, the pungence of garlic.

Legs folded backwards and forwards.
Daddy pushing, pushing.
Up in the air and over the wall.
Daddy headless on a ladder.
No.
Up in the air so blue.
The lurch of the tree-house when you were in it and someone climbed up.
Oh I do think it's the pleasantest thing
Ever a child can do.

'Here we are.'

I start as Vassily comes in with two plates of pasta and mushrooms. It smells divine. We sit side by side on the sofa, plates on our knees.

'I've got some wine,' I say.

'Good.'

Red wine, blue-red in this light. As we eat we talk about food. A safe topic. I don't speak of Foxy but he mentions his wife Caroline several times, and the difficulty of coaxing their daughter to eat anything except sausages and Battenberg cake. 'First she peels off the marzipan and rolls it into a ball. Then she separates the squares, builds a tower, knocks it down, eats the white squares, then the pink squares, then the marzipan.' He is proud of this infant eccentricity. I don't ask why they give her Battenberg instead of healthy food. I'm sure it's not that simple. I don't pretend to understand children. The pasta is delicious, lots of garlic, torn basil leaves, black pepper, slivers of fried mushroom. We're drinking the wine too fast. Vassily's lips are stained blue.

When we've finished eating he shows me photographs: Caroline and little Naomi. 'Don't say she looks like me because she doesn't.' He has a shred of basil caught between his front teeth.

'What about you?' he asks.

'What about me?'

'Not married?'

'No. I was engaged once . . . but it didn't work out.'

'And now?'

'Alone.' I feel Foxy's fingernail dragging down my spine. Well, it's true isn't it? From now on, probably, I am alone.

He waits for elaboration but I offer none.

'Huw?'

'Oh, a string of girlfriends, can't see him settling down for a while. If ever. Hazel's the only one who's settled and she . . .' has settled down too easily, I want to say, has attached herself to safety. Colin is safety, as far as a man can ever be. But I don't say.

And silence. Too long.

What's wrong with safety? Who the hell am I to mock?

'Well I'm glad Wanda's married. He looks nice.' I nod towards the wedding photograph.

'Stan the man.' Vassily slides his index finger round inside the collar of his shirt, a soft pale blue shirt under a soft pale grey sweater. I wonder if he chooses his own clothes or whether it's Caroline who has such exquisite taste. 'He's a good bloke,' he says. 'Mum likes him, that's what counts.'

'And you?'

'She's happy.'

If I am not going to go tonight, there's something we have to break through. There is a membrane between this small talk and the real things we could say to each other. The real things I feel compelled to say, at least. It is only nine-thirty. I can't politely go to bed for at least an hour. But how can we go on spinning out this meaningless conversation for another hour? *I* can't. If we don't say something real I will have to go.

I want to be on the promenade under the bleaching lights, walking fast and hard. I want to jump on the shifting shingle and run to the lip of the sea and hear it breathe, smell it, feel it. No. Liar. I want to go into the phone box by the pier and ring Foxy and tell her . . . I don't know what. I want to hear her voice so badly that I ache. But I don't want to hear anything she might say.

A long silence. Vassily holds the wine bottle up to the light – empty. He unscrews the whisky, looks at me, I hesitate, then nod.

'I didn't know until today . . .' I say in a rush. Too fast, he leans towards me to catch my words. 'I didn't know until today that . . .' the words have turned to pebbles in my mouth. 'That your Mum . . . that Wanda was a . . .' I cannot say it.

198

LICK

'Prostitute?' His eyebrows are raised.

I try to breathe in but the pebbles are banked up in my chest and throat. Where I was empty now I am full of hard, heavy words, so heavy I can hardly move.

'You didn't know?' He watches my eyes as if to catch a lie. He doesn't believe me. 'What did you think she did then?'

'I don't know. I didn't think. She was just your mother.'

'Money has to come from somewhere.'

'I didn't think.'

'No.' I don't like the way he emphasises this negative, the sour little shake of his head.

A gulp of whisky goes down the wrong way. I choke and splutter. He doesn't pat my back like Foxy would. He sits and watches, coolly he waits. I struggle to regain control, feeling, oh feeling such a fool. 'And that my dad . . .'

'Sorry?' He leans towards me.

'My dad,' I repeat.

He nods, then: 'I thought that was why you hated me.'

'Why?'

'Because my mother was a whore . . . and because of her and Ralph.'

I sort of laugh. 'I didn't know what a whore was!' Too late I realise that I should have said I didn't hate him. I can't say it now, a beat too late. And was it even true? I can't remember. The little spook looks down at me from his frame on the mantelpiece. Yellow, cheesy wedge of a face.

I wonder what Foxy is doing? If I rang she might not answer and that would mean that either she is out or that she has unplugged the phone. If I rang and there was no answer I would feel worse.

'I loved him,' Vassily says. 'And so did Mum.'

'Yes.' Can I say the same?

He leans back, stretches his legs, then bends forward and unties his shoe-laces. I curl up on the sofa, my feet, that are still cold, tucked underneath me. Superficially, he looks relaxed but his hands are clenched and there is a little tic in the muscle above his jaw.

'I used to . . .' I begin. I'm not quite drunk enough to break through this. Vassily pours more whisky. As he does so he catches my eye as if he understands and will force me through. I am almost scared. Amazing that words that are nothing but air and vibration can be so hard. Words evaporate once they are spoken but their meanings can scorch very deep into your tender soul. *Sticks and stones might break my bones but words will never hurt me.* What a lie.

'Go on.' It is unnerving, the intensity with which he waits and watches. I take another swallow of the whisky. It is like a game of dares. Elaine and I used to play dares sometimes with some wild girls I wasn't supposed to play with. I dare you to cross the railway track. I dare you to steal a packet of Love-hearts from the shop. I dare you to kiss Puddle-duck. No one ever said that – but they might have done.

'I used to be very jealous of you.' I wait for his surprise.

'Go on,' is all that he says.

'How Daddy seemed . . . almost to prefer you.' He watches me closely but I cannot read his expression. I wind my hair round my finger. 'How he cared about your feelings and not ours, mine and Hazel's. How he hardly even *noticed* Huw.'

The light is too bright in my eyes. The single central light-bulb under its pleated shade casts a bleak uniform light. Keeping my face tilted so he can see my mouth dazzles me. I feel a little lurch inside that warns me I should drink no more. Vassily keeps his eyes on my face. He communicates so well I keep forgetting that he needs to watch my lips.

'The pond . . .' I want to rid myself of the pebbles that shift and grind in my chest. What ever can it matter now? I am thinking of the ants. He must forgive me.

'The pond and how . . . it was your pond and his pond and . . .' I am starting to sound childish. I laugh a bit, a brittle laugh that snaps off halfway through. Daddy's hand over his little hand patting the beautiful white sand flat. He doesn't laugh. Inscrutable, that's what he is. 'Even when Hazel and I went to get the pond-weed it didn't work . . . and you helped him make it.' Christ, I am *not* going to cry. I gulp more whisky, blushing and squirming under his cool gaze as if I'm on the end of a pin, or pinioned underneath his foot. The more I say the stupider I sound. And the less honest. Although I am trying to be honest.

'I feel as if . . .' But I am stuck. His green eyes are clear and cold.

'As if . . .' he prompts.

Something occurs to me. 'Tell me . . . after we moved away did you see him again, my father?'

'Of course.' He looks surprised.

My feet are cramped underneath me. I uncurl. 'I . . . I had no idea.'

He shrugs. 'That's how it was.'

A swelling sensation, the germ of what I knew expanding in my chest, a wait while it does so. 'When?'

'What?'

'Did you see him?'

He looks at me as if at an idiot. 'Evenings, weekends. Summer holidays.' My nails are in my palms. I close my eyes, think. *Yes*, he was often away: work, golf trips. We didn't miss him. The rhythms of the house so much easier, the atmosphere lighter in his absence. I never thought about where he was. I feel betrayed. Betrayed? *Me*? Why? Did it hurt me? The swelling in my rib-cage and throat has grown so great I'm almost choked. I gasp in a big breath. The electric-fire is baking the stale air. 'Mind if I open the window?'

I've got pins and needles in my foot. I get up and stamp it on the floor, wincing against the excruciating fizz. Behind the curtains is a blur of wet orange light, glittering drops on the glass, the movement of a dark tree. I didn't know it had been raining.

'Won't open,' Vassily says. 'Painted solid.'

'But I can't breathe.'

He shrugs his shoulders.

'I'll go in the kitchen.' Walking about makes me realise how much too much I've drunk. I'm clumsy as if wearing giant boots and boxing gloves. I go upstairs to the bathroom, moving quietly as I can so as not to disturb Wanda. The bathroom is cool at least, the shelves crammed with medicine bottles, pills, essential oils; the turquoise plastic bath smeary. A thick blue candle is stuck to the side of the bath in a solidified cascade of drips. No possibility of opening this window either, sealed up with a sheet of polythene taped to the frame, inside a scatter of dead flies, the skeleton of a lace-wing. I will suffocate.

Downstairs, I reach for my coat. 'I'm going to get some fresh air.'

'It's pouring with rain.'

'Just five minutes.'

He looks as if he couldn't care less, which, probably, he couldn't. I go out into the icy streaming night. As usual, I'm wearing stupid shoes for walking, low-heeled – but they pinch my toes. Sleet smashes from the sky and jumps halfway up my legs. I've no umbrella and no hood. Cold needles prickle my skull, my hair will be ruined. In my hurry to escape I've turned the wrong way, I have to walk along the muddy edge of the dual carriageway before turning into quieter streets. The juggernauts thunder through the wet orange and black and send sheets of freezing oily water, waves of it, sloshing up from the gutter, soaking me to the waist. It's only fifty yards or so to the corner – but I turn back. Too vain to ruin my hair? Too cold and wet to think? You cannot breathe in such rain.

5

Vassily smirks when I burst back in. He regards my soaking skirt and the gritty wetness of my stockings. 'I'll get something of Mum's.'

He runs upstairs and brings down a pair of tie-dyed leggings and a sweat-shirt.

'I'll change upstairs.'

'Stay by the fire. I'll do the washing up.' He takes the plates out into the kitchen. My fingers feel huge and they are trembling as I fumble with the buttons of my dress, undo my stockings, laddered, the thin nylon stuck to me, the sensation like peeling off the top layer of skin. My legs are red and blotchy as salami. Wanda's clothes smell of a sickly fabric conditioner, not my sort of clothes at all, but soft and dry. The mirror shows me that my curls have gone, the wetness frizzing my hair into its old bushiness. My nipples are screwed up tightly with the cold, they hurt as if someone is pinching them between their fingers and thumbs, not a loving squeeze, spiteful. Dog-belly's nipples in my mind now. Does he still have them? Of course, he must. Dog-belly. What did I used to say running along to school . . . *Dog-belly, Puddle-duck, Puddle-belly, Dog's muck.*

Oh but it was only a game. My stomach lurching like the lurch of the tree-house. I was only a child. I didn't mean it. He doesn't walk like that any more with his feet splayed out, slap, slap, slap. He doesn't walk like a duck.

I'm not sure that he is Puddle-duck at all.

Except that he knows what I am.

He comes back into the sitting-room, drying his hands on a tea-towel.

'Better?'

'Yes, thanks.'

He sits down and pours more whisky. 'Not for me,' I say, but he doesn't hear me. 'Vassily, I'd rather have a cup of coffee.'

'I think you should drink with me.' I am chilled by his tone. No smile in his eyes. I sit down. There is a smell of detergent now and his hands are very pink. My stockings and suspenders are sprawled on the arm of the sofa, I inch them towards me, tuck them down the side of the sofa cushion.

'I knew you were jealous,' he says. 'I liked it.'

'Oh.' Since I'm probably going to be ill anyway, I swallow more whisky. He liked it. Not such an innocent then. Nothing quite makes sense. 'I don't ... didn't ... *don't* understand. Why he seemed to prefer *you*.'

He presses his lips together, then runs his tongue round his front teeth. 'I didn't – at the time.' He is sitting so close to me I can feel his breath. 'Maybe not a matter of *prefer*,' he muses. Or maybe it's my imagination, not his breath. A trickle from my hair runs down my neck. He does not like me – no reason why he should and ample reason why he shouldn't. So why am I suddenly so aware of him? What is this sudden tension? To make love to Vassily ... Puddle-duck ... Dog-belly ... Dog's muck. 'No!'

'What?'

'Oh!' I was not aware that I had spoken aloud, the edge between inside my head and outside blurring. I cannot think straight. I shake my head to try and dislodge the thought but that only makes the room spin, makes it worse. Someone makes love to him, someone takes off his shirt and presses her breasts against his dog's-belly. Caroline does, they have a child to prove it. Does she kiss them every one, lower and lower, does she kiss each one of those nipples in turn?

Oh Foxy, Foxy, save me from myself. She is on my side, Foxy is, whatever she says, whatever she does, she is on my side.

'What?' he says again.

'Just . . . nothing.' I must stop drinking.

'Do you remember . . .?' His voice is very quiet. Goose-pimples on my arms although I am hot again now. I grasp the wet bushiness of my hair to keep awake, keep sensible, hold on. Remember what? Did I say it or not? I remember the jam smeared on his body, ants at the corners of his eyes, feeding at his lips, falling in his mouth when he opened it to scream.

I don't know what he wants of me. What is his intention? I cannot read his face which has grown indistinct.

'I didn't understand, then, why Ralph, sort of . . . took me on.' His own speech is becoming hard to follow. Is it me or is it him? I swallow whisky in a hot gulp. He lifts the bottle, I try to put my hand over my glass but miss and he pours more in. Does he want to ravish me? I smother a giggle. He ignores me, perhaps he doesn't hear. 'But now I do.'

'Because of Wanda.' That much is obvious to me. Wanda with her luscious body under the filmy nylon. A sudden flash of Daddy on the landing at night, wild-haired, the squashy purple acorn glimpse, a shudder, the whisky rising in my throat. And she was a whore, God suddenly I love that word. When I was little I used to love the words hoar-frost, raspy cat's tongue harsh, made me shiver with an unidentified longing. Associated with hips and haws and sticky rose-hip syrup, sticky, sweetie syrup. Whore. And Daddy so prudish that he left the room or hid behind his newspaper when animals mated on television. Now I'm being naive again. It's not as simple as that. It never bloody is. I pull hard at the hair at the back of my skull with both hands, pull to keep myself present.

Another question, like what? Some neutral thing. Oh. 'Does Caroline drink?'

A funny look. 'A bit.'

'How long have you been together?' He doesn't even bother to answer. 'Happy?'

He puts one elbow on his knee, leans his chin on his hand. 'We have our moments.' Then reconsiders. 'Very happy, very happy, yes. She's wonderful.' I feel put in my place. His voice is louder now that he is drunk, the careful edges of his words dissolved, he looks more intently at my face as I speak. The way he looks up at me, his chin cupped in his palm, makes him seem more vulnerable. I feel better, not better, I feel dreadful . . . but what? Less threatened. It's nice to be wearing the leggings, to have the freedom to sprawl, put my legs anyhow. I had these winceyette pyjamas, inceywinceyette, little ducks on them and a frill round the neck. Mummy said they were a bugger to iron and that is the only time I have ever heard her swear. My usual clothes, calculated, circumscribe my movements, why do I do it? Dress like that? Christ knows.

'Explain then,' I say.

'What?'

My hand goes to his knee. The fine wool fabric of his trousers is both soft and rough, cat's tongue again, hoar, whore. He straightens up. What am I doing, touching him? I can't pull my hand away, don't know how to move it now. We're so close together on the sofa. What does it signify? Only a touch.

'Explain what?'

'That you understand . . . Daddy.'

'Because I am deaf.' I pull a face at him, flooded with a woozy fondness. 'And I was . . . I was a poor little thing.'

'Little spook,' I say and I am caressing his knee while part of me peels away, aghast. I force my hand away and pick up my glass. My hands are trembling, everything outside our hot circle of breath is out of focus.

He smiles, lop-sided. 'Yes. Little spook. He used to talk to me, you know.'

'Daddy?'

'On and on. He used to tell me things.'

'What things?' An awareness of the heat of his thigh but at the same time my eyes prickling. He never told *me* anything.

'About . . . all sorts . . . about the war. About when he was a prisoner-of-war.'

A chilliness. What I want to know. Maybe now I can. But from him? I am quiet, we both are. Lorries roar past, silent for him, or perhaps he feels the vibration.

'He talked to me because . . . because I couldn't hear him.' I want to cry but I won't. Instead a drop of sweat from my arm-pit meanders down my side. 'I did catch some of it though. And then . . . he did talk to Mum.' And was that worse, more unfaithful, more a betrayal, than the sex? How can I possibly puzzle such a thing?

'She loved him,' I say.

He nods. 'She was broken up when he died. "He was the love of my life," she said.'

'She said that? But Stan . . .'

He smiles. 'Mum's nothing if not a pragmatist. She was getting on. Wanted not to be . . . on the game. And Stan the man came along . . . offering her the stars.' He extends his hand ironically to indicate the miserable proportions of the room. 'And anyway, Ralph was married, wasn't he? He wasn't about to leave.'

'Did he think of it?' Now the salty creep of a tear on my cheek. Though would it have been so terrible? I am more amazed than upset. Astonished, dizzied by how much I did not know. I stick out my tongue and catch the tear as it passes my mouth. Only one tear. Vassily shakes his head: because he doesn't know? Because he thinks he's said too much?

'So he talked to Wanda?'

'He told her just about everything, I should think. She's a good listener, Mum. She let him talk. I think, I think *now* that for *him* that was what was between them more than . . .'

'Sex?'

'Yes.'

A moment of clarity in the booziness, something I will know. 'I know a bit . . . about Vince.' I focus on his face.

'Yes.'

'You know who I mean?'

'Of course. Poor Ralph.' I wait, but he stretches. 'Oh dear, drunk too much. Coffee?' He turns from his stretch and his face is very close to mine. I don't know what I'm doing. It's not what I want, I want to know about Vince. It's not me doing anything now it's the alcohol animating my limbs and my lips. I kiss him.

His response is ambivalent but he does not pull away. His lips are firm but I cannot feel his tongue, I feel the rough edge where his bristles start. He lets me kiss him. There is heat in my belly. I push away the tangle of thoughts, motives, turn my body against his. I put my leg over his leg, I rub my hand on his thigh, slide it up the inside. I brush his groin but all is cool and soft. Nothing. He lets me kiss him, that is all. No response, no heat. I don't stop immediately, I'm too embarrassed. I rub some more but nothing happens. This is nothing but a cool man allowing himself to be kissed. I remove my hand, my leg, my mouth from him.

He wipes his lips on the back of his hand. 'I'll make that coffee.' He staggers a bit when he gets up. I stare at the whisky bottle which is empty to just below the label and my face grows fatter and hotter with each beat of my heart until I fear it will burst. My lips itch. Blood is beating in my ears. I scrub my crawling lips with the sleeve of Wanda's sweat-shirt. I kissed Dog-belly. *I* kissed him, not the other way round. No, no, not me, the loneliness and the desperation kissed him; the whisky and the wine in me. Not me. But stupid, ill-judged. Why do I always do that? Misjudge everything.

I wish the floor would open up and swallow me . . . such a cliché but I do wish it, I really do. I want the flowered carpet to stretch and rip, thread from thread; the rusty blossoms to split; the floorboards to rear up and splinter; the foundations to crumble and the raw black earth to yawn open and take me in. And all to close above me.

I cannot move. I hear him on the stairs, gently opening and closing Wanda's door. I hear him in the kitchen, the rush of the kettle coming to a boil, the sound of pouring. He brings through the glass jug and two mugs.

I can't even look up, until, when he speaks, I do so with surprise. 'Remember Hiroshima?' he says.

'What?' I laugh, almost a real laugh, a momentary relief from humiliation.

'Hiroshima – and Nagasaki for that matter.'

'Yes. Terrible. But what's that got to do with the price of fish?' My words slurring. The prishe of fish.

My nostrils flinch at the dark snarl of the coffee as he pours it out.

'Black OK? Without Hiroshima, *you* would not be. Ralph would have died – along with thousands more.'

'Well yes, but . . . so?'

He says nothing for a moment, then: 'Just that there are two ways of looking . . .'

'Only two!'

He opens his mouth as if to reply, then closes it again. Why has he brought up this, now? He is as drunk as me and I am unequal to a logical sequence of thought. The coffee scalds the roof of my mouth. I don't like it so strong. I pull one of my feet up on to my lap. The sole is very pink and slightly shiny. I pumice my heels every week so as not to snag my fine stockings. I run my finger over the heel, smooth and cool.

'So . . . so what are you saying?'

'Just a thought.'

'*Would* he have died?'

'He was near death. Starving of course, cerebral malaria, tropical ulcers . . .'

I let my foot go. I've never considered that Hiroshima had anything to do with me. Hiroshima – I used to think it was a lovely word. A sudden slotting into place, an awkwardness never explained: Christmas again, must have been, we only played such games at Christmas. 'Favourite words Grizzle?' A quick-fire round you had to answer on the count of three, or pay a forfeit, funny how the mind goes blank, all of them pointing their fingers at me and chanting together one, two and as they reach three I cry out 'Kamikaze' which was, still is, a favourite word – not for what it means, just for the sound of it. A grey pall falling sudden as a blanket and Daddy, the life and soul only moments before, leaving the room. The game over, the atmosphere soured. Never an explanation. Japanese word. Surely that wasn't really why?

'Forget it,' Vassily says. 'Time to turn in. I'll be off first thing so you won't see me again.' He stands up, yawns, stretches his arms above his head. His finger-tips almost touch the ceiling.

'Where will you sleep?'

'Here.' He indicates the sofa, though it's not half long enough for him.

'No, you must have your room. I'll sleep here.'

'No.' Very firm. 'I'll get my head down for a couple of hours to sleep off the . . .' He indicates the bottles on the table. I think it will take more than a couple of hours. 'Then I'll get on the road, miss the traffic, take Naomi to nursery before work.'

'OK.' I get up and go to the foot of the stairs. There are more things I want to ask him, there is more I should say. There is something but it eludes me. I feel low and sluggish and slightly sick. Straight into a hangover. I fill a mug with water in the kitchen and go upstairs. 'Good-night', I call, 'Good-bye', but I call it from the stairs and he doesn't hear. It doesn't strike me why he didn't answer until I'm shivering in the bathroom.

6

The bed is double and the sheets aren't clean. Not quite dirty but not fresh either. When I pull back the duvet I see that they are rumpled and that there are hairs on the pillows. Whose? Too cold to undress, I climb straight in and pull the duvet over me. The bed feels dampish – or maybe it's just that it's so cold. The room rocks and swirls about me. I lie very still on my back waiting for it to stop. And who *would* wash the sheets? Not Wanda, not Vassily on one of his flying visits, probably not Stan. There is no hope that I'll sleep. Foxy's warmth is what I would need for that. Oh how I lie to myself, I would be warm, but still I would lie awake. I could have her still. I could go back tomorrow and say, yes, I love you and I want you to stay – and I want you to be free. The drink makes it seem *half* possible. The drink – or the cold space beside me – make it seem impossible that I'll ever have the strength to leave her or to throw her out.

'Foxy, I love you. Do what you like, come and go as you like, I will always be with you.'

Doesn't that make me sound like an albatross? Can it really be what she wants me to say?

'Foxy, there is someone else ... don't be hurt, we can still be friends, still live together if you like, but this is something I must explore ...'

If only there bloody was someone else.

Maybe when I get back she will be gone and I can toss and turn all night, pace around in the blazing light without disturbing a soul. I can have the curtains open and all the windows and the doors . . . though the thought of all that draughtiness does make me shiver.

I do not switch off the light. The 60-watt bulb is a dull fruit above me, cobweb strands across the shade. My cheeks blaze with the sudden memory of that kiss, my heart squirms and my body writhes, so mortified I don't know where to put myself.

Occasionally when I kiss Foxy her lips do not move. She lets me kiss her but does not kiss back. Smiles at me vaguely when I draw away, lets me take something from her while her mind is elsewhere, burrowing in a past that's not her own.

Nonsense she says in my ear, the warmth of her breath on my cheek, *the past belongs to everybody, it's a part of everybody*, she looks at me in an intimate way that seems to say *especially you*. She would if she was here.

Vassily. Oh no. My heart contracts again. Stop it.

Kamikaze, Mitsubishi, Sushi, Sake, Geisha.

Vassily. I could have said – forgive me.

Both icy cold and stuffy in this room, a camphorish smell like the inside of old wardrobes. So many of the clothes I buy for the shop smell like that and it's almost impossible to dispel, even after washing and drying them in the sun you can still catch a whiff of it. Perhaps Connie does me a favour with her Gauloises. More exotic than the moth-ball reek, at least.

Look, I need never see Vassily again. No one will ever know that I kissed him. That he . . . Forget it, Grizzle. No, no, Zelda, forget it. Imagining Hazel's face . . . ha! I will not even tell Foxy.

Pink and grey flowers close to my eyes, slightly textured, a scrape where furniture was carelessly moved. Walls against my face. The wall by the bunk, Hazel's bottom bunk, her list of dates. The dates of Daddy's dreams.

To sleep in a strange house is impossible. Vassily's feet on the stairs, the bathroom taps running.

I snuggle down. A little warmth leaking from me now into the mattress, into the duvet. I can smell my own sour boozy breath. Although it is *him*, a man who despises me, at least there is someone awake. What did he mean: Poor Ralph? About Vince? Question marks like twists of wire, sharp in my brain. Wanda through the wall in her drugged sleep. Wanda dying and all evening my head full of myself, yes, myself in relation to Foxy, Daddy, Vassily.

Oh the ants again and comfort gone. Only a game. Oh shut up, that lie is wearing thin.

It was not their fault but they had to die? What?

Kamikaze, Mitsubishi, sushi, sushi, sushi.

The splatter of rain on the window.

My thumb in my mouth. Well why not? No one to see, no one to know. Christ, I'm nearly thirty. Soapy tasting thumb-pad hooking into the ridged hollow, teeth catching just below the knuckle. A little squeak in my ears with each suck.

And I do sleep. Not long, but a soft, deep, oblivious slice of it, a small portion but a portion still, digested. I wake and grope for my watch. A flicker of pride. I slept two hours in a strange bed.

What woke me?

The drink is burning me up. I sip some water, very cold as if it has been in the fridge and almost drop off again but then I am disturbed by a groan. Wanda. The roar of traffic, the reek of camphor and exhaust fumes, the dull electric-light, the cold. Why does she live here?

Wanda, Wanda, what a place to choose to die.

I wait for Vassily's feet on the stairs but they do not come. More groans. Maybe he has already gone. She cries out and I am wide awake, my skin prickling with the cold as I sit up. Her cry is one of pain, there is no mistaking it. I stumble up, my head crashing, trip over something, bash my knee on the end of the bed. I open her door. The bedside lamp is on and she is turning this way and that, her head on the pillow rolling from right to left as if trying to escape something, her scarf pulled half off, her face grey and sunken. I don't know what to do.

'Wanda?'

Vassily should have told me what to do. I stand, stupidly. My eyes hurt, dry and scratchy. I must look appalling. Stop thinking about yourself.

'Should I call the doctor?'

She gives no sign of having heard me. I don't even know if she knows I'm here. Vassily's feet on the stairs at last. Of course he cannot hear. He zips up his trousers as he pushes past me into the room. I want to creep back to bed but don't, don't want to seem heartless.

'Mum, all right, there, there, Mum . . .' His voice is loud but gentle, soothing, like a father soothing a child, *some* fathers. There is the bitter smell of part-excreted alcohol coming off him – and me too I suppose. He tips out a capsule from a pill bottle, scoops her head up in one palm, coaxes her to swallow it with a sip of water, dabs the trickle of water off her chin with the edge of the sheet. Then lies her down again. 'All right, Mum,' he says, 'just hang on in there.' She lets out a long moan. 'Morphine,' he explains to me, 'takes a while to kick in.'

'I'll go back to bed,' I say.

Wanda waves her hand at me. 'No . . . stay.' I look at Vassily but he shrugs. It is so cold in the room, if I'm going to stay there is nothing to be done but to get into bed with her.

'OK.'

The mattress tilts with my weight, so much greater than hers though I am not big. The pillow smells slightly of man, or maybe it's my imagination, the thought of Stan beside her. I cannot help but wonder: do they still make love? Her poor body, thin and swollen at once, could it bear such use? We lie together in the lamp-light. I listen to her breathing, little hard, tight breaths that at last begin to loosen. I wonder if she has forgotten I'm here, whether she'll drift back to sleep now, but she hasn't forgotten a thing. She looks over at me, her eyes bright.

'Better?' I say, stupid as ever.

She struggles to sit up. I get out of bed and help, plump the pillows behind her. She reaches for the glass of water by the bed, takes tiny sips, her hand trembling. The skin is papery thin, in the yellowish lamplight you can see the green and ivory of vein and bone, you can see her workings.

'I'm sorry,' she says.

'Sorry!' I sit down on the edge of her bed and take the thin hand.

'For waking you.'

'Don't be silly.' I smooth the tissue of skin, one of her orange nails has gone, the bed of it raw and caked with curds of glue. 'I never sleep.'

'You and Vass been chewing the fat?' The gleam in her eye is almost mischievous. I wonder what she thinks? Her hand goes to her head. I help her straighten her scarf.

Vassily comes up the stairs, puts his head round the door. 'I'm getting off soon,' he says. 'I'll make a cup of tea before I go. Anyone?'

'Please,' I say.

'What I fancy,' Wanda says, 'is a proper cup of PG Tips or what have you. Proper tea. None of that herbal slop.'

'Right you are.' Vassily goes downstairs. I look at Wanda's clock – three-fifteen.

'Shall I tidy you up, start again . . .?' for the scarf is still lop-sided. She nods and tilts her head towards me. I slide the scarf off the faintly bristly skin of her scalp, undo the knot, smooth it with my hands. To my surprise I feel almost content. In what? In being in a house full of people wide awake in the dead of the night, the worst hour of the night, the hour too far

215

from the shore of evening or the shore of morning, the drowning hour. I would feel content if the whisky was not a dirty taste in my mouth, a burn in my throat. I long for the tea. My eyes sting, my temples throb.

I fold the scarf round her head and tie it, a cotton paisley scarf, brown and yellow. The skin at the nape of her neck is fine and soft as silk, softer. I tie the knot flat so that it won't dig into her when she lies down again. Her make-up is smeared and clogged into the lines around her eyes. On her dressing-table is cleanser and cotton wool. I pour some cleanser on a ball of cotton wool, fresh smelling cucumber stuff, and I wipe it over her cheeks and round her lips, scoop gently under each eye, smooth it over her forehead.

'That's beautiful,' she breathes, her eyes closed. 'I always said I wanted a girl.' She opens her eyes a slit and smiles at me, 'A boy would never think of doing this . . . not that my Vass int an angel.'

'He's very good.'

'And I've got a daughter-in-law now – and a grand-daughter. Oh she's that bright.' She looks past me into her grand-daughter's bright future, into her own oblivion, and her eyes cloud.

'How about some perfume?'

'Don't bother much with that any more.' She lifts her index finger to the corner of her eye, presses, as if forcing a tear back in.

'No?'

'That seem to make me feel queasy.'

'I've got some eau-de-Cologne in my bag, that's refreshing.'

I fetch it, dab a little on her temples, her thin beating wrists. I straighten the covers, rearrange her pillows. Feel a little seep of satisfaction – I've made her more comfortable, I've given her ease. A feeling inside me like a small ripening. It strikes me I've never done this before, this motherly thing, looked after a person in such a tender thoughtful way. Maybe with Huwie, a long long time ago, but never since. It's Foxy who looks after me – mostly it's that way round. I had never thought.

'I'll go down and help Vassily with the tea.'

She nods. She looks tidy, composed, almost childlike, her skin sheeny in the light from the lamp.

He drops a couple of tea-bags into the pot.

'What would have happened if no one was there?' I say.

'Stan is here mostly. If not I try and come – she rarely has a night alone. She doesn't wake like that every night.'

'But what if?'

He shrugs.

'How long?' I ask, but his head is bent over the tea-pot. 'Months, weeks, what?'

'Sugar?' he says.

7

Five o'clock, back in bed, Vassily gone. I won't see him again. Unless, possibly, at Wanda's funeral – if I'm asked. Hearing the door slam behind him, I felt lost for a moment, found my hands were grasping at the empty air.

I want him to like me – but he does not. Why should he? Once he wanted me to like him. Oh, why do I care?

I stayed in bed beside Wanda until she fell asleep again, her breath inflating her lips, escaping in little puffs. I edged out of her bed, carefully, carefully, so as not to wake her and crept back into this cold room, drank water, swallowed a couple of paracetamol from my bag. It's not so bad – the far side of the night. I can be alone. The lorry noise has never ceased but I am starting not to hear it, not to hear every separate vehicle that thunders past. Closing my eyes I imagine the faces of the men, mostly men, high up in their cabs, radios blaring, sandwiches and fags on the dashboard, eyes eating the road, minds on their wives or their children or lovers, on whatever makes them feel at home.

I said a last good-bye to Vassily, once before, when we were children. I hadn't seen him since the ants, or only in the distance at school. For the last couple of weeks of the half-term, I was ill, said I was, I think I *was*, with a dull hard ache in my stomach as if I had swallowed a stone. I could hardly eat. The doctor found nothing wrong, but because we were moving and starting a new school anyway after the Whitsun holiday, Mummy let me stay at home.

My eleventh birthday had been in the time between the ants and the move, a horrible birthday. Hazel and I were still half in disgrace so there was no party. Mummy took us to see *Oliver* and then for a posh tea in a hotel – minute sandwiches and fragile cakes off a china stand. I didn't think it was much of a feed but didn't dare complain. I'd had clothes and a watch and a Spirograph. I'd wanted a chemistry set but Daddy had said, No, giving no reason but looking at me as if he thought I was too dangerous for a chemistry set. I had enjoyed *Oliver* – but the birthday had been all wrong and sour. Hazel had come into my room at bedtime and said, 'Bad luck, old bean.' 'Thanks, old bean,' I'd said, comforted that she understood. 'Good-night.'

The day we moved: a heat-wave – temperatures in the eighties and the air stifling with the scent of wallflowers and creosote. The removal men stamped and shouted brutishly through the house in their string vests, sweat trickling down their faces. There was banging as they heaved boxes of our belongings and furniture into the van, the roar of the vacuum cleaner in empty rooms, shuddery sounds as the metal sides of the van vibrated. The house filled with the smell of the men's sweat and cigarette smoke. Hazel and I were taking turns – an hour each – keeping Huw out from under everyone's feet and helping Mummy clean each room as it was emptied.

I took Huwie out into the garden, my eyes averted from Vassily's window in case he was behind it, looking down. Huwie had refused to wear a T-shirt and his tender shoulders were pink from the sun. He had scribbled on his tummy with a Biro and was very proud of the result. We peered into the pond. 'Look, Huwie,' I said, 'a frog.' It was the first. The first tadpole to do the whole thing: lose its tail, grow legs, lose its gills, grow lungs; become nothing but a frog. 'Fog,' Huwie said lying on his belly and making a grab for it, but the frog swam to the far side of the pool, its splayed legs scissoring it away in rippling surges. A frog the size of my thumbnail. The most perfect thing I'd ever seen. We'd done diagrams at school, the metamorphosis from sticky blob to frog, smudgy black pencil on sugar paper. But we had not drawn the wonder of it. I had not understood. Huwie tried to get in the pond and I carried him away into the cool and strangely echoey house.

'The men have almost finished, Grizzle,' Mummy said. 'Daddy's loading the car. Will you take that book back to Vassily?' she nods at a curled-up reading book lying on the draining-board. 'I found it down the back of the sofa – and you can say good-bye to them.'

'Why don't you?'

'Just do it – we haven't got long.'

'Hazel?' I looked at her pleadingly.

'I saw them yesterday,' she said, tossing her tidy head.

'Don't be long though,' Mummy said. She was emptying the vacuum cleaner into a bin bag, blinking and pursing her lips against a rising cloud of dust.

I walked round the corner. It was five o'clock, still blazing hot. The air was still and golden, almost syrupy with the sweetness of heated grass and flowers. I dragged my feet and stuck my bottom lip out. I felt about five. My shorts were too short and tight and my blouse was dirty, but all the clean clothes were packed. Away in the distance I could hear the Brahms's *Lullaby* jingle of an ice-cream van.

The garden in front of Wanda's flat was overgrown. The old pram was still there but grass had grown up around it and bindweed twined round the hood. Dandelions and their fluffy clocks grew up the sides of the path. I kicked one and a cloud of fairies bloomed up into the air. By the door a cluster of cloudy milk-bottles stank sourly.

I went up the stairs and knocked at Wanda's door. No answer. Relieved. I started to turn away but then I heard movement inside. The handle turned and Vassily's face appeared in the gap. I understood then that a smile need not be friendly. He was not wearing his hearing-aids and his hair hung in his eyes. He did not ask me in.

'I've brought this back,' I said loudly, holding out the book. Wanda appeared suddenly behind him, wrenching open the door with one hand, holding her dressing-gown together with the other.

'Thanks.' She took the book and gestured me inside. 'You off then?' I entered reluctantly and stood in the hall. On top of the incense scent and patchouli oil I could smell bubble-bath. Wanda's hair was wet around the bottom, the fuzz turned to solid darkish curls. She hugged me against her velvety dressing-gown, overwhelming me with softness.

'Thanks,' she said.

I disengaged myself. 'For what?'

'For playing with my Vass.'

'That's all right.' I looked at the floor. Was she serious?

'You look boiled,' she said, 'have a drink.'

I was tempted. Everything nice had been packed away in boxes at home and we'd only been able to have water since lunchtime. She gave me a coke, the bottle misted and icy from the fridge. 'Vass?' He shook his head. I drank it as fast as I could, the bubbles hard as grit as I swallowed them, my teeth turning soft and furry.

'Thank you,' I said.

'I'm that choked you're going.' She did look sorry. Obviously she did not really know me. She put one arm round me, one round Vassily, and hugged us both so that he and I were almost pressed together. 'Do keep in touch,' she said.

When I left I had to run up and down the road shaking my arms and legs to get rid of a mass of horrible creeping twitches. I don't know what it was. The sweat under my arms was smelling horrible, it had just started to do that, a grown-up complicated smell and wisps of hair were growing there too, so that I had to keep my arms down if I was wearing anything sleeveless.

'Whatever are you doing?' Mummy called. She was standing by the car holding Huw. The van had gone. It was time for us to go. I climbed into the back of the car. The hot seat burnt the backs of my thighs. The car was cramped, crammed with the five of us and pot-plants and my father's bad temper.

I had a rubber-plant on my lap and was squashed up against Hazel who wriggled irritably but dared say nothing because of the colour of Daddy's neck. All I could hope was that she wouldn't be sick. The windows were wide open and as we drove away Mummy called out, 'Good-bye house, Good-bye The Nook', and Huwie, sitting on her lap, waved and called 'Bye-bye' too. But I, my face hidden by the thick rubbery leaves, did not even look back.

8

The air in the room is thick and frowsty. I approach the bed warily with Wanda's tea. She is absolutely still. My heart is a stiff wing against my ribs. It is the only movement in the room. I am frozen mid-way through a step. Outside, a lull between lorries lets in the regular high chink-chink of a sparrow.

Then Wanda opens her eyes, two bright slits, and I breathe again. I put down the cup of tea, dizzied by a hot rush of relief. She tries to raise her head from the pillow to squint at the clock.

'Eight-thirty,' I say. 'I looked in before but you were asleep.'

I do not say that she was so sound asleep I was afraid then that she had gone. That I had crept downstairs, taken more pills for my pounding head, drunk my way through a pot of tea, crouching by the electric-fire, terrified, trying to distract myself with breakfast television. Telling myself not to be silly, that she was not dead but only sound asleep, deeply, deeply asleep. But hearing in my head at the same time, the granite grave-stone words: *she is not dead but sleepeth*. Crossing my arms across my chest, clutching myself, rocking, clutched by the fear that I was alone in a house with a dead person and that it was up to me to do the things that must be done, things I had only seen in films or on television, had only the haziest idea about – to bend over Wanda's body, to feel for her pulse, lift her eyelids, to touch her chilly skin. To hold a mirror to her face to check for breath.

I made her tea in defiance of all that – and I am proved right to have done so. She is alive, and now her eyes are opening wider and she is smiling at me. She is alive for today – and how precious life seems suddenly, how precious and precarious. If only there was a God I would give thanks.

I turn my face away to hide my expression which must be crazed with relief. I open her curtains to let the grey light in. *Sea-link, Geest, Ferrymaster*, say the sides of the passing lorries. 'How about a bath?' I say.

There is a spider in the bath, a big palm-sized crouching one. At home I would ask Foxy to remove it. Not that I'm scared of spiders, not at all, it's just touching it . . . just the idea that it might run up my arm, up my sleeve. Too big to wash down the plug-hole. There is a plastic beaker by the sink, opaque with toothpaste splashes. I nudge the spider inside it with the end of a tooth-brush, stuff a handful of toilet paper in, not tight enough to kill it, just to trap it while I take it downstairs. On the back steps I pull out the wad of paper, the spider clinging to it, fling it as far as I can, slam the door and run back upstairs. It's *not* that I'm frightened of spiders – what is there to be frightened of? It's just that they are so delicate, so fragile, I do not want to do them any harm.

I want this bath to be lovely for Wanda. I wipe the bath which is none too clean, put in the plug, turn on the taps, slosh in some bath-oil. The smell of roses fills the room. I am reminded of Foxy running me a bath, six months ago, the morning after my father died. Foxy bringing me breakfast in bed after that terrible night, caring for me so well. I light the blue candle on the edge of the bath. The cold air fills with scented steam. The radiator is hardly warm. I take the towels downstairs and hang them over chairs in front of the fire.

Wanda is sitting on the edge of the bed when I go in. 'Ready for me?'

'It's chilly in the bathroom,' I warn, suddenly anxious. I don't know anything about nursing, whether this is the wrong thing, whether she'll catch cold. I don't want to make her worse. Her hand on the landing wall, steadying herself, I hover behind her. I don't know how much help she needs, whether to let her be private, but she starts to take off her nightdress with no embarrassment. I help her slip it over her head and untie the scarf. Her body is so changed I want to look away but she is watching my face so I only look into her eyes and smile.

'Always fancied being thin . . .' Her smile is rueful and invites me to look. Her flesh is yellowish in the candlelight and clutches her bones. Her breasts have pleated themselves against her but her belly is swollen. Her pubic hair has gone and the blunt white place looks so vulnerable I want to moan. I bat away the thought of my father. I hold her arm and she steps into the bath, eases herself down into the water.

'Not too hot . . .?'

'Ahhh . . . that's bliss,' she breathes, her eyes closing. I can almost feel her pleasure. The candlelight is grainy in the steam. Condensation trickles down the cold window glass but the scent of the bath-oil and the candle have almost masked the smell of sickness and of damp.

'What would make it even better?' I ask. 'Music? Tea?'

She opens her eyes. 'This is as good as it's going to get,' she says. 'Just let me be.'

I put my hand on the door-handle.

'But don't go.'

'You can't relax with me here. Thought I'd change your sheets.'

'No, stay a bit.'

'Course.' I sit down on the lid of the toilet.

'There's things I want to say. There's things *you* want to say, int there?'

I frown at the water. The turquoise of the bath and the pink oil cast a surreal sheen of rose and verdigris on her body. The heat has brought a tinge of colour to her cheeks. Her nipples are the colour of copper.

'Things you want to know?' She watches me, a half smile of pleasure on her face from the warmth of the cradling water.

'Yes.'

She shifts herself, the water rocks around her and the candlelight blooms in it. There is a spatter of cold rain against the window. I am unnerved by the weird unworldly beauty of her, hairless, glossy, looking up at me from the watery capsule of the bath. She knows the things I want to know but suddenly I doubt it, doubt I do want to know, have any right.

'Daddy didn't tell me . . . I suppose he didn't want me to know.'

'Why do you reckon?'

'I don't . . . don't understand.'

Her fingers move under the water as if she is trying to grasp something. There's the glint of nine vivid nails. 'Well, don't you reckon he might . . . he sort of wanted to . . . protect you?'

'Maybe.'

'And your mum.'

'But then . . . why would he talk to you . . . and Vassily?' A childish whine in my voice I can't quite suppress.

She waits, rolls her head against the back of the bath and a little trail of bubbles rise. 'Well, this is what I reckon . . . He talked to me because I wasn't as *good* as your mum in his eyes. I wasn't as . . . as clean.'

'Clean?' I almost laugh at the irony of this from Wanda's bath.

'No . . . Mum says he . . .'

'What?'

A drop of blue wax escapes from the candle and runs down the side of the bath, setting above a cluster of older runnels and drips. The flame is reflected in each tap, in the water, in its circle of melted wax, and, when I look back at Wanda, in her eyes.

'What?' What pleasure it might give her if I tell her that my mother said he loved her. But she continues before the words will gather on my tongue. 'I think he was sort of overawed by your mum . . . and me!' She laughs and the thin skin on her lower lip splits. She licks away the sudden bead of blood, I wince, thinking how sore that must be, how very fragile her skin. 'I might be wrong. That wouldn't be the first time. But anyway, what *I* reckon is, he wanted to keep her away from all that, her and you too, all that horrid stuff. Whereas me and Vass . . . well . . .'

'But he came to you as a prostitute!' I didn't mean to shout. Looking at her sheeny body, utterly naked, utterly, utterly vulnerable, I feel a sudden surge of rage, the lovingness gone. Bodies. His purply penis, his woolly chest all gone now, up in smoke and hers a ruin. Vassily's body. My ants . . . oh I don't know. Fury. Foxy with her hands, her mouth, on someone else. Too angry to sit down any more I stand up; see at once how easy it would be to press her down under the water, no violence required, just the steady pressing of my hands until she breathed in the oily pink water and filled her lungs. No one would ever know it wasn't an accident – or suicide.

Life so precious.

I leave the room before I can, run down the stairs. Think I will leave the house. Leave her to it. She can get herself out. I don't trust the anger in my hands. Or maybe she'll drown without me, drown or die of cold. Buttoning my coat, I catch my face in the mirror again, my hair a sight, a frown that will harden as I grow old, lines that will deepen, the corners of my mouth dragged down. I stop and make it pleasant, smile, see Vassily again, the little one, that small, snaggle-toothed face. Teeth straight now, must have worn braces after I knew him, must have looked worse before he looked better.

Some memory of a kiss: I think I must have dreamed it.

I cannot leave Wanda in the bath. As if I ever would. I take off my coat and go back upstairs.

'Ready to get out?'

She looks at me warily. 'That's getting cold.'

'Shall I just wash your back?'

'Mmmm.' I help her sit up and she leans forward. There are red marks on her skin where the bath has pressed against her. The skin is loose. I put soap on a flannel and start rubbing roughly, not too roughly. She says nothing, but I see the marks I'm making. I'm sorry. The anger drips out of my fingers with the water from the flannel. I stroke gently from the nape of her neck down the bumpy ridge of her spine. Little moles on her shoulders, a couple of tiny scars, pearly soap bubbles clinging to her shoulder-blades that are sharp as wings. Goose-pimples rise on her arms. 'I'll fetch the towels,' I say.

9

Dirty clouds are lumbering over the sea, but at least the rain has stopped. After her bath, Wanda was exhausted. I got her back into bed and then the district nurse arrived, so I left them and came for a walk by the sea. My stupid shoes are pinching but I'm warm – Wanda's trousers that I borrowed, Vassily's sweater, Wanda's coat. I go into the Oxfam shop – out of habit – to see if there's anything for Second Hand Rose. I find a pair of purple Doc Marten's, Foxy would like them but they're my size, not hers. I slide my feet into them, not my style, but I feel solid and rooted and my toes are happy. They spread out with relief. I hesitate over the purchase, but they're cheap enough and anyway I can always sell them on. On my way out I spot a shawl, fine soft wool, a deep foggy green, a delicate lacy pattern, and I go back and buy that too. I stop again and get myself a pair of woollen socks.

Sitting on a bench on the promenade I remove my slim Italian shoes, withered and muddy from their soaking last night, put on the warm socks and the boots. It reminds me of being a little girl, cold from the sea, how tickly and wonderful when my mother dried between my toes and put my socks on me. The boots feel heavy and odd. Foxy bought me these shoes in Milan. My best shoes, narrow, fine tan leather – but they've never been comfortable. I've never admitted it to myself before now.

With an alarming rumble of wheels, two boys shoot past on

skateboards and my heart is suddenly in my mouth. A fat gingery dog skitters past, followed by a man in a tweed overcoat and trilby. 'Cold enough for you?' he says. 'Yes.' I look after him, stunned, something about his voice – Daddy. Since he died I see him everywhere. In one man's posture, another man's voice, the smile of another. And sometimes, when I'm driving or being driven, I see him on the pavement, I'm sure I do, I really see him, really him. If I stopped and ran after him, called him, the man who turned would wear a stranger's face. Of course I know that, but still, since he died, I do see him everywhere.

I put my hand in my bag, bury it in the cloudy softness of the shawl. I want to know what made Daddy scream in the night. I want to know what was in his dreams.

'Nothing,' Mummy used to say, 'just the past.' *Just* the past! And she didn't know, he couldn't tell *her*.

And is Foxy just *my* past?

Why should that sound like less than the future?

There is a public telephone near the pier. I could ring her. I could be speaking to her in a few minutes. I can picture her, at the other end, picking up the phone. By now she will be worried, but she will be working – nothing would put her off her work. Her hair will be knotted loosely back, her glasses on the end of her nose, a pencil, maybe, behind her ear, lipstick smudged. Does she wear lipstick when nobody's there? I think, yes. In the early days I used to nip home from work unexpectedly and drag her into bed. She'd laugh and protest – but not too strongly. And once, I can scarcely believe this now, once she came to the shop when I was there alone and got me to shut the shop, pull down the blinds, and made love to me under my low wooden desk in a scramble of clothes she'd pulled from their hangers, and then she'd pinned up her hair, re-done her lips and sailed out like a snooty customer leaving me dozy and melting – with a pile of ironing to do. But nothing like that for a very long time.

I get up and walk away, leaving my shoes on the bench. Gulls are bobbing on the sullen sea that is the same grey as the sky so you can hardly see the line between them. I stalk, hands in pockets, towards the pier. No children on the big rippled slide. The candy-floss kiosk shut – but I can smell chips. Even though it is too early for lunch I am seized by a sudden urge for chips, more to warm my hands on than anything. They come not wrapped in real newspaper but in a cardboard cone printed to look like newspaper. That would make Foxy laugh and she'd hold the cone up to read the text, trying to work out whether it was genuine news or pastiche. Fancy that, she'd muse, fancy writing imaginary news stories to be printed on artificial newspaper for the sale of fish and chips. She might even use the word post-modern. Wanda wouldn't think that, Wanda wouldn't think anything, she'd just scoff the chips. She would have done, once. I douse them with vinegar and frost them with salt. Delicious.

I walk along past old couples, muffled and clinging to each other or to sticks; people in wheelchairs; mothers with push-chairs; the boys on the skateboards back again; scampering dogs. A wind is picking up, slits of cold sunshine escape from rips in the sky, glint on the sea.

I swap the chips from hand to hand to warm them both. The taste of vinegar is strong and withers the insides of my cheeks. The wind is in my face, icy, my eyes water. I turn back towards the pier, go into the amusement arcade. Dim inside, lights blink from the machines, an oily smell. Colours flash and pictures roll, dice and naked women, guns firing straight at me, lasers. The carpet is tacky under my feet. A cluster of teenagers round a machine, nudging. It's a schoolday, so, a cluster of truants. I would never have dared. A man watches them, narrow-eyed, oil-slick hair pushed back, leather jacket, the sort of man that lurks in the nightmares of parents I should think.

I have ten pence change in my pocket from the chips. I put it in a slot. If I win I will go back to Foxy and we will try again. Everything will be all right. Colours, a siren noise, a roll of dice, buttons to press. I don't know what I'm doing, I press something, a blast of noise, now and then a chunter, chunter, chunter as the coins spill out, spill and spill and the kids crowd round. 'Fuckinell,' they say in one voice. I fill my fists with silver but it is too much. I'm embarrassed by these sudden riches, find I didn't want to win.

I hold out my hand to a girl in a mini-skirt and bare mottled legs. 'Want it?' I say, as some of the coins scatter to the ground. I breathe her smoky teenage cheap and glamorous smell. 'Cool,' she says, grinding out her fag on the carpet with her heel and holding out her hands. There's a phone number written in Biro on her wrist and she wears a puzzle ring.

I blink in the brightness of outside. The sky is in shreds now, the sun blowing through the tatters. I walk back to my shoes, still poised, pigeon-toed, on their bench. An old pair of stranger's shoes – who would want them? I could take them to the Oxfam shop. But instead, and with a sort of smile in my body, a burst of energy, I jump down on to the shingle, run and hurl them into the sea, one then the other, two twizzling arcs, two splashes. I walk faster in my new purple boots. I walk fast back to Wanda's house, stopping to buy food to tempt her with, home-cured ham and fresh white bread, yoghurt, a tub of chocolate ice-cream.

After I've eaten my sandwich and Wanda has failed to eat hers but toyed with a tiny bowl of ice-cream, we sit by the fire. Wanda is done up ready for Stan, a different scarf on her head, her eyes made up, her lipstick glossy, some eau-de-Cologne on her wrists. Close up, I notice that she has drawn her eyebrows on in green, wonder whether or not it's deliberate. She is snuggled in the shawl which suits her, as I knew it would. Sometimes a garment is just right for a person, you see it and you think of the person to whom it should belong. In the shop that happens, someone walks in and before they've said a word I know what they will go for. And Foxy too, of course, I always know what's right for Foxy. Wanda wears red velvet leggings, too loose on her thin legs, but she looks good, quite sexy. She is excited about Stan's return. I'll stay until he comes.

The television is on, some old black-and-white film, but neither of us is concentrating on it.

'I reckon that was just an excuse,' Wanda says suddenly.

'Sorry?'

'The sex . . . I reckon that was a way of seeing me. What he really wanted was to talk.'

'But you did . . .?'

She smiles and looks down. Is that a blush? Then angrily: 'How could he do that? Top himself. I couldn't could you? Even like *this* I couldn't.' Her hand goes gingerly to her swollen belly. 'That's such a shit thing to do. And if he were here I'd tell him.'

My stomach gives a startled flip at this outburst. If we cannot avoid referring to my father's death – my family, even Foxy – we refer to it now as if it was somehow natural. The shocking violence of it, the self-inflicted violence, glossed over as if it was bad taste on his part which we have politely overlooked.

I smile weakly, nod. 'He used to have such terrible dreams,' I say. 'I mean, he used to wake us.'

She gives a little grunt. 'He never knew that. "Fortunately they all sleep like logs" is what he used to say.'

I almost want to laugh, she mimics him so well. It never occurred to me that he might not know he woke us. But how could he have known since no one ever talked about it, no one ever said? Our eyes go back to the screen. Something about the heroine of this film is like Foxy – the way she holds herself, the way she tilts her chin. My heart contracts.

'Let her go,' Wanda says suddenly, sharply, making me start.

'Sorry?'

'Your . . .'

'Foxy?'

'First law of human nature . . . what you can't have you want. If you really want it, of course.'

I snort at her sensible nonsense.

'Me and Ralph . . .' she looks wary, not sure if this is dangerous ground. I'm not sure either.

'Yes?'

'If . . . if he'd of *had* me, I mean split up with Astrid and left you all for me then odds on he would have . . .'

'Regretted it?'

'I would have lost my . . . my . . . allure.' We are both quiet then simultaneously burst into laughter. 'Alllooooor,' she repeats with relish.

'But . . .' I wipe my eyes, laughter feels perilously close to tears today, 'but it wasn't just your . . . allure . . . it was . . . he could *talk* to you.'

Her eyes shift back to the screen. The woman appears to be on her sick-bed now, firelight flickers dimly on her face, the background music is loaded with doom.

'Let's turn this over,' I say, picking up the remote control, finding the end of some quiz.

She watches for a moment. 'And you want to know what he said?'

I nod.

'Why?'

'You sound just like Mum. She doesn't understand.'

'I reckon she does.'

I consider. 'I don't know. She certainly doesn't approve.'

She shifts in her chair, easing the elastic on the waistband of her leggings and wrapping her shawl more tightly around her.

'Don't you think it odd that I never wondered why he had such terrible dreams?' I say. 'I mean it was just . . . just part of him . . . like playing golf or wearing glasses. I was just beginning to wonder . . . and then he . . .'

'Did away with himself, the bugger.'

Despite myself I'm laughing again, and crying too.

Wanda gives me a moment, then says, 'I think we need a cup of tea.'

'Yes.' I stand up, pluck a tissue from the box on the table, wipe my eyes, blow my nose. 'Anything else . . . you've hardly eaten . . .'

She sighs impatiently. 'I don't know what I do want any more. That's the worst of this . . . that's the worst of this, this . . . disease, you can't *fancy* anything any more. You know what that's like to fancy something, a bit of chocolate or a cake . . . how lovely that is . . .'

'Yes.' I think of the fat golden chips, how gorgeous it was to cram them in my mouth, to lick my salty lips. I pick up our plates, Wanda's ham sandwich untouched, a pool of melted ice-cream in her bowl.

'There's nothing in the world that I could fancy. That's the saddest thing,' Wanda says. She draws her knees up to her chin once more and hugs them like a child. Her knee bones are sharp through the dark red velvet.

I don't know what to say. I don't know what to offer her. Something else. 'I did see some bits of his diary . . .' I begin.

'No . . . from the war?' Her green eyebrows rise. 'He said he kept a diary but that got lost, or stolen or something.'

'Yes.' I grimace thinking of the fate of most of the diary. 'Well it turned up, some of it – half-eaten by ants – you couldn't make much out but there was something about a friend, a good friend . . .'

'Ah, that'd be Vince.'

A juggernaut rumbles outside and the window trembles in its frame. On the television is an advertisement for dog food, red-setters bounding.

'Yes, that's right, Vince.'

I wait, breath held, the plates balanced on my hands but she says nothing else.

I go into the kitchen to make tea, camomile for Wanda, PG Tips for me. While it brews I run upstairs to the toilet. My stomach cramps, I don't know why. Nothing she can say can make any difference to *now*. Whatever happened happened.

And now he's dead. The flushing cistern is a roaring in my ears. There's a ring round the bath, I wipe it away, snap off a brittle nugget of blue wax.

Wanda's tea is too hot, she puts it on the table beside her. I don't know where her thoughts are now.

'The shawl looks lovely,' I say, 'it almost matches your eyes.'

'Australian chap,' she says. 'They hit it off . . . how sometimes you do.'

'Yes.'

'Well this chap, Vince, got injured . . .'

'An explosion . . .'

'You know?'

'That's all.'

'So, the Japs made him work, if you could stand you could work sort of thing . . . such pain. No pain-killers, of course.' She stops, clutches her arm, her eyes widening with the thought that there could be no pain-killers. 'I don't know all the ins and outs of it, half of what he told me went straight in one ear, out the other . . .' She is looking at the TV screen as she speaks, not at me. The light changes on her face, some programme about vets now.

'And?'

'He told me dreadful things that'd make your blood run cold. But he couldn't tell me everything.'

'But I thought . . .'

'He couldn't speak everything. Say it. Even to me. So he wrote it.'

'Wrote?'

'He wrote me a letter.' There is a pause. She nods towards the television. 'Shall we switch that off?' A cat is being held down on an examining table, its tail lashing. I turn it off and the room is instantly gloomier, the traffic noise more intrusive. I get up and switch on the light. She needs a lamp in here. If I stayed any longer I would buy her a lamp with a pink shade to cast a rosy softening light, rather than the harsh white bulb that strips the life from her face -- and mine too I'm sure. I wait but she seems miles away.

'Wanda, the letter . . . what did it say?'

'There's a chocolate-box in Vass's . . . in the spare room. That's got photos and cards and stuff in, but if you look under everything you'll find it.'

'Can I . . .?'

'Bring it down.'

I stand in the bedroom the letter in my hand. Addressed to Wanda, of course, not to me. I don't know what to do, attacked by a sudden scruple about his privacy. But I am so close to knowing now and she said I could read it. I take the letter downstairs and give it to Wanda. She removes the pages from their envelope, smooths them out, glances at them and hands them to me. I would rather take the letter away, away from her eyes, but that would feel somehow rude, so I sit down on the sofa. The paper is blue Basildon Bond and Daddy's handwriting is familiar and cramped, written in fountain-pen, probably the gold fountain-pen, which, when I left after the funeral, Mummy let me keep.

Dear Wanda,   6.6.75

Why should I burden you with my memories? I have no excuse for my cowardice in doing so, just this rather ridiculous notion that somehow to tell someone, to tell you *might make it better. This is hardly rational. But I can't tell even you the worst thing. Indeed now I have pen and paper in front of me I can hardly bring myself to write the words. Do not feel compelled to read what follows. Maybe it is enough that I write it and address it to you.*

I told you some of Vince's horrific injuries after the incident with the dynamite. He lost several fingers, suffered terrible flesh injuries to his torso and worse, worse perhaps for a man, certainly a young virile man, such injuries to his private parts that, well, that it was unlikely that he could ever father a child.

This was the lowest ebb for many of us. I escaped severe injury but was constantly plagued with disease, tortured by the deep tropical ulcers on my legs that refused to heal. We were all – Japs as well – close to starvation. On Christmas Eve Vince collapsed. He was in agony. Have you ever been with someone in agony? Someone you care about? Until that moment I didn't understand what helplessness was. We had some hooch that someone had brewed from rice. Being so starved it took very little to make us immediately very drunk. In his agony Vince begged me to help him die. At first I refused but I thought it only a matter of time anyway and he was in such anguish. In short I killed him by suffocation. It took longer than you might believe to make him die, weak and co-operative as he was. Thus I am a murderer. I meant it well, but still I am a murderer. Sometimes I can't look at my children without remembering that.

Worse. Next day, Christmas Day, we were given extra rations of fresh meat. Not till after we had eaten, the shreds of pink meat with rice and cabbage did we wonder what kind of meat it was. Unlike most of the bodies of our fellows which we prepared for burial ourselves, the bodies of Vince and another couple of men were buried by the Japanese before we held our services.

Writing this makes me sick to my stomach.

Oh Wanda, what would I have done without you?

With my dearest love to you and Vassily,

Ralph

The letter is held in both my hands. My eyes stay on the last word, his name. I can feel Wanda's eyes on me. I swallow a mouthful of saliva. She is waiting for some response but what can I say? I feel almost embarrassed. What *is* there to say? I experience a sudden fierce itch between my shoulder-blades. I reach my thumb up backwards to scratch.

Oh Daddy.

There he is, suddenly, at the table, lifting the bottle of Tabasco, banging it with the heel of his hand, smothering the taste of his food, ruining it, Mummy said. I swallow hard, hug a cushion to my stomach, lean forward. I close my eyes and hear the trace of a scream, the rushing of water. My nostrils fill with the sickly air-freshener sweetness in the bathroom in the middle of the night.

'You all right?' Wanda leans towards me.

My blood is beating in my ears.

'Don't pass out on me for Christ's sake.' Wanda sounds frightened.

'No, of course not.' I force a smile, remember to breathe. 'I'm all right . . . really.'

'I shouldn't have . . .'

'It's all right.'

'Sure?'

I look up. Something bright is caught in Wanda's shawl. I shudder, realising that it's another one of her nails come unstuck.

'That he thought he was a murderer . . .' I feel a rush of compassion, a rush of . . . love? His face so closed in, the glasses a shield hiding his eyes from my eyes, a bright glassy shield, his hair wild in the night like the texture of his screams.

So hard, so impossible to marry the two men, the tortured soul who thought himself a murderer, who feared he had eaten the flesh of his friend, and the grumpy man I knew, the man behind the newspaper, the man forever at work or at the golf course. The man I didn't really know.

Wanda watches me anxiously. She picks up her tea and cups her hands round the mug as if to warm them, then she puts it down clumsily, slopping tea on the table as if it is too heavy to hold.

I am ashamed. I have been forgetting her pain. I squeeze my eyes tightly shut, try to squeeze away what I have learnt. 'Shall I help you upstairs?'

She shakes her head. 'I *am* knackered, but I'm not going up stairs without Stan.' She looks up at the wedding photograph and the ghost of a smile passes across her face. Then she looks back at me. 'Sure you're all right? I feel bad letting you . . .'

'Wanda, don't . . .'

'That might *not* have been Vince . . . that might not have been human meat at all . . .' she says.

'I'm sure it wasn't . . . and if it was . . .'

'That wasn't his fault.'

'No,' I say, 'and anyway . . . that's not the point.'

'But in his dreams . . . well you know what dreams are like.'

My nails are sharp smiles in my palms. 'Yes,' I say, 'yes, I do know what dreams are like.'

Upstairs in the cold, cold room I open the chocolate-box to replace the letter, and take out a slippery handful of photographs. On the bed I sort them into two piles, those that feature Daddy and those that do not. Then more slowly I browse through the images of Daddy – the man I knew and did not know at all. Here in his shirt-sleeves on some beach with Vassily grinning beside him; here with his arm slung casually round Wanda – a happy couple; here gazing into some unspecified distance, one hand shielding his eyes from the sun.

And here, young Daddy in his uniform, not a father then, young Ralph in his uniform, smooth face, eyes big and lustrous dark behind his spectacles. A smooth and hopeful face looking forward into a future he could not guess.

I stare into the bright darkness of his eyes. Twin points of light in each one.

LICK

I swallow, gorge rising in my throat. Poor Daddy. With all that inside him. So horrifying, so . . . there is no word for it . . . and yet . . .

I am taken aback to discover – now that I *know* – that I had thought it would be worse.

How worse?

What could be worse?

What worse than the killing and eating of a friend?

But what could be darker than imagination?

What could be worse than guilt?

And whatever could equal forty-five years of nightmares and the shattering of sleep?

What possible equation could there be?

I want to ask Wanda what they said after she'd read the letter. I go downstairs to do so but she is so tired she cannot speak. I will not bother her any more. I feel a curious looseness inside, as if something has given, though I am not sure what.

Wanda will not go upstairs no matter how I urge her, so I draw the curtains, bring a pillow downstairs and she curls up on the sofa, the shawl covering her. I change her sheets and put the stale ones in the washing machine, tidy up the kitchen. In the bathroom I wash my face and pick a shred of ham from between my teeth, meeting my own mirrored eyes with a shudder and a flinch. I take my toothbrush and scrub my mouth minty fresh, spitting white froth over and over into the turquoise basin.

I change into my own crumpled clothes, odd with the boots but it can't be helped – a little pang of regret for the Italian shoes. I retrieve my stockings from down the side of the sofa, and I bend over Wanda for a few moments watching her sleep. Her face is very smooth and blank, the lashless lids waxy as petals, above them one of the green eyebrows rubbed off. The light glints on the rings in her ears. I kiss her very softly on her forehead, hardly a kiss, a brush of the lips. I catch the bitter breath of her disease. And I know I'll never see her again.

I wait, as I promised, for Stan to get home. When he arrives – rough, stubbled, donkey-jacketed – she is still sleeping. He greets me gruffly, goes straight to her, scared of what he will find. He kneels down beside the sofa and with his thick gentle oily finger strokes her cheek. I go upstairs and collect my things.

I leave before she wakes again.

10

Wanda's funeral. Foxy beside me in a little netted pill-box hat. 'I don't think I could bear to lose you,' she said when I got back, four months ago, on a freezing February night. 'Funny,' I said, 'because I've just realised that maybe I *could* do without you.' She was quiet for a moment, thinking before she spoke. 'Well,' she kept her voice calm, but I saw the flare of her pupils, felt the small intake of breath, 'that's good, that is healthier, don't you think?' And she's still with me, though whether forever I really do not know. What is forever? How can one contemplate forever standing by an open grave?

I wear just what I wore for my father's funeral nine months ago. The day is as bright as that day, hotter, more golden; the fat green and gold of early June. Many more people present than at Daddy's funeral. Vassily, of course, with his daughter and his wife, a tiny dark woman who looks up at him with eyes that are both loving and critical. Who looks sideways at me. She's sharp. What does she know about me? Vassily's daughter, rosy and dark-eyed, noisy in the church, singing her own song. Stan dressed in his wedding-suit, wet-eyed and reeking of whisky. Many strangers. In the graveyard, in front of my mother, in front of everyone, Foxy holds my hand.

After the church we make our way to a pub on the seafront where Vassily has booked a room, a small glass extension with wicker chairs and puffy Roman blinds. Not at all suitable for a funeral, but Wanda would have liked it. It is blazing hot, greenhouse hot inside, despite a whirring fan, and open windows through which come shouts from people on the beach. There's the occasional thwack of a beach-ball hitting the glass. Caroline wears white, not black. She's the only one who looks cool. Stan's drunken face seen too close, open pores, a flake of puff-pastry caught in the corner of his mouth. Mummy is very quiet. She has come with her friend John. I look at the two of them and wonder. They sit very close together sipping sherry.

Naomi trips over and bangs her head, she screams, unbearably piercing in the little room. At a sign from Caroline, Vassily scoops her up and carries her outside.

Despite the fan and the windows there is no air in the room, it's suffocating. Foxy has fallen into conversation with an elderly woman in a black straw hat. I see her fumble in her handbag for her notebook and pen. I follow Vassily out. I need fresh air, the grief and the sherry and the hot June sun through glass are too much.

I find them on the beach. Naomi has recovered from her bump. She's barefoot, her dress tucked in her knickers, splashing about at the edge of the sea. Vassily has loosened his tie, rolled up his shirt-sleeves. He sits on a breakwater watching Naomi, her little shoes and socks beside him. A few couples sprawl on rugs, some teenagers throw a beach-ball from the beach to the sea and back, brown skin, dripping limbs, shouting as if with joy.

In this heat the sea itself seems almost too lazy to move. It makes contented sounds, softly sucking and sighing, just the occasional refreshing plash when it summons the energy to send a small wave washing up. The child is singing again, I can't quite hear what, just a soft high note now and then, sweet. But Vassily can't hear the sea, or Naomi or the sound of my feet scrunching on the shingle as I approach.

I touch his arm and he jumps, turns round.

'She's lovely.' I nod towards Naomi. I sit down beside him

on the rough concrete of the breakwater. 'Vassily, I'm so very sorry about Wanda.'

Sitting so close to him, looking at the long brown hairs on his forearms where he's rolled his shirt-sleeves up, I'm suddenly hit by a humiliating memory: a drunken kiss. The sun on the sea makes me squint.

'Daddy look,' Naomi, limping up on the shingle on her wet pink feet brings him a stiffened starfish. 'Is it deaded?'

He nods. 'Yes, sweetie, it's dead.'

'Poor lickle star.' She goes back to the sea, cradling it in her two hands.

Vassily is a good father I can see that. I am glad for the little girl. The bottom of her dress has come down and is dark and wet from the sea. But it doesn't matter.

I touch his arm. 'Vassily, I'm sorry.'

He nods.

'I mean . . . when we were children.'

His face hardens. He has not forgotten. I thought maybe the game, the childish game may have been forgotten. His eyes are just the green of his mother's, small tobacco-gold flecks round the pupils which are tiny in the brightness. The skin on the back of my neck is hot and itchy, this sun would burn you in an instant. Tears come into my eyes.

A little muscle twitches in his jaw. I cannot know what he is thinking.

'Do you forgive me?' I ask. The tears spill.

He watches my face for a long moment. His face is quite inscrutable. Then he puts his index finger on my cheek and catches a tear. He holds it in front of his eyes and examines it there on his finger-tip, a bright bead of wet reflecting the sun, reflecting too minutely to see the shape of his own head.

The child runs up the beach dragging behind her a giant ribbon of wet brown weed. 'Look Daddy, it lasts for *miles*.'

Vassily licks the tear from his finger before he smiles at me.

A NOTE ON THE AUTHOR

Lesley Glaister was born in Wellingborough in 1956.
She teaches a Master's Degree in Writing at Sheffield
Hallam University, and writes regular book reviews for
the *Spectator* and *The Times*. She is the author of *Honour
Thy Father*, which won a Somerset Maugham and a
Betty Trask award, *Trick or Treat*, *Digging to Australia*,
Limestone and Clay, *Partial Eclipse*, and most recently,
The Private Parts of Women. She lives in Sheffield.